A SCIC

THE FORGOTTEN
LEGACY OF GODS & MEN

JAY REACE

First published in the United States of America by FJR Publishing LLC, 2024.

Text copyright © 2024 by Jay Reace

FJR Publishing supports copyright. Copyrights encourage and fuels, creativity and diverse voices while allowing free speech and various cultures to shine. Thank you for buying a legal edition of this book and for complying with any and all copyright laws by not reproducing, scanning, or distributing any part of this book in any form without permission. You are supporting writers and allowing FJR Publishing to continue publishing books for every reader.

ISBN 978-1-7348990-5-4

Library of Congress Control Number 2024909998

Book edited by Kaitlyn Brown

Book written by Jay Reace

WWW.JayReace.Com

"*A grand adventure to stop the end of the world that tests the bonds of family.*"

-Alfred Muller, Author of the Water Crystal Series

"*It's a fantastic continuation, with brand new obstacles and epic characters.*"

-Rosaly Aponte Author of the Dragonlord's Daughter

"*The world Jay has created is beautifully crafted and the story woven is gripping and highly addictive.*"

-Nicklous Adams II, Author of the Zanthia Series

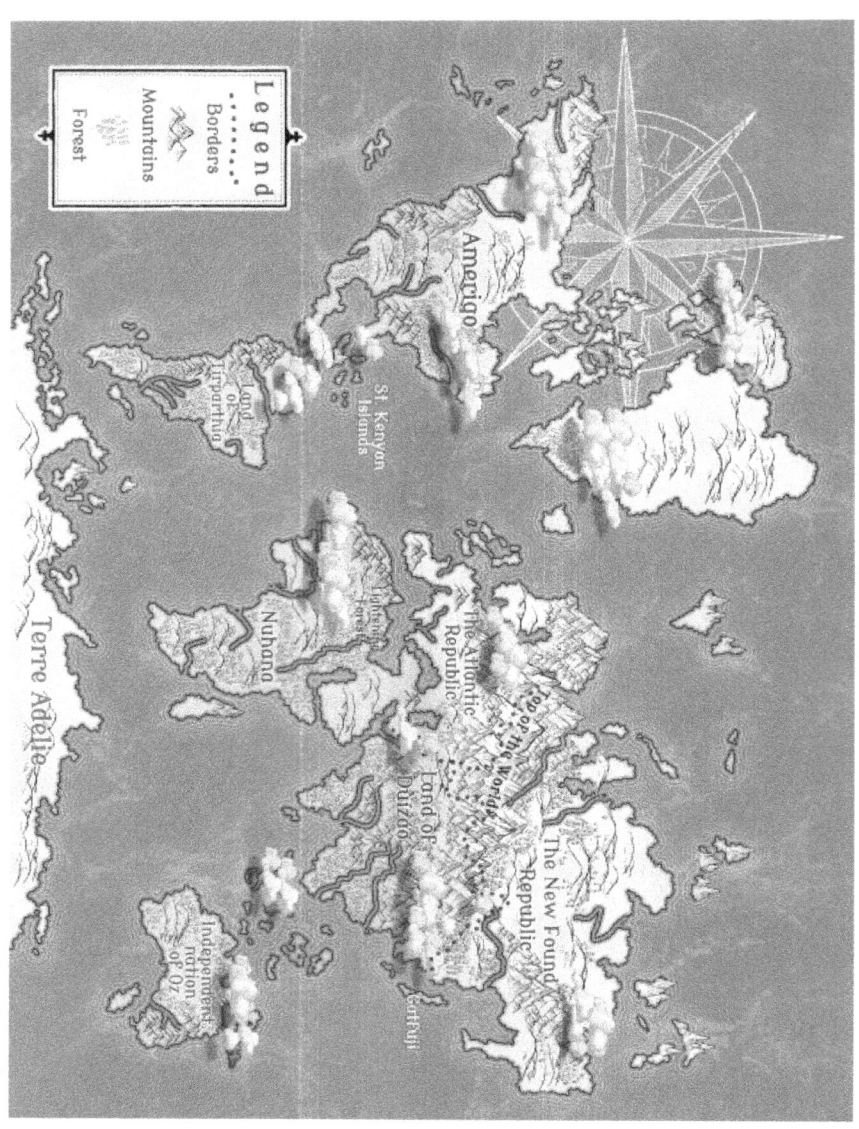

This book is dedicated to all those wanting to share their own stories, go ahead, I dare you. Not for me, but for yourself and all those waiting on your gifts.

Table of Contents:

Last Time In the Scion Universe:
C1: Mommy Dearest - Part 1
C2: Alpha
C3: Mommy Dearest - Part 2
C4: We keep our promises
C5: He's back
C6: Time flies
C7: More than meets the eye
C8: Meeting of the minds
C9: Reunited
C10: What happens next
C11: All in her head
C12: What lays underneath
C13 Angels, demons, or gods
C14: They don't say
C15: It's not what you think
C16: They walk among us
C17: The Plan
C18: Buckle up
C19: A sibling revelation
C20: The cabin on the lake
C21: Dead men don't talk
C22: Rock, paper, scissors, snakes
C23: My old friend
C24: If you ever met a god
C25: It can't be that
C26: The lost boy
C27: You can't be serious
C28: Don't forget a gift
C29: Sibling Rivalry
C30: We have to go
C31: The Scion Contention
C32: Next Challenger
C33: Yin & Yang
C34: Reunited-ish
C35: Wake up
C36: Give them the room
C37: Keep thinking

C38: The Hag
C39: A whole new world
C40: Save yourself
C41: Gangs all here
C42: In the final moments
Thank You To:
Final Thoughts:

A SCION BOOK SERIES

THE FORGOTTEN
LEGACY OF GODS & MEN

JAY REACE

Last time in the scion universe...
Disclaimer, this is not a substitute for reading previous novels within the Scion Universe. This is merely a brief recap of previous events related to this story

We left our heroes Raine, Xolani, Keon, and Niya as they just finished bringing peace to Nuhana and the world by stopping King Xerxes's plan to use the Lumastar, (a star like being from another plan, with unlimited power), to power Nuhana at great cost to the earth. Unknown to them, Xolani's brother Xaden, (previously thought to be dead), was working with King Xerxes and used his gift of mind control to take over Niya, Keon, and Miss Lupita, while trying to kill Xolani and his family. But Xaden betrayed King Xerxes for his own selfish gains only to be killed by Xolani's best friend Rashid. Now with the King dead, a royal family member must step up to take control of the country before anarchy reigns.

All fingers point to Xolani, but Raine and Xolani want nothing better than to take their family back home. But will they be able to live a dream of returning home or will they have to live a nightmare of royal life, as the responsibilities of leading a country, raising kids, and marital disagreements drive them apart? So Xolani and several other venture the royal grounds of the Tree Palace, better known as the Mother Tree to find his and Haygena's mother to ask, who will rule? Not knowing, what's lurking beneath.

Elsewhere in the realm...

A lone shadowy figure waits in the chilly dark void. The faint sounds of screaming agony echos throughout. Another dark figure appears in the distance, before floating closer to meet.

"Report," the shadowy figure commands with a devilish voice.

"Mission unsuccessful," the other says in a sinister voice. "But the Lumastar is in the Tree Palace and the Scion was located."

"Excellent, where is the Scion now?"

"On the royal grounds, and now that the Scion is there . . . your plan will not be stopped."

"Everything is coming together. Is the Scion ready?"

"Yes, and awaits your orders."

"The time draws near, and I will finally be able to take my rightful place."

"What should we do with the Lumastar?"

"I will call the Lumastar home when the time is right. So, it can stay in the Tree Palace for now. We've waited this long, we can wait a little longer. Return and I will summon you when I am ready."

"Yes, Mistress," the sinister voice says as they both fade away, leaving the void empty.

Chapter 1:

Mommy Dearest - Part I

Outside, on the Tree Palace grounds of Nuhana; Raine, Xolani, and their kids, Niya and Keon, walk with Haygena toward a cabin that rests on the inner ring wall. Xolani holds Raine's hand as his sister, Haygena, walks in front with the children.

Raine clutches at her purple shirt as she says, "Do you think we should be taking the kids to see your mother?" Raine asks.

"Of course, she's my mother."

"I know," she says, "but with all they've been through in the last few days, your brother Xaden kidnapping and brainwashing them, Keon getting his abilities while saving you and fighting your dad—"

"You don't need to recap, I was there."

Raine lowers her voice to a mere whisper, "And Niya being there when Rashid killed Xaden."

"Raine, I know."

"Sorry, I'm just worried about the kids. Niya still doesn't seem to be herself. And Keon, well to be honest, he seems okay but I don't want to overlook him just because he seems okay."

"Raine, it's my mother. I'm sure you're nervous about meeting her."

"I'm not nervous," she shouts, bringing brief attention from the others before lowering her tone, "I'm just not sure it's wise to take the kids to see her prior to us seeing her first."

"I hear you my love, but it's my mother and I'm sure it will be fine." They all continue to walk in silence until they near the cabin and Keon suddenly asks,

"Dad? When Miss Lupita was protecting us, she mentioned her job was to take us home. What did she mean? Because we were already home, right?" They reach the cabin and Xolani knocks on the door as he answers Keon,

"I will tell you later what that meant, but first, it's time to meet your grandmother."

The door opens and standing in the threshold of the door is Lady Neyma, a tall, beautifully-aged woman. Her shimmering green dress is only overshadowed by her caring, grayish-blue eyes and her warm, inviting smile. She quickly gazes at each of them before asking,

"May I help you?"

Xolani opens his mouth but a lump of emotions prevents the words from forming. He tries to hold back the flood of emotions but his beaming expression of joy penetrates the surface as his usually stern hazel eyes have now become glossy. He turns slightly to Raine but notices her gaze is centered on Haygena. Xolani whips his head to see Haygena, normally the stoic warrior, weeping uncontrollably. He gathers his words and with a voice choked with tears says,

"Mother, it's us. Xolani and Hay, I mean Xalen and Ada."

Lady Neyma mumbles, "Can't be." Her face written with scrambling thoughts while she processes the possibility of her long-lost children still being alive. She takes a step back as the weight of this revelation hits her. Soon joyful tears stream down her face as her loving smile returns. She extends her arms and without a second thought, Xolani and Haygena run and embrace their mother.

Niya, Keon, and Raine stand contently as they wait patiently for the joyful hug to end. Raine smiles at the affection displayed in front of her and decides to look at her own children. Keon with his head down, softly kicking at patches of grass beneath his feet, oblivious to his mother's gaze. Raine gently strokes his hair and is met with an unapproving stare from Keon. Raine breaks eye contact to look over to Niya, who says with her head hanging down,

"I'm good Mom."

Raine silently mimics Niya as she looks back toward Xolani. But is quickly taken aback by the icy stare from Lady Neyma. A smirk inches its way across Lady Neyma's lips before a joyful smile returns and she breaks away from Xolani and Haygena.

"Thank the Creator you're alive," Lady Neyma says enthusiastically before asking, "where's your brother?"

Xolani and Haygena glance at one another before Xolani says, "Xaden... he," Haygena steps closer and says,

"How about we come in first, would that be okay?"

"Of course, come, come," Lady Neyma says as she hurries them inside. "You must tell me everything. But wait, pardon me, who are these beautiful young people and this gorgeous lady with you?"

Xolani hits himself in the head and says, "I'm so sorry, I don't know if you remember Raine, I mean LaRaina."

"I don't," Lady Neyma says flashing a cold smile.

"Well, she's my wife now and these are our wonderful children Niya and Keon."

Lady Neyma says with a heavy sigh, "I've missed so much." She leans down to the kids and says, "Call me gram gram. I have plenty of sweets in the cabin if you two would like some."

"I would!" Keon blurts out while Niya smiles politely.

"Well, good," Lady Neyma says, "follow me then." She straightens up and leads the way into the cabin. The kids follow closely behind her. Haygena and Raine walk in behind them as Xolani enters last.

He is surprised that the modestly, run-down cabin's exterior does not match the luxurious interior. His eyes bounce from the gorgeous chandlers to the stunning red drapes flowing from the high ceiling to the floor and to the stunning, white marble floors.

"Mother," he mumbles, "How is this, I mean, I wasn't expecting, well, all of this."

"It's too much, isn't it? I'll change it," Lady Neyma says apologetically as the luxurious walls and fixtures morph into a rustic cabin with a quaint table and rustling fireplace. The group stands dumbfounded as the extravagant environment changes all around them.

"What just happened?" Haygena says. With a satisfied smile, Lady Neyma exchanges stares with Xolani and Haygena. But then her smile fades as she reads the confused faces and without making further eye contact, she speaks to the air.

"Oh no, you've forgotten. You've forgotten my gifts. It's been so long, why would you remember?" Lady Neyma makes her way over to a modest table by the fireplace. They follow behind her concerned, and take seats around the table.

"No one has forgotten you, Mother," Xolani says while placing a gentle hand on Lady Neyma's. She smiles and pats him with her other hand.

"I know you haven't forgotten me, my child. I just didn't think you'd forget I was a mental morph."

"What's that?" Keon blurts out. Niya, with an almost normal-sounding annoyance for her brother, rolls her eyes as she replies,

"Why do you spend so much time with Ms. Shay if you're still going to be so dumb?"

"Niya!" Raine and Xolani's voices exclaim in shock. "You apologize to your brother right now!" Raine commands.

"I, I, I'm sorry Keon. I don't know why I said that," Niya says with her head lowered.

"I'm sure the little angel meant nothing by her remark," says Lady Neyma as she tries to make light of the comment, "teenage hormones. Plus, she's obviously been through a lot. Keon, a mental morph can shift what your mind sees into whatever they choose for you to see."

"An illusionist, basically," Raine says as she crosses her arms. Lady Neyma narrows her gaze and with cold eyes stares at Raine before continuing.

"To simplify it, yes, but so much more. I can sense the gifts in others and know what they are." She pauses for a second as she looks at each of them, "See, your father, being of royal blood, is an elemental. His gifts control natural elements like fire, water, earth and even air." She turns to face Raine with a smirk, "While your mother is only an empath and can... wait, let me see, sense others locations and you can absorb an item's properties, fascinating. And, what was your name again dear? Niya?" She asks sweetly as Niya nods her head shyly. "You are a, oh my. You are a Tele-mental and truly regal, rare indeed. Not often is there more than one in a family for generations, but your uncle Xaden he's a Tele-mental too." Niya's lip curls in disgust at the mention of Xaden, but quickly catches herself and smiles politely before Keon interrupts and asks,

"What about me, what are my gifts?"

"You are a..., wait," Lady Neyma closes her eyes and places a hand on her head. "You have great physical control over your body but you are, unclear. I'm sorry Keon, I can't say what you are because you haven't come into all your gifts yet."

"So I'm going to have more abilities?" Keon says enthusiastically before Niya smugly mumbles under her breath,

"Of course you are."

"Niya!" Xolani and Raine shout stunned at her remark. Lady Neyma waves her hand and says with a big smile,

"Oh don't yell at the poor baby. It's just a little sibling rivalry. And I'm sure she didn't mean anything by it." She says as she turns to Niya and asks, "Did you, honey?"

"No, ma'am," says Niya with her head hanging down.

"See, no harm done," Lady Neyma says as she turns back towards Xolani and says, "And if I may ask, Xalen—"

"Mother, it's Xolani now," he says politely.

"Oh come now, Xalen, why would you change your name? You and your brother were named after your great-grandfather and his brother, the twin defenders against the realm. They defeated the thousand-man militia against the sovereign province all by themselves."

"It made it easier to stay hidden while we lived in exile," Xolani replies.

"Well, you're not in exile now, Xalen," she says before turning to Haygena, "I supposed you changed your name as well, Ada?"

"No, I mean, my name was changed. But by the warriors I stayed with during my youth, as a way of honoring who I had become." Haygena replies.

"I've missed so much being confined to this cabin. And Xaden, why isn't he here and has he changed his name too?" Lady Neyma asks.

"No, Xaden is still Xaden. But Xaden's..." Xolani says slowly. "Xaden is dead."

"So it's true, you did kill him the night of your Scion Contention."

"No, I was framed for Xaden's death that night and we have lived in exile ever since. But after he killed King Xerxes," he glances briefly at Niya and Raine, "he killed for trying to kill us."

"My poor, poor boy," Lady Neyma says.

"Your poor boy brainwashed tons of people, killed several others, and tried to take over the world," Raine says bluntly.

"Nobody's perfect, he was still my son," Lady Neyma says as she takes in a deep breath then continues, "perhaps we can discuss this in more detail later..." She looks down and says, "Xalen, where oh where did you get that lovely red sash?" She says as she points to the red and gold-tipped sash tied around Xolani's waist. He runs the tattered fabric through his fingers as he recalls that fateful night.

"Xalen," Lady Neyma says, but Xolani's mind wonders back to that night as he fails to respond...

Chapter 2:

Alpha

A young Xolani, stands in the darkness of a jail cell. The smell of old sweat and mildew hits his senses. His fingers examining the cold stone wall causing a shudder to run down his spine. He jumps as the heavy iron bars slam shut behind him. A digital locking sound blends in with the fading echo of the guard's boots hitting the hard floor as they walk away.

"What's your name?" a rough voice whispers. Xolani, feeling the weight of the uncomfortable metal armband the guards placed on his wrist before escorting him back, lifts his heavy hand slowly over the top of his eyebrows to help pierce through the darkness of the cell. He inches forward stuttering as he replies,

"Xalen",

In an unnaturally deep voice while his eyes continue to adjust. Light trickles in from the hall but, leaves most of the cell cloaked in darkness.

"Thought that was you," the rough voice says. Xolani's eyes dart in the direction of the voice to see a scruffy-looking man sitting comfortably on the floor with his back propped onto the corner of the cell. "Didn't think a prince could be arrested," he adds with a smirk.

"You're Alpha, leader of the rebellion?" Xolani asks with surprise. Alpha rubs the stubble on his rugged chin, bringing attention to the bruises on his olive skin. "What happened to your face?"

"Let's just say, your dad has a heavy-handed way with words." Alpha replies and continues, "He didn't take kindly to me saving my sister from this place. Or maybe, it was all the people uprising against his rule. Either way, the King's Five caught me and now I'm here."

"Serves you right," Xolani says.

"Excuse me?" Alpha says.

"My dad only wants what's best for Nuhana and you rebels are too stupid to see that." Xolani replies and then asks, "Wait, if you're the leader of the Rebels, why was my father holding your sister?" Alpha smiles as he rises to his feet and says,

"I will ignore the insult, but I'm not sure I should burst such an innocent bubble." Alpha says as he steps forward. Xolani inches back as the distance between him and Alpha is noticeably shorter now. Alpha's almond-shaped eyes narrow, focusing in on Xolani. "Your daddy has been experimenting on people with unique gifts, including my sister and a few others for starters. We broke in to save them."

"My father is a lot of things, but he would never do something like that," Xolani says as he bumps into the back wall. "Just like a filthy rebel to warp the truth." Alpha steps forward while sizing Xolani up and down.

"There you go insulting again," Alpha says sternly, "luckily for you, I had a vision about this night." Xolani's rises a brow and says,

"Visions? Yet you were still caught?"

"The interesting thing about visions, no matter the end destination it cannot be changed. Trust me... Fate will find you, no matter the path, we still must walk it and your path is long Xalen, and ends in sacrifice."

"That's very, um, philosophical," Xolani says with hesitation.

"It's okay, you don't need to understand or believe me," Alpha says with a smile, "but you will in time... How'd your fight go?"

Xolani looks off and begins to fidgets as he stands. Alpha eyes grow wide as he suddenly realizes why Xolani is there and says,

"You killed Xaden."

"It was self-defense." Xolani snaps, before softly saying, "I didn't mean to kill him, he left me no choice."

"I believe you," Alpha says in a reassuring tone, "I'm sorry, killing your brother couldn't have been easy. Even if he was a dick." Xolani quickly replies,

"Takes one to know one, right?"Alpha snorts and says,

"I guess you're right."

Rushed boots hit the floor and fill the jail as sounds begin to ricochet against the walls.

"Quick," Alpha whispers as he grabs and pulls Xolani's arm, "to the wall, sit down! And shut up!" They rush over and slam themselves to the floor. Alpha sits back in his original position, with his head tilted into his arms as they rest on his knees. Xolani hurries to copy Alpha's every move.

"Prisoner 3958?" A guard shouts nervously as he repeats it through the halls.

"Crap," Alpha utters in a whisper, "that's not good."

"Why?" Xolani asks. Alpha glances over to Xolani's wrist,

"Look at your armband," he replies, "that's you." Xolani looks and swallows hard before asking,

"Wha, what do I do?"

"I suggest you respond and then pray. It's always worse if you don't answer them."

"Worse?"

The sounds of boots hitting the linoleum floor stop as a lone guard stands in front of their cell. The ceiling lights turn on, blinding Alpha and Xolani. The guard's imposing silhouette stands threateningly still.

"Prisoner 3958!" The low-voiced guard commands before continuing, "Stand!" Xolani quickly glances at Alpha before rising to his feet. "Hands through the feed slot." A slot slides open as Xolani walks cautiously toward the front of the cell. The guard bangs the bars and barks, "Move it, 3958!"

Xolani picks up the pace as his feet shuffle. He places his hands through the feed slot as instructed. The guard grabs Xolani's wrists and with his free hand waves it over Xolani's. With a click, the armband pops open and drops. Swiftly the guard catches it before it hits the ground. With a confused expression on Xolani's face, he looks up to see the guard is his long-time friend Rashid.

"What are you doing here?" He asks.

"Looking for a summer home. Really?" Rashid whispers sarcastically. Xolani smiles while rubbing his wrist. Rashid pulls a white card from his pocket and waves it over a panel on the wall, causing the cell to open with a loud clank. Xolani turns back to Alpha and motions for him to come with them. As Alpha stands, Rashid clears his throat and says, "Xalen, the key card is only coded for me and one prisoner's exit. I can only take one of you."

"Can't you just reprogram it?" Xolani pleads.

"There isn't enough time for that," Rashid says.

"But enough time for you to play solider?" Xolani mocks. Rashid lowers his head slightly, then raises again to say,

"I am sorry, but we need to hurry if we are going to make it out. I took my dad's spear uniform and someone will notice if we don't move."

Xolani turns to Alpha but before he can utter a word. Alpha raises his hand and says,

"Don't worry about me. I've gotten out of tougher spots."

"We can't just leave you here to rot, Alpha. Leave with us," Xolani protests. Alpha smiles as he replies,

"Remember, we often find our fate on the road we chose to avoid it. I've seen my fate and it is here, but take this," He unties the red sash from around his waist and hands it to Xolani, "it will help you in your journey." Xolani hadn't noticed the weird writing embroidered on the gold tips of it. He looks back up to Alpha and with a confused face says,

"I don't understand."

"You will in time. Kle a louvri nenpòt pòt, the key to open any door."

"You've had a way to get out this whole time, why didn't use it?" Xolani says.

"The key is not a means to escape but a means to help you along your path." Alpha says, "And this is where my path leads."

"Take it back, you need it." Xolani insists.

"You will need this far more than I will. Now go while you and your friend still have time."

Xolani gives Alpha a look before tying the sash around his waist. Xolani solemnly walks out of the cell and Rashid motions for him to follow. They move swiftly through the prison halls. As they turn a corner, they briefly see a small orange metallic ball bounce toward them. Rashid pushes Xolani while screaming, "Get Down!" But it's too late. It goes off with a blinding bright light and thunderous boom that ripples through their eardrums.

A deafening silence covers Xolani's ears as a slow piercing hum begins to amplify in his head. He wipes his blinded eyes, trying to restore his vision. The growing sound of Rashid yelling hits his ears as he stumbles around.

"Xalen, Xalen, Xalen..."

Chapter 3:
Mommy Dearest Part II

"Xalen!" Lady Neyma shouts, bringing him back to the present. "Are you okay? You seem to have zoned out for a second."

The gentle caress of Raine's hand rests on his as he works to avoid her gaze and says, "Yeah, I'm fine. Lost in thought, I guess. What were you asking me?"

Niya and Keon chuckle softly. Lady Neyma says, "I asked about that lovely red sash?"

Xolani lets his fingers play with the old tattered fabric before responding, "It was a gift from a friend long ago." He doesn't notice the cold glare from Lady Neyma's grayish-blue eyes before she smiles and says,

"That must have been some friend to give you such a nice gift."

"Yeah, he was."

With a clear of her throat, Haygena says, "With all due respect, Mother, Xolani, we should get to the matter at hand."

"Yes, you're right. Mother, King Xerxes is dead, making you the Scion."

A coy smile rolls over Lady Neyma's face before she speaks, "I cannot take the throne. The heir has to be blood born and I am simply a girl from the southern province who got lucky to marry a king. Xalen, you are the oldest, the throne belongs to you."

Xolani looks to Haygena, who bows her head. He looks to Raine, who gives a subtle nod.

"My family and I want to get back to our lives," Xolani says with a bit of hesitation, "but under the circumstances, I suppose the responsibilities of the crown falls to us, or more accurately, me."

"So, we're going to stay?" Keon asks enthusiastically. Raine answers as she places her hand back on Xolani's.

"Yes baby, we're staying,"

They both smile before Haygena says,

"Mother, why don't you come live in the Tree Palace? I'm sure there is more than enough room."

Lady Neyma wrings her hands together saying, "I don't know. I've been in this cabin for so long, I'm not sure if I know how to live in the Tree Palace or anywhere else anymore"

"You couldn't have been happy here alone," Haygena says.

"Yes, Mother stay in the Tree Palace," Xolani chimes in. Lady Neyma replies softly,

"Let me think about it, okay?" They both nod in agreement before starting to get up. "Oh wait, you can't go yet, you just arrived. Can't you stay for a little while longer?"

"Sure," Xolani says with a smile. "Perhaps we can tell you more about our lives away from the palace."

Lady Neyma with a light voice and warm smile says, "I'd like that".

Chapter 4:

We Keep Our Promises

The morning sun reaches high atop Nuhana's royal Tree Palace, more commonly known as the Mother Tree. Raine, stands on the helipad with her young son, Keon, who is leaned against one of the many royal fleet's prize black hover sedans surrounding them, talking to their beloved friend Miss Lupita as she prepares to head back to Port Ambit.

"I don't know why you insisted on meeting out here Raine?" Says Miss Lupita, "We could have easily said our see you laters on the ground floor."

"Are you sure you have to go?" Wide-eyed Keon asks as he tugs on Miss Lupita's simple outfit. She looks down and into his saddened green eyes before gently wiping a falling tear off his soft light brown skin. Warm crinkles form in the corners of her eyes as she smiles and replies,

"I made a promise to our animal friends Francine and Fransisco, remember? If they helped pull our carriage, I would take them back home and return them back into fish. You wouldn't want me to break a promise, now, would you?"

Keon looks down at the purple granite of the helipad's surface as he fidgets with his leg and says,

"No."

"Good," Miss Lupita says before reaching over, taking his chin in her hand and nudging his head up, "You shouldn't worry though. I'll be back before you know it."

"I know" he says before jumping up and hugging her tightly.

"We'd love to go", Raine says, "are you sure you don't want one of us to go with you?" Miss Lupita simply shakes her head before Raine adds, "at least take some of the royal guards with you."

Miss Lupita takes Raine by the hand and says, "I appreciate that my dear, but you have so many new responsibilities to the throne now,"

"I wish," Raine says, "I'm mostly just exploring the Mother Tree while Xolani is in meeting after meeting."

"Either way," says Miss Lupita, "It would be unfair to ask you to come with me. Besides, I will be fine, I promise... But speaking of his royal highness, I thought Xolani was going to see me off."

"You know Lani hates to be called that." Raine says, "He and Rashid got pulled away to discuss more reports of rebels blocking shipments. However, he did send his love."

"I understand," She replies, "heavy is the head that wears the crown." Miss Lupita looks around and then says, "Wait, where is Niya?"

Raine scans over the enormous area before saying, "Actually, I'm not sure where she might be. She knows you're leaving, I can't imagine why she isn't here."

Keon replies, "She said her head was hurting, when we came up and turned back to her room".

"Oh," Raine says but is quickly interrupted by a voice yelling from across the huge circular surface,

"I'm here!" They all turn in that direction to see Gibbon's lanky frame running from inside the Tree Palace toward them. Once he's near them he pants out, "I'm sorry," as he bends over to catch his breath, "took longer than expected to get clearance for take-off."

"Clearance?" Miss Lupita says, "Raine, is that why you insisted on meeting here? I said not to make a fuss. I'm happy to walk back to Port Ambit."

"Nonsense," Raine says, "It would take you months to get back there. With the Skyways, you'll be there in a few hours. And Gibbon doesn't mind."

"It's no trouble, Miss Lupita," Gibbon says, "I'll use any reason to fly."

Miss Lupita thinks for a moment and then says, "Well I guess, but Port Ambit is a rustic seaport, stuck in more traditional ways. They don't take kindly to any modern technology." She points a finger at Gibbon, "You'll need to drop me off far outside of town."

Gibbon tightens up and stands at attention as he says, "Yes sir... Ma'am." Keon giggles before Miss Lupita says,

"I was hoping to see Niya before I left, she has been seeming a little off lately."

"I agree, but I'm sure she is just homesick," Raine says.

"I'm sure you're right." Says Miss Lupita. She then takes Gibbon by the arm and says, "After you, my good sir."

They both walk off to a black sedan. Raine and Keon watch as Gibbon opens the door for her and then hops over to the driver's side. The car's engine begins to hum as they stand and observe. It starts to levitate before the wheels fold under themselves. Keon and Raine watch it as it continues to rise high into the sky and take off, leaving a small jet trail in its wake.

"I BELIEVE WE ARE ALMOST near Port Ambit," Gibbon says. Miss Lupita smiles and replies simply,

"Good, there is a forest just before we get to there. You can land on this side of the forest edge, and I will walk the rest of the way."

Gibbon clears his throat before saying, "I can't just leave you, why don't I just fly to the border of the town and come with you?"

"I appreciate the gesture, Gibbon," Miss Lupita says in a sweet voice, "but I'm not sure yet how long I'm staying. Also, technology is not welcomed in Port Ambit, and after being in that stuffy Tree Palace, I could use some time to myself, no offense."

Gibbon attempts to keep his facial expressions neutral as he says, "None taken, I guess. But what if there are bandits or robbers in the forest?"

"I guess it's a good thing I'm not carrying any money," she jokes.

"Seriously, someone your—" Gibbon starts to say but stops as she gives him a strong glare and asks,

"Someone your... what?" Gibbon quickly looks over the dash, points, and says,

"Oh look, we're here." Miss Lupita gives Gibbon a sideways glance before their landing. He toggles several switches before the car begins to hover. He eases the steering wheel back to gently lower the car down. It lands with a soft thud and Miss Lupita quickly unbuckles herself. Gibbon reaches into the center consul and pulls out a small metallic circle. He extends it to Miss Lupita and says,

"I'm staying here for about an hour. But even after I've left, if you press this button I will return."

"Gibbon," Miss Lupita says before he stops her and says,

"I know you won't need to but it will give me peace of mind. Okay?"

"Okay," she says and places it in her pocket. She leans in and hugs him tightly. Gibbon stands and watches her as she fades into the forest.

———◉———

MISS LUPITA STROLLS with a smile on her face as she is serenaded by birds chirping and the faint sound of small critters frolicking on the forest floor. A small breeze warms her face as she moves along. The sun peaks through the canopy, touching her every so often.

"Stop!", she hears a voice shout in the distance, "You have no right."

Miss Lupita with her head up and alert, she hurries toward the voices to find a young boy being held by two goons, one oddly pudgy and the other comically tall and lanky. While another somewhere physically between the two, stands off to the side counting coins from a bag.

"That's my money Shade!" the boy shouts.

"Not any more," Shade says as he continues to riffle through the brown bag, "think of it as a donation."

"Enough!" Miss Lupita yells, "Unhand the boy and give him back his money."

The three of them frown in confusion before bursting into laughter. The tall and lanky one says,

"Listen here you crotchety old hag, you better mind your business before we mind it for you."

Miss Lupita approaches them with ease while saying, "I will give you all the money in my purse if any if you can lay a hand on me."

Their eyes widen before Shade, their leader says, "All right," and gives the other two a look to signal to unhand the boy as he continues, "we don't mind hitting a geriatric."

Miss Lupita bends down and picks up a twig. "We will see," she says as the twig grows and stretches into a bow staff.

The overly pudgy one yells as he charges at Miss Lupita but is swiftly met with a whack to the head with her staff. Shade runs toward her but she quickly knocks the wind out of him as she connects the staff painfully to his stomach. She swirls the staff to throw him off as he tries to pivot past her defenses. She trips him as she gracefully slides the staff through his legs. He lands face-first onto the forest floor. He moves to get up but Miss Lupita slaps the staff against his back. Forcing him back down every time he tries to get up. Tall and lanky goes to catch Miss Lupita off guard and starts to wrap his arms around her. She pulls the staff and forces it into his sternum. He quickly falls as he grabs his chest. She turns to the pudgy one, who throws his hands up and runs over to some nearby horses. He stumbles onto the horse and then gallops away through the forest. The sound of the leader grunting catches her attention. She goes to face him and says,

"Give him his money back" His lips purse together as he stares at her. Miss Lupita swings the staff to point it inches from his face, "Now!"

Shade reaches into his pocket and flings the bag at the boy. "You don't know who we are?"

"Nor do I care," Miss Lupita fires back, "now go before I beat you like your father should have."

He stares at Miss Lupita as he limps up and walks over to the other goon that's still holding his chest, "Come on idiot, let's go." They both manage to hobble over to the remaining two horses and clumsily climb onto them and gallop away. Miss Lupita watches them leave until she feels a tug at her side,

"Thank you, miss?" the boy says. Miss Lupita can't help but notice his unusually pale skin and skinny frame for such a young teenager before she replies with a smile,

"Miss Lupita." He returns her smile with one of his own. He runs his hands through his messy black hair in an attempt to fix it. Then says,

"Hi Miss Lupita, I'm Yosé."

"Hello Yosé, it's nice to meet you. Are you okay, did they hurt you?"

"I'm okay," he says with a smile before continuing, "I really hate those three."

Miss Lupita looks at him and says, "It doesn't seem like they make it easy to love them, do they?"

"No," Yosé replies quickly. Miss Lupita returns her bow staff into a twig and places it back on the forest floor, then says,

"I'm heading into town if you'd like to walk together."

"That's okay," Yosé says, "I was heading home. I'm sure my dad is wondering where I am."

"Well," Miss Lupita says, "you shouldn't keep him waiting then. It was a pleasure meeting you Yosé, and may our paths cross again." She sticks out her hand as Yosé does the same. They shake hands and go their separate ways.

Miss Lupita continues onward as the air's familiar forest scent changes to a crisp salty breeze. And with that hint of being closer, she picks up her pace toward the town. Miss Lupita ascends a hill to see the beautiful vista displaying the town of Port Ambit overlooking the sea.

She winds through the town peacefully, smiling at the kids running through the streets as they kick a ball to one another. She waves to the sailors getting their ships ready for a day of kelp harvesting at sea.

But just as she sees Jo's familiar dark blue sign, Miss Lupita hears a commotion just around the bend.

She rounds the corner and sees a gaggle of people standing around a few others. In the middle stands a tall beautiful dark-skinned woman with long purple locs braided into a single strand flowing over her shoulder. Miss Lupita inches closer to get a better view as she whispers to herself,

"*Jo... wait, is that the...*" she sees Jo's hands pointing furiously at the same goons that Miss Lupita sent packing, only hours ago.

"Jo!" She yells over the crowd but Jo doesn't hear her. She yells again, however, Jo is too involved with the goon in front of her.

"This whole phase you're going through was cute at first. But this town is sick of your thuggish attitude, and trying to extort money from us!" Jo shouts, "So get back on your horses and ride, until you're ready to act more civilized, Wacoby"

"My name is Shade and you best remember that Josephi... Jo," he says catching a stern look from Jo. "We are the Ambit Triad and if you don't want nothing to happen to your little watering hole, you'll give me what we want, or else."

"Or else what?" Jo says with a smirk. Shade takes a step back and says,

"Boys," before raising his hand above his head and snapping his finger. His companions from earlier, stand beside him and rush forward to grab Jo's arms, holding her in place.

Miss Lupita sprints forward but quickly stops when Jo lets out an enormous laugh and pulls her arms together causing them to collide into one another. They let go. She then swiftly turns low with her leg extended, knocking their legs from under them. They fall flat with a loud groan.

"Idiots!" Shade says before he sees Jo open to attack. He quickly leaps onto her. Sliding his arm around her neck, he places her into a chokehold. She instinctively grabs his arm and pulls to free herself. To no avail, she can't seem to break from his grasp.

"Uaf!" Shade says as his grip loosens and grabs his head in pain. Jo gives him a well-placed elbow to the stomach. Causing him to fall to his knees.

"Lupita!" Jo says as she sees Miss Lupita standing there with a staff in hand. They hug tightly before hearing Shade mumble,

"Krikes, not you again."

"I see you didn't learn anything from earlier," Miss Lupita replies. Jo with a wrinkled brow asks,

"You know him?"

"Not really," she answers, "but I did give him and his boys a free lesson in manners earlier. Oh, did you get my sparrow?" Jo just laughs at the question before replying,

"I did. Those odd-acting horses are fine, however, this conversation will have to wait. I need to give them a refresher on the course you gave them earlier."

"Who do you think you're talking to?" Shade says as he worms away, still holding his stomach, "We are the Ambit Triad and you will give us what we want!"

Jo simply rolls her eyes and says to Miss Lupita,

"See what I mean?"

"Ya, I know," Miss Lupita says, "I thought they learned their lesson."

"Listen here, granny!" Shade shouts.

"Is that the best insult you have, kid?" Miss Lupita asks. He stomps his feet and shouts,

"I'm not a kid, grandma!" Jo and Miss Lupita laugh hysterically.

"Enough! This has gone on long enough," Shade shouts but they continue to laugh as he pulls out a small flat black circle. It begins to display tiny little silhouettes of people before he presses a button on the side and they all disappear back into the circle. Shade places the device into his pocket and says, "You'll be sorry now."

Miss Lupita and Jo start to settle down as they notice all the surrounding shadows getting longer and reaching toward them. They look at Shade, who is smiling maliciously with his arms stretched out wide. Jo and Miss Lupita take defensive stances as they watch black humanoid figures begin to morph from out of the shadows. Shade's goons join behind their leader as they move slowly toward Miss Lupita and Jo.

Miss Lupita and Jo stand firm in their positions as the black figures emerge from the darkness and burst into these incredibly small white clones of Shade. They both erupt into laughter again.

"Get them!" Shade commands and his little clones make their way toward Jo and Miss Lupita.

Jo begins to step on them. Miss Lupita follows suit. They keep stomping, but the barrage doesn't end. They soon find themselves almost completely covered.

"Guess this wasn't that funny, huh?" Jo says chuckling to Miss Lupita, who replies,

"It's still a little funny. Perhaps we should stop playing around now?" Jo nods in agreement. Jo begins to spin, causing the little clones to fly off violently. They splatter as they hit the cobblestone street and the nearby crowd who move frantically to avoid the little critters. Miss Lupita simply shakes and watches them fall as they spatter on the ground. "I think you may need to work on your gifts a little longer Wacoby," Miss Lupita says.

"My name is Shade!" he says through gritted teeth. But then feels the familiar sting of Miss Lupita's staff as she swiftly knocks him in the head. He grabs his head and yelps as Jo grabs him by the collar and says,

"Enough is enough. I think it's time you and your motley crew find a new place to play before you really make us mad"

He squirms as she holds him there. He looks back for help but quickly sees the other goons have long left his side. Jo then drops him back to the ground. He briefly looks at Jo, then at Miss Lupita, who says softly,

"I don't know you but, you are better than this." Shade looks up with his head down. He starts to speak but his chin quivers. And without a word he gets up and runs away.

They watch him for a moment before turning to one another. Jo then says,

"Come, let's head into my place." Jo leads the way as they walk through the dispersing crowd and into Jo's Tavern. She stops at the first table, only to pull out a chair for Miss Lupita. She then takes a seat beside her and says, "Thanks for your help."

"Like you needed it, but you're welcome," Miss Lupita replies with a smile. "I didn't see Fransisco or Francine tied up outside."

"You wouldn't," Jo jokes, "they're out back so no one would mess with them."

"No one's hurt them, have they?" Miss Lupita asks.

"No, no," Jo says as she stands, "they're just a little odd and thought it might be best to keep them out of sight." Miss Lupita stands to follow Jo through the bar and out to the backside of the tavern. Once outside, Jo stops and says, "See what I mean?"

They stand for a second observing Fransisco and Francine. Two beautiful golden brown stallions with long blond manes lay on their sides, doing their best to swim through the weeds and sand. Miss Lupita chuckles and says,

"That's not odd, it's just their nature."

"That is not in a horse's nature to do that," Jo says as she points in Francine and Fransisco's direction.

"But fish do," Miss Lupita replies,

"Lupita," Jo says in disbelief, "You can't be serious, those are not fish."

"They are, or at least they were. I didn't mention it in my letter but they were fish that were nice enough to help me and the kids on our previous journey. I'm here to make good on my promise and take them home."

"Home, being?" she asks.

"A stream back in the Aberrant territory," Miss Lupita says with a coy smile.

"The Aberrant Territory?" Jo says in amazement, "I know you like to rough it, but I think that's a little extreme."

"It's actually quite peaceful."

"I bet," Jo replies with a sarcastic tone before being interrupted by Francine and Fransisco, who have noticed Miss Lupita and have barged in between them to start nuzzling her. "I think they missed you."

"Perhaps a little." Miss Lupita says smiling. Jo watches for a second before asking,

"How long are you staying?"

"Well," Miss Lupita says as she thinks, "I shouldn't make these two wait any longer. Because I'm sure they would like to return to their homes as soon as possible... But I am happy to return for a visit once I have completed that task."

"I would like that," Jo says, "can I at least offer you a room for the night?"

"I appreciate that Jo," Miss Lupita says, "but I have a small cottage there and it shouldn't take me more than a few hours to get there."

"Good" Jo says. Miss Lupita replies,

"Hey do you still have some of those old relics up in the attic?"

"Of course, why?" Jo asks.

"I'd like to look through them if you don't mind."

"Of course. I'll make sure to take them down before you return."

"Also, will you help me get Francisco and Francine ready, please?" Miss Lupita asks. Jo nods and they begin packing some small assortment of supplies and placing them on the satchels of Francine and Fransisco.

They lead them through and out of the tavern. Miss Lupita and Jo hug quickly before Miss Lupita hops onto Francine's back and gently nudges her to go. Francisco feels the tug on his harness as Miss Lupita pulls him along beside her. Jo looks on for a moment before heading back into the tavern.

MISS LUPITA TROTS PEACEFULLY as she makes her way back out of town. She finds her way back into the forest. The sun beams through the cracks of the leafy canopy. With its vibrant colors of oranges, greens, yellows, and reds dancing through the trees. Miss Lupita continues onward, enjoying the scenery until she sees Yosé resting at the bottom of a tree.

She dismounts and walks Francine and Fransisco over to Yosé. The back of Yosé's head rests on the tree as a beam of light shines on his face. His eyes remain closed as Miss Lupita approaches and says,

"Yosé?" He opens an eye to glance at her. "I thought you went to check on your father, why are you out here all by yourself?"

Yosé stretches his arms wide as he lets out a long yawn. Rising to his feet he makes steady eye contact with Miss Lupita's gaze. His somehow comforting large pupils catch her attention as he says,

"You were so kind to help me before. I didn't want to just let you leave without giving you something for your trouble."

He stretches out his hand. Miss Lupita is shocked as she sees the bag he's holding is almost as big as her head. She smiles and says,

"Thank you Yosé for your generous offer, but I didn't help you for a reward. It was the right thing to do." Yosé laughs to himself and says,
"He said you'd say that but I needed to offer it to you anyhow."
Miss Lupita stands with narrowed eyes for a moment before asking, "Who said I'd say that?"
"My father," Yosé says before clearing his throat and continuing, "I can't really explain right now, but know a debt is always paid. Miss Lupita, and I will be sure to keep an eye on you."
Miss Lupita puts her hand to her lip before asking, "Are you okay, Yosé?" He laughs again and says,
"Yes, I'm fine. Well, almost. Since you won't take my gift, I will have to find another way to repay you." Miss Lupita scratches her head as he continues, "I'll be seeing you, Miss Lupita."
Yosé begins to twist until his body is a blur of a vortex and tiny little particles begin to fly and dissipate into the ground. Miss Lupita stands there in awe, not really knowing what to say or do as the particulars disappear into the earth.
"Fascinating," she whispers to herself before turning to Fransisco and saying, "you don't think he was a... Naw you're right. Why even worry about it?" She shrugs her shoulders and hops onto Fransisco before motioning him forward and nudging Francine with her harness.

THEY ARRIVE BACK TO Miss Lupita's little cottage in the Aberrant Territory. She shuffles off Fransisco and removes his and Francine's satchels. They both begin to jump and neigh excitedly as they prance through the flowing stream.
"Hold on," Miss Lupita says kindly, "I can't return you to your original state until you settle down." She smiles as they nuzzle her and lick her face. "Let's get close to the stream," she adds.

They move close and she touches them on their manes, after a second of Miss Lupita focusing, Francine and Fransisco begin to morph. Their legs grow shorter as their bodies shrink. Fins and gills sprout from various places as their horse bodies begin to resemble fish. They flay about in Miss Lupita's hands as she places them into the flowing stream. They swim in circles as they seemingly dance within the water.

Miss Lupita smiles as she watches them enjoy their home. She breathes triumphantly before turning to look at her cottage. She begins to walk toward it before catching something moving in a nearby bush. She crutches down and says softly,

"Don't be scared little one. You're safe with me." A small black and white dog-like animal cautiously peaks its head out. "that's it," Miss Lupita says as it continues to slowly find its way out. It wanders over to her and she picks it up gently and says,

"Now aren't you the sweetest little thing," she strokes it on the head and down its back as she makes her way into the house and says, "I bet you're looking for a good home, aren't you? And I know the perfect place."

Chapter 5:
He's Back

Xolani's body falls through the darkness. His limbs move helplessly through the air, his heart pounds in his ears. He feels the force of his frame falling faster and faster. His muscles tighten, anticipating his final moments. Then with a violent shake, he's frozen in place. Unable to move. An intense tightening grips his chest. His lungs hunger for air as it becomes increasingly difficult to breathe. Xolani yells in silent agony, with breathless sounds leaving his lips.

"Your time draws near Xolani," a dark voice echoes in the blank void. Xolani's body drops to the ground suddenly. He gasps for air, resting his hands on his knees. His breath, shallow at first but deepens as he takes a few long and deep breaths before standing.

"Who are you?" Xolani demands authoritatively.

"Come now, you haven't forgotten me this soon." The sound of the dark voice slithers through the air as it continues, "It wasn't but mere months ago that you killed me for the second time."

"Xaden?" Xolani ask before yelling, "Enough with the games. Show yourself."

"You can't see me?" Xaden laughs, "Maybe that's because you're not looking hard enough!"

Xolani does his best to angle his body defensively but it's too late, a shock of pain runs through his side, causing him to lose focus. Fighting through his body's breathlessness, he clutches his side and places his free hand up in defense. Xolani tries to focus but feels off-balance, as though the room is spinning. Gathering himself he says,

"Xaden, I will not play your games this time around!"

"You won't?" Xaden says smiling, "But you already are."

Xolani suddenly feels the impact of a blow to his stomach and lets out a gasp of air. He hunches over, clutching his belly in pain. Dropping to his knee, Xolani fights to breathe. Struggling to stand, he feels the hurt radiate throughout his body. His fist glows like embers before igniting the dark void around him with fire. Xolani stands tall in the fiery glow of his fist before taking a defensive stance.

"Try that again," Xolani taunts.

"My pleasure," Xaden retorts as he steps into the flickering light. The red and orange hues from Xolani's flames wrap around Xaden's dingy and tattered white suit. The vibrant hues lessen as Xolani's hands wrap in flames and return to a bright glowing ember. Xaden dashes forward with a combination of kicks. The glow illuminates the fight as Xolani blocks each advance. The force of each kick radiates through Xolani's body. His feet anchor down as his arms begin to get heavy. He sidesteps, avoiding a Xaden's knee sweep. Xaden pounces forward, catching Xolani off balance. Xolani falls back as Xaden tackles him to the ground. They violently tussle before Xaden is engulfed in flames from a blast of fire from Xolani. Xaden flies back in agony as he screams and falls to the floor. Xolani works to catch his breath as he stands up. He watches Xaden roll in pain. Xaden's body flays about until it slowly ceases to move and fades away in a transparent cloud of smoke. Laughter rains throughout the void before Xaden says,

"That was fun, ready for round two?"

Xolani is swept up by a giant hand and smashed into a wall. The impact knocks the wind from Xolani's lungs. Xolani gasps to refill his lungs but the increasing pressure on his chest from the enormous hand prevents his chest from rising. The immense pain running over Xolani builds up until he screams out in pain. The slithery voice of Xaden rings in his ear, "No matter the place, no matter the time, no matter whom you pretend to be, you can't beat me Xolani."

Like a rag doll, Xolani is pounded repeatedly against the wall. His helpless body shakes furiously with each impact. He feels his body being lifted higher and higher. Until the force changes direction and his worn-out body flies full force back toward the wall. His heart pounding out of his chest as the wall gets closer and...

Chapter 6:

Time Flies

Xolani wakes in a panic on the floor. He quickly realizes it was just another dream. He notices the room violently shaking as Raine sits up and peers over the edge of the bed asking,

"Are you okay, what happened?"

"Must have been tossed out of bed by Niya's tremors," Xolani says as he makes his way off the floor.

"She's having another night terror, I'll get her," she says as she yawns and wipes the sleep from her eyes.

"I got it," Xolani says, "I'm already out of bed, you try to go back to sleep." He kisses her gently before wobbling over to grab his robe from the bedpost. Wrapping it around himself, he stumbles through their bedroom door and down the Tree Palace's shaking halls. The displayed works of art tremble with the wall's violent movements. His feet fight against the gold marble flooring as he makes his way down to Niya's room. Her screams of turmoil and anguish can be heard. Xolani nears her room but is slowed by an invisible force. He pushes through slowly as he reaches through the invisible barrier keeping him from the doorknob. He forces his way through the invisible barrier and into her room. Moonlight peaking through her bay window shows her innocent sleeping face as she squirms in torment, floating above her bed.

Xolani continuing to push through the force, places an arm underneath her as he gently lowers her back down onto her bed. He slowly moves to gently rub her cheek and wake her, as he's grown accustomed to doing over the past month. Niya's eyes slowly open before she says,

"Dad?"

"It's okay my star, you're safe now. Go back to sleep," Xolani says with a soft but tense voice.

"I did it again, I'm sorry. I don't know what's happening to me."

"You're okay. Back to sleep and we will talk more in the morning."

She closes her eyes while Xolani kisses her forehead. He begins to leave her room but takes a moment to watch her fall back asleep before closing her door slowly. He travels back through the halls toward his room but doesn't enter. He continues onward down the deep purple hall to a small balcony overlooking Nuhana. The city's tall canopy of mighty trees intermingled with massive skyscrapers, light up the vista with its neon-glowing fauna and flora.

Xolani stands watching multiple lanes of hover-cars whiz in the distance, through the city forest skyline before the gentle hand of Raine caresses his back. She leans against him and asks,

"How is she?"

"Same, screaming uncontrollably, and has no idea she's shaking this palace apart."

"I see," she says. Raine stands for a moment while rubbing her pants leg and crossing her arms. She does this a few times before looking into the night sky. Xolani takes notice of Raine's movements and says,

"You okay?"

"Of course, why do you ask?" Raine says, with a sudden fake smile. He laughs to himself before saying,

"You have that face."

"You mean, my face."

"Yes, that wonderful face," he says as he moves closer to Raine, "what's wrong?" She thinks of a witty retort but chooses to be vulnerable and says,

"I feel blessed to have someone that loves my children as much as you do but..."

"But," Xolani adds, "they are my kids too, you know."

"That's not how I meant it, forget it." She says with her lips pursing together. Xolani then nudges her playfully and says,

"Come now, what is it?"

"It's silly..." Raine says as she smooths down her regal robe, "I just wish she needed me like she needs you."

He smiles and hugs her tightly and says,

"It's not silly and she does need you. They both do. It's just different. I'm busy most days and she doesn't get to see me much but you, you are always there when she needs you."

Raine smiles and says,

"I didn't mean to make this moment about me. It's just my feelings, I guess. You always know how to put everyone at ease."

"Except myself," Mumbles Xolani.

"What do you mean?" She asks.

"Nothing, just tired." Xolani's says as he stretches his arms and pretends to yawn.

"Lani."

He turns to stare off into the vista and says,

"I had another dream about Xaden." She directs his face to hers and says softly,

"Your brother is dead, you can't keep letting him live rent-free in your mind."

"Trust me," he says, "if I could control my dreams, I would. But, it's almost as if he's still here, lurking behind the scenes somewhere."

"You saw him die."

"Wouldn't be the first time I saw him die, only for him to re-emerge like a virus and infect those we love."

"I know it's not easy to believe. Especially after what he put us through, but he's gone."

"Yeah," Xolani says with a sigh, "I just, in a weird way, miss the bond he and I used to have so long ago. We used to be thick as thieves. And when we would fight together in training, it's like we could read each other's minds."

"I get that," she says as she lays her head on his arm, "My sister and I used to have a similar bond before we left. And Xaden was your brother after all."

They both become silent for a moment as they bask in the moonlight and the orchestra of tree-top creatures singing in the distance.

"Xolani," Raine says, "maybe being here is too much for all of us." Xolani already knowing where this conversation is starting to go, remains silent as she continues, "I didn't want to bring this up-"

"But you will," Xolani says smiling,

"Being here seems to bring up a lot of painful memories for you. Keon seems homesick. I know I definitely am and Niya, well Niya isn't herself. Perhaps it's time we went back home?"

"Raine, we've been through this. We agreed to stay and rule. We can't just leave like we did before. Not with so much going on..."

"Yeah," Raine says with a long sigh as Xolani continues,

"The civil unrest, the rebels,"

"I know," She adds.

"U.R.A. questions, the Lumastar" Xolani says but Raine, surprised asks,

"Wait, why is the United Regime Assembly questioning anything here? They have no authority in Nuhana."

"They are stating since I left," Xolani says while pinching his nose, "and I renounced my royal name, I gave up any rights or claims to the throne."

"You already know they are a bunch of pompous old windbags that puff hot air at any old thing. Don't worry about them... But what's wrong with the Lumastar?"

"It's giving off some sort of radiation." He says, "Rashid and his team have been unable to fix or slow it down."

"What do you think?" Asks Raine.

"If it was up to me, I'd take it back to where we found the cursed thing. But again, so much else is going on I couldn't leave if I tried."

"Well, maybe a vacation is in order. We could visit my parents and sister. They still live just beyond the outer ring. It would be good for you, Niya, all of us to get out of here."

"Raine, I just said... I can't pick up and leave right now. And besides, Niya's fine."

"Fine?" Raine says with a raised voice.

"Not fine, but she's okay here. I believe her talks with Dr. Katear are going well."

"Lani, I don't think her speaking with a therapist again is the answer. Dr. Katear is great, particularly with what she's done for Keon but Niya's night terrors are getting stronger and she is getting worse." Raine says with concern.

"The night terrors are getting worse but she's getting better." Says Xolani, "Plus, we have Keon's Dynamism Day in a week. That we've already put off twice. It would be unfair to him to move his celebration again. And, I have a meeting with the U.R.A. and several other world leaders in the morning as well, to discuss foreign policies and aid relief to help the people of Nuhana. Hopefully, they will help put an end to the civil issues that have been plaguing the city. So, let's make it through this week and I'm sure I can find the time to break away."

Raine gives him a stern look of disapproval and Xolani adds, "I will look over my schedule today and find the time. Is that better?"

"Yes," she says with a smile before kissing him, "now, let's go back to bed and try to get some rest."

"I don't think it's rest we will be getting," he says as he pulls her close and kisses her passionately. Soon they are interrupted by the growing sound of Rashid's footsteps. Xolani lets out an audible sigh as Rashid appears distressed and out of breath.

"Sire, Sire," Rashid pants out. "I've been looking all over for you. Hello Raine."

"Rashid, how's the cure for the Mother Tree coming along? And for the thousandth time, please don't call me 'sire' or 'king' in private. It's just us."

"But you are the king. Your majesty," Xolani rolls his eyes, while Rashid looks at Raine and winks after saying, "He really loves it when I call him that. And yes, we have been able to isolate various compound combinations that have given some promising results in our initial trials."

"Good," Xolani replies, "it's great to hear you and your team are making headway on the damage to the Mother Tree. Outside of losing this palace, I don't think our country could withstand losing its connection to her. I'm glad you'll be able to heal her and fix what my father has done."

"Thank you Xolani, but that's not why I've come to find you."

"What is it?" Xolani says,

"The Lumastar was shaken out of its containment."

"Its radiation hasn't gotten worse, has it?" Xolani asks.

"No, we don't believe it to be."

"If it's radiation hasn't gotten worse, then put it back into its containment."

"It's just... It's gone dark." Says Rashid with shrugged shoulders.

"Dark? What do you mean dark?"

"I think you should take a look." Xolani looks to Raine as she returns his gaze. They both quickly follow behind Rashid as he makes his way through the deep purple halls. He snakes left down a corridor, then right. They follow him down a flight of stairs to a pair of steel doors. Rashid pushes through them and they make their way past glass beakers resting on lit burners. Every few steps is a rack of test tubes with various colored serums. They make it to the back of the room where a black door with a keypad resides. Rashid begins to use the keypad when he stops suddenly,

"Uh, could you please turn around?"

"Are you serious? Rashid, I'm the," he's stopped by a nudge in the ribs by Raine. Xolani rolls his eyes and turns reluctantly. Rashid looks to Raine, who remembers she needs to turn around too. He continues and the pad beeps with each press. A gush of air can be heard as Rashid punches in the last code and the door pops open. He holds the door and motions for Raine and Xolani to enter first.

They enter the sterile room with its blinding fluorescent lights bouncing off white walls and the absurd number of white coats huddled and crutched together in the middle of the room. Xolani loudly clears his throat and a few of the scientists peek over the shoulders of the others. They immediately move to address Xolani and Raine.

"Sire, Lady Raine, we were not expecting you."

"I noticed," Xolani says with a stern voice, "what's happening with the Lumastar?"

"Nothing to worry about Sire," a balding old man says. The man nudges his circle—framed glasses further up his nose as he continues, "We told Rashid, he was overreacting and not to bother you. It could easily have waited until the morning."

"I've placed Rashid in charge. So his authority is like my own. If he saw fit that I needed to be called, then you should listen." Xolani pauses for a second before narrowing his gaze toward the others still huddled over the Lumastar, "You too!" They all snap to attention as Xolani continues, "Now, what is going on with the Lumastar?"

Rashid steps forward and makes his way to the poly-angled star resting on a square pedestal. "It's like I mentioned before, the star has gone dark. We hypothesis that the actions of the previous King, King Xerxes, trying to harness the Lumastar's energy, contaminated the lightning within the Lumastar with the same virus that was infecting the Mother Tree. Causing the lightning that was rampant within to become a flicker of embers."

Xolani and Raine move in closer to examine the Lumastar before Xolani asks, "I don't agree with King Xerxes's methods, but I understand him trying to provide an alternative power source to the people of Nuhana. What does the Lumastar, as you put it, going dark, mean?"

A short woman with a peachy-fair complexion steps forward as she speaks. "Our first hypothesis was that the Lumastar was simply getting weaker."

"King Xolani, this is Lead Scientist Marsella Obi." Xolani looks to Rashid and asks,

"Your life partner?" Rashid smiles from ear to ear and quickly says, "Yes, she officially joined the team yesterday."

"We have heard great things about you. Marsella. I haven't been able to step away from my duties to properly greet you. I must make it up to you both, but please, continue."

"Of course, your majesty." Rashid holds in a laugh as Xolani cuts him a look while she continues, "Because we thought the Lumastar was getting weaker, we ran tests to find its electron count, however, the Lumastar's energy level is still the same from its initial testing upon its arrival to the lab. And all of our tests conclude that it still has enough condensed energy to level Nuhana or worse."

"Which is why something so powerful, that can level a major city, is merely resting on a stool?" Xolani says as he motions toward the Lumastar.

"I can see how that looks sire," Marsella says, "but it's freed itself from every container or confinement we've placed it in. That's the only place it will stay still." She moves to grab a chart from a nearby table and presents it to Xolani and Raine. Raine takes hold of the chart as Xolani peeks over her shoulder. "We have also made sure to detect and possibly identify any radioactive materials and/or ionizing radiation coming from the Lumastar."

"We were under the impression its radiation is harmless," Raine says.

"At its current levels, yes." Marsella says, "But, as you can see from the chart, we've tracked the Lumastar's levels and they are slightly increasing since its arrival a month ago."

Xolani steps back as he nods slowly and says, "Increasing how slightly?"

"It was recorded that the Lumastar was giving off about 3.27 Millirems and currently, it is giving off more or less 8.29 Millirems of radiation. That's a 5.02 gain in a very short amount of time. However, the radiation is at safe levels but if it keeps increasing at this rate, it will reach a point of no return and... go critical." Raine steps forward and says, "I wonder if... You don't think it misses home, do you?" With a raised brow Xolani says,

"I don't follow."

"Remember what Malkum said." Raine states

"Who's Malkum?" Marsella asks. Rashid then says,

"This real prick of an angel that is half demon. Or maybe the demon is half angel..."

"Rashid," Xolani exclaims.

"Right, either way, he's the guy we got the Lumastar from."

"Thanks, Rashid," Raine says before continuing, "Malkum, said the Lumastar is a living creature. So maybe it's just lonely and wants to go back to where it came from?"

"Possibly," Xolani says and then turns, "Marsella, your background is trans-species biology, correct?"

"That is correct your majesty."

"I want you to keep monitoring the radiation of the Lumastar and to start looking at it as a living creature. I know you arrived only yesterday but find out why the Lumastar's radiation is increasing and report your findings to Rashid by the end of today." Marsella bows her head in agreement before he continues. "You all are doing great work and I know you will figure it out. Rashid, follow me please." Raine turns with Xolani as he exits, with Rashid closely behind them. Once they leave the lab Xolani faces Rashid and says,

"I see why you came and got me. If there are any more issues, get me immediately."

"Yeah sure Lani,... was that it? You could have said that in the room."

"I wanted to ask, are you sure you enjoy being in the lab? I really could use you in the throne room, helping me with the council."

"I appreciate the offer your majesty," Rashid bows in jest and continues speaking as Xolani playfully elbows Rashid in the ribs, "I mean I love researching but after being in the royal records for years under your father's rule, reading dusty manuscript after manuscript, I would rather get back to my first love."

"Science or Marsella?" Xolani asks jokingly. Rashid smiles as he says,

"Probably more so Marsella"

"I understand." Xolani says, "But if I may say, it's not easy working with your spouse."

Raine nudges Xolani and says, "What is that supposed to mean?"

Xolani smiles at her and says, "Nothing," as he gives Rashid a telling look and then continues, "Just do me a favor and don't set your eyebrows on fire again, okay?"

"Everyone has to learn. And they grew back just fine, didn't they Raine?"

"I'm just going to go over here." Raine says as she walks away.

"You don't have to answer, I know my brows are sexy." Xolani pats him on the back before saying,

"Sorry pal, the left one grew back a little crooked." Xolani exits with Raine by his side as Rashid stands there rubbing his left eyebrow.

Chapter 7:

More than meets the eye

Arrows violently slam into a concrete wall. Niya glances behind her at the arrow's new home, refocuses, and yells before twirling her spear toward Keon. He reaches into his quiver and pulls out several arrows before firing them directly at Niya. One by one, she easily knocks them out of her path until she's in striking distance.

Shifting her weight to the balls of her feet, Niya leaps forward to bring the full force of the spear's staff on top of Keon. But he dodges to her right. The air flows around his young fist as it grows in volume to surprise Niya with a direct punch to her stomach.

She expels a gasp of air as she stumbles back to recover. Her body is numb with pain as she struggles to breathe. Keon sprints to tackle her. Niya catches him inches before he wraps his arms around her. She grabs his wrist and tosses him over her hip. Keon tumbles through the air but regains his footing by decreasing in size. Landing on the ground, he quickly grows back to size before launching himself toward Niya. They grapple for a moment to break free from each other's grasp. They begin to trade punches for kicks, kicks for punches while blocking each other's best blows.

Niya reactions begin to slow, not from a lack of fatigue but more so from a delayed response of some sort of internal conflict. Keon sees an opportunity and lands a push kick into her armor-plated chest. She staggers back but her eyes are filled with confusion. Keon sees her struggle and quickly places a single arrow between the two small sheaves and lets it lay into the rest. He takes in a breath. His fingers tighten around the handle's finger rings as he pulls back the rubber cable. He places Niya in his sight before exhaling as he fires. The arrow whistles through the air straight and true.

Keon's eyes grow large in surprise as the arrow stops moments away from Niya. She stands straight, looking at the arrow as it slowly spirals in the air. The arrow starts to turn back toward Keon while she tilts her head to one side.

"My turn," she says with a smirk. The arrow darts forward. Keon cartwheels out of its trajectory. The arrow scrapes his cheek, stinging his face, speed past him and impale the wall behind him. Keon stands and proclaims, "Playtime is over Sis, you're going down." He grips the rings of the handle and pulls to produce a pair of taser brass knuckles. Niya chuckles,

"Sure I am, bighead."

"I'll show you a bighead," Keon screams as his body, clothes, and weapons grow four times their original size to dwarf Niya. She takes a step back as Keon towers over her. His clothes, stretch as they work to keep up with his growing size before his gigantic hand swipes the floor to grab her. She leaps forward, sending a swift kick to Keon's jaw before bouncing back and landing softly. His deep laugh echoes through the room as he says,

"That tickled." He goes to grab Niya again. She vanishes to reappear on Keon's shoulders before moving to give a quick kick to his ear. She suddenly finds herself falling back to the floor as Keon's body shrinks until he disappears. She vanishes mid-fall to gracefully reappear on the floor.

"I know you're still here Keon, I can hear your thoughts" she says. Keon springs up in front of her and quickly replies,

"That's cheating Niya! You're not supposed to do that!"

"Fooled ya!" She shouts and gives him a barrage of kicks. Keon puts his hands up in defense. He blocks kick after kick, until he sees an opening and grabs Niya's foot and twirls her backward. He grows rapidly to continue his assault. Pivoting around her to engulf her in both his now enormous hands. Soon he feels a force pushing against his hands. He fights to keep his hands together until the force is too great and they explode apart. Niya floats eye level to Keon and he begins to gasp for air as she extends her hands, using her telekinesis to strangle him.

"That's enough," a soft voice announces overhead. But Keon continues to struggle for air while shrinking back to his normal size. "Niya!" The voice echoes through the intercom system.

Keon's hands clasp at his neck as he struggles. Niya looks on with cold eyes as Keon falls to his knees. Like a hunter observing their prey, Niya slowly walks over and towers over Keon. He reaches out to her but she ignores his pleas. She feels the weight of a hand fall on her shoulder as they whisper.

"Niya!"

She shutters and blinks furiously as the weight of the hand on her shoulder catches her attention. Keon takes in a huge audible breath.

"I-I-I don't know what happened," she says as she turns to see Kaleo, one of the King's five and their current fight instructor. His Polynesian accent shine through his hushed tone as he speaks,

"You lost control, again,"

His massive dark-tanned muscular skin was partially covered in tribal-inspired armor, and the rest, a beautiful display of tribal tattoos. He looks down with his hypnotic green eyes, extends his hand to Keon, and with a low voice asks,

"You okay?" Keon grabs Kaleo's hand and nods. Kaleo pulls him up and turns back to Niya. "What was the trigger this time?"

Niya stands silent with her head hanging down. Kaleo lets the moment linger, in hopes she will verbalize her inner struggle. She shifts her body weight to one leg before rubbing her arm and saying meekly,

"I'm not sure, I-I just remember Keon's large hands pressing against me and then nothing until feeling your hand on my shoulder."

"Interesting," Kaleo says softly to himself as he lifts his wrist and taps the screen of a purple band wrapped around it. The weapons Niya and Keon used begin to pixelate and vanish in a purplish haze. The walls around them follow suit to expose black panels aligning the walls, floor, and ceiling, exposing a wide double door with gold trim in the distance. "Everything in this room is simulated, well, except for us." He chuckles at his own joke, "Do you feel you were stressed little one?"

"I don't think so... Keon has had me in that move before because that's all he can do."

"That's not all I can do! I can also shrink and..." Keon protest but Niya interrupts him as she continues,

"I just meant I'm used to that kind of pressure."

"Both of you," Kaleo says gaining their attention, "you did very well today. It's good to see that fabric left over from your grandfather's collection was able to keep up with you growing abilities, and Niya. The next time you start to feel that way again, I want you to-" Kaleo stops mid-sentence. Straightening his posture as he notices Haygena entering the room. Her shoulders are back with her chin held high, as she walks toward them.

"Haygena!" the kids yell simultaneously as they run and hug their aunt. Kaleo stands serenely and in a low tone says,

"Is everything okay, Security Director Haygena?"

"Yes, I need to end the children's training for today, Kaleo. There is a guest dying to see the children." Keon quickly begins to bounce on his toes, with eyes that dance with curiosity and asks,

"Who is it?"

"You will see in a moment little one." Haygena says with an upturned face. Keon quickly grows taller than her and says,

"I'm not little,"

"Keon," Haygena says with the loving, playful authority of any good aunt. Keon shrinks back to his normal hight before Haygena looks to Niya. Niya's gaze seems to be wondering around the room before she notices Haygena staring. She fakes a smile and Haygena passes it off as preteen angst. She looks to Kaleo and says,

"I will take the kids. Return to your post with the rest of the King's Five."

Kaleo bows respectfully as he replies, "Yes my love."

"Ooooh!" Keon and Niya say as they begin to make kissy faces and sounds. She looks at them disapprovingly and says,

"Walk." They all begin to move forward before Kaleo touches Haygena's arm and says gently,

"Before we go, may I speak with you in private?"

"Of course. Niya, will you teleport yourself and Keon to the royal study? I will meet you there momentarily to take you to our guest."

"Yes," Niya says.

"Do not go anywhere else without me," Haygena says sternly.

"Yes," Niya says with a roll of her eyes. She snatches Keon's arm and then they vanish. Haygena shakes her head and says,

"What is it?"

Kaleo, unsure of the right words to say, finally says faintly, "I'm not sure how to tell the King but, something isn't right with Niya. She is getting more and more aggressive with Keon."

"No more than Keon's electrified brass knuckles, I'm sure." She says dismissively and continues, "I'm sure that's just sibling rivalry."

"It's more than that. I've noticed over the last few sessions she is using attacks that I haven't taught her... Life-threatening attacks."

"Did she do something today?" Haygena asks. Kaleo begins to rub the back of his neck and then says,

"She choked Keon with her mind and would stop until I intervened."

"Are you sure? Because it's possible she just got caught up in the moment of the training exercise."

"Haygena, you know my background and you know my gift is telling people's true intent. She was going to kill him."

"Come on Kaleo, that's her brother! Do you really think she would?" she retorts. He steps closer and with a low soothing tone says,

"Yes, I do. I know this isn't what any of us want to hear and unfortunately there is more."

"What?" Haygena says and then stares at him waiting for an explanation. He catches her stare and proceeds,

"During the exercise... her movements changed like they weren't her own. Almost as if she was acting or being controlled by someone else."

Haygena thinks for a moment. Her head in her hand. "Do not worry about telling the king. I will discuss it later this evening with him."

"Better you than me," Kaleo says with a coy smile.

"Well, he is my brother." She starts to leave when she feels Kaleo's hand on her wrist pulling her back. She turns to face him as he leans in to steal a kiss.

"There, you may go now," he jokes. Haygena smiles as she says,

"You should show more respect to your superior officers."

"I do. That's why I did it," he says with a smirk. Haygena rolls her eyes and casually begins to leave. "Don't forget to go report...actually, follow me."

"Yes Sir," Kaleo replies before proceeding closely behind her out of the room.

Chapter 8:

Meeting of the Minds

Xolani hurries through the corridor, rushing past various members of the royal staff. He pivots and dodges as he nearly misses those in the hall casually walking to their destination. All the while saying excuse and, pardon me as he makes his way through, before he turns a corner and bumps into Lady Neyma.

"You startled me," she says as her hand flies to her chest. Xolani tries to side step her as he says,

"My apologies Mother, I'm running..." But she blocks his path as she replies,

"A king never apologizes, my son."

"I was merely, you're right." He replies with a sigh, "Now if you will excuse me, I'm a tad late."

"Actually, I need to speak with you."

"Can this wait Mother? I have to go," Xolani begins to walk briskly as Lady Neyma hurries closely behind him.

"I promise this won't take long... You walk fast," she pants out.

"Mother, I told you. I am in a rush. I am heading to a council meeting with the United Regime Authority."

"Oh, that sounds serious. What do they want?"

"You know I can't tell you that."

"You can tell your mother anything Xalen." Clenching his jaw, Xolani says,

"It's Xolani now and certain matters of state I cannot discuss."

"I bet Raine knows."

"She is an advisor to the king and I am not having this conversation again."

"So, she does know," Lady Neyma says accusingly, before almost running into Xolani as he comes to a dead stop to face her. He rubs his brow as if warding off a headache while saying,

"This is not the time, nor the place, to question what I do or do not tell my wife, the queen, if you would like to wait, I can speak with you after my meeting Mother." She sinks her head as she looks down at the dark cherry wood floors.

"I-I, just missed so much of your life and I don't want to miss any more of it," she says tearfully. Xolani lets out a remorseful sigh before saying,

"I know, and I shouldn't have snapped. But please, I have important people waiting on me and I need to go. Okay?" Lady Neyma nods her head in understanding as she slowly replies,

"Okay."

"Good," Xolani says. He kisses her on the cheek, and starts to head down the corridor again. Lady Neyma follows behind and says,

"Xalen, I mean Xolani, I know you have to get to your meeting but, I've been planning an event for weeks and I want to make sure I tell you that I've invited everyone for a Grand Ball tonight." He stops again. His fingers release a cracking sound as he stretches them into a fist and says,

"What do you mean, you've invited ev-er-ry one, for a Ball tonight?"

"Well, I was thinking. You've been so stressed lately and this may also be a great way to help relations with our allies in a more social atmosphere." Xolani takes in a deep breath before saying through clinched teeth,

"Cancel the Ball and un-invite all the guests." Lady Neyma looks on with flushed cheeks and clears her throat before her words stammer out,

"I couldn't do that. How would that make us look?"

"I don't care!" He shouts then recomposes himself. People stare as he then says, "Cancel the Ball."

"But Xalen, it's tonight," she pleads. Xolani with nostrils flared says, "Cancel the Ball."

"I'm only thinking of you. We need to show the world we are still powerful and..."

"Who cares what the world thinks!" He snaps, "I am this close to losing my mind with meetings, policies, and keeping my family together, and you want to throw a Ball for show? Cancel it, and cancel it now!"

"Yes, your Highness," she says in a flat monotoned voice as she bows. She walks away staring down at her feet. Xolani, sees her and pinches the bridge of his nose, and sighs loudly before saying,

"Don't cancel the Ball, but tell Kasmine immediately what is happening tonight. And have the staff do whatever is needed to get the main hall ready. And Mother, this behavior is unacceptable. Things like this need to be cleared through me, and Kasmine well before they are finalized. Understand?"

"I'm not a child Xalen, um Xolani," she says. He sighs heavily before asking sarcastically,

"May I go to my meeting now?"

"Of course, you may. Don't be late," she says with a smirk as she hurries off. Xolani stands there for a moment shaking his head and mumbles to himself,

"I'm supposed to be the king."

He brushes off his thoughts and continues quickly down the hall. As he closes in on tall double doors, he hears delegates shouting over one another. He stands by the door listening for a second as he can already picture all the members of the United Regime Authority sitting proudly to one side of the round table shouting as various royal council members shout back. He takes in a few deep breaths and smiles as he opens the door to walk in and says,

"Thank you all for your patience. I appreciate you waiting. Shall we begin?"

Chapter 9:

Reunited

Carved out bookshelves line the wooden walls, from the marble polished floor to the high vaulted ceilings of the huge room. Staircases leading to second levels and beyond as the sun shines through a large far off circular window, with the Uwani royal family seal of a roaring lion. A few reading nooks are tucked in the corners as well as few amber plush couches and chairs.

Raine and Miss Lupita stand chatting about how the weeks have passed and what they've missed.

"It sounds as though you had quite an adventure, Miss Lupita. The Ambit Triad, I don't want to mess with them," Raine jokes before asking, "And how was our home?"

"Everything is fine," Miss Lupita replies, before pauses, then continues, "Well, your garden has seen better days."

"Yeah, I figured as much. Us being gone this long, it wouldn't surprise me if my little garden was a complete forest by this point. But we'll get back there soon. Lani and I just have to make sure Nuhana is thriving before we go."

"You mentioned that earlier. How is that going?"

"I can't mention too much but to be honest, not as well as I expected. I believe Lani is meeting with the United Regime Assembly now to discuss the affairs of civil unrest and several other things they feel like sticking their noses in. Um…, the kids are well, considering the torture Xaden put them and you through. Keon is seemingly very well. Niya, she is having some sort of night terrors that shake the Tree Palace violently."

"Do you think it is repressed trauma from Xaden? After all, she spent the longest time under his influence."

"Perhaps, but she won't talk about it, not to us, not to her therapist, no one."

"She's young and young people don't like to talk," Miss Lupita says, "they like you to beg them until it annoys the information out of them." She and Raine chuckle.

"That's very true, however, this is different. I can feel it. I'm just not sure what to do yet."

"What does Xolani think about it?"

"He's acknowledging something's wrong. I just feel he's downplaying what's going on with her. I've been trying to convince him that we all should return home but,"

"The responsibilities of the throne won't let him leave," Miss Lupita states and Raine nods in agreement. "That is a tough one, my dear. However, I wonder if,"

"Miss Lupita!" the kids shout as they burst through the library doors and into her arms. She embraces them tightly as smiles light up the room.

"I missed you both so much," she says with gentleness in her aged face. "I'm sorry it took so long. But I had a few challenges getting Francisco and Francine from Jo's Tavern."

"Refresh my memory, who were Francisco and Francine again?" Raine asks as she takes a seat in a plush chair by the corner.

"They were these two amazing horses that were helping us," Keon says enthusiastically, "actually they were really fish that Miss Lupita turned into horses for us."

Raine looks to Miss Lupita, who simply smiles back with a shrug.

"Children, it's been so long! What have I missed?" asks Miss Lupita.

"Nothing, it's so boring here. I'm ready to go home." Niya says then notices her mother's stare and quickly says, "I mean, it's not boring, I just miss my stuff from home."

"Well, I'm sure we can find something around here that would entertain you two. Let me see," Miss Lupita turns to reveal a long white box and a box that's covered with a black cloth. "For you Keon I have some books."

"Books?" Keon says with a mixture of disgust and disappointment.

"Yes, books," Miss Lupita replies, "but not just any books. These books are special. I believe they were called funny pages. They're about heroes with amazing abilities, fighting against all manners of evil." She knocks the lid off the white box and pulls out a colorful, thin book in a transparent protective cover. Keon's eyes light up with excitement as she begins to speak, "This one is Aceblade. He's a vigilante who wants to make the world a better place." She places it on the table and pulls out another, "We also have E.X.O: The Legend of Wade Williams, Luberjax, Harlem, or... how about, Konkret Comic's, Odina?"

"Wow," Keon shouts, "these are for me?"

"Of course, they are. The whole box," Miss Lupita replies, "Just be careful with them. They are quite old."

"Yes, Ma'am!" Keon dives for the box, slides it across to the other side of the table, and starts flipping through book after book. Haygena and Kaleo quietly walk into the room and stand next to Raine.

"And I have something for you as well my dear," Miss Lupita says with a big smile to Niya while motioning her closer, "This my dear, is a Sissykat."

Kaleo's eyes enlarge with worry as Miss Lupita pulls off the black cloth covering a beige box, revealing a cute but small and slightly older Canine. "You must be gentle, she has been around for quite some time." Niya's face begins to glow as a smile travels across her face.

"I love her!" Niya says while squeezing gently on the gray and white Canine. "What's a Sissykat?"

"She's like a companion that is there when you need her," Miss Lupita replies.

"She's perfect," Niya shouts, "can I keep her?"

"Of course, you can," Raine replies but is quickly questioned by Kaleo,

"Madam, no disrespect to you or Miss Lupita but is it wise to give a Sissykat to a child?"

"Oh, come now," Miss Lupita scuffs, "Sissykats are no more dangerous than a newborn baby goatpher."

"That may be," Kaleo says in his low tone, "but Sissykats have a history of attaching themselves to their owner's emotions and can become..."

"Go on Kaleo," Raine encourages before realizing what he might be implying and says, "I believe you may be right, but I understand they also stabilize emotions as well. Besides," Raine stands as she continues, "There's nothing wrong with a child having a companion, is there? Now what will you call her?"

Niya thinks for a second and says,

"Sissy."

"How original." Keon says under his breath.

"I think that's a beautiful name," Raine says before kissing Niya and Keon on their heads. But then like a streak of lightning she says, "I almost forgot I have a meeting. I will return shortly." Haygena and Kaleo walk to intercept Raine. Haygena says,

"Lady Raine,"

"We've been over this Haygena, you don't have to call me Lady Raine, we're family." Raine says.

"I know, I'm still getting used to our dynamic. But if you have a moment, Kaleo and I would like to have an official word with you."

"Oh my, an official word, sure. I was about to check in with Kasmine. She has been keeping me updated on Qarinah's rehabilitation but I'm sure she can wait a few moments."

"Yes," Haygena replies, "she'd mentioned you were keeping tabs on Qarinah's progress or the lack thereof. If I may ask, why?"

"Why? No real reason, I guess." Raine answers, "I didn't really know her before Lani, and I left Nuhana. I had only heard the stories Lani would tell me about her and Xaden. But even when she helped Xaden kidnap the kids and Miss Lupita, I can't help but feel her remorse. Like it's pulling on me. If that makes sense."

"Not really, but guess it doesn't need to" Haygena says. Raine begins to leave again before Kaleo says in a low tone as he rushes to intercept her,

"We would like to speak with you in private, your Highness," and bows politely. Miss Lupita notices and says,

"Um kids, I haven't gotten a tour of this lovely Tree Palace since the last time I was here and blew a hole in the outer ring wall." Miss Lupita laughs and continues, "How about we take your stuff to your rooms and you both show me around if that's okay with Lady Raine and Security Director Haygena?"

"I know the king and queen trust you but," Haygena states as she crosses her arms "I'm going to need...,"

"Lighten up Haygena," Raine says, cutting off Haygena in the process, as she playfully hits her on the shoulder, "Miss Lupita is family and is always welcome in our home. Wherever that may be"

"Thank you, Lady Raine," Miss Lupita says jokingly, "Come on children, let's go have some fun." Keon grabs the box and strains for a second while trying to lift it, but instinctively his body grows in mass, and he grabs the box with ease and heads for the door while Niya grabs the cage Sissy is in and follows behind him.

"Hold on," Raine snaps, "I think you both forgot something." Both the kids' faces instantly grow with disgust before walking over and kissing Raine on the cheek. "Much better, even if you act as if you don't love your mother." The kids roll their eyes after turning away from Raine,

"I saw that," She states. The kids hurry out of the room with Miss Lupita trailing behind them. "So, what is it you two would like to talk about?"

Kaleo steps forward saying softly,

"Niya."

Chapter 10:

What Happens Next

The mixed smell of strong perfumes and colognes, line the plain colored walls of the now empty boardroom. The air heavy from the weight of decisions made. Xolani sits in a plush chair with his arms leaning on the long wooden table and his head in his hand. Raine walks in with her body tilting in his direction. She asks.

"How'd it go?"

"Abysmal," He replies.

"I'm sure it wasn't that bad," she replies, only to have Xolani shoot her a sideways glance. She acknowledges the look with one of her own and proceeds. "You just got out of a meeting, but do you have a moment?" she says while leaning on the back of the chair closest to him.

"Of course, for you my moon, always. Wait, is this about Qarinah?"

"No, I delayed my meeting with Kasmine. However, I did just speak with Kaleo and Haygena. They brought up concerns about Niya," She pauses as if waiting for Xolani to interrupt but then keeps going. "Kaleo mentioned that during the kid's training, Niya has been growing increasingly aggressive. So much so he is starting to worry. He thinks Niya may be a danger to herself and others."

"I'm sure it's not that bad Raine," he replies and rises from the table. Raine straightens up before saying,

"Lani, we can't keep ignoring whatever is going on with her."

"I'm not ignoring anything," he says with an even tone, and a forcibly calm demeanor, "I know something is off with Niya but do I think she is a threat or dangerous, no. She's, my daughter. I think you and Kaleo are overanalyzing the situation." He begins to walk away but Raine follows him as she shouts,

"Overanalyzing! She is my daughter too Lani!"

"I know Raine."

"Then act like it!" she shouts as she wipes a tear from her eye. She then takes in a deep breath and says , "I understand the weight of Nuhana is on your shoulders right now, I really do, but this is our family. And I thought our family would always come first."

"Of course, our family comes first I just…" Xolani takes in a deep breath and exhales slow to calm himself before continuing, "Niya is one of my many top priorities. And each priority will get its time… The U.R.A. is threatening to put sanctions on our trade agreements if we don't get a handle on the civil unrest that has increased dramatically since I became king and intelligence tells me that rebels are planning to overthrow the monarchy, meaning at any moment, there may or may not be trained assassins coming to kill us. And what was the other thing… oh yeah, my mother decided it would be a great idea to throw a party with royals and dignitaries tonight. I think that may about cover it," He says with a touch of sarcasm. "So, at the moment, I'm sorry, Niya isn't the highest priority." Raine places a gentle hand on his as she says,

"Look, I know you are doing your best. Because that's who you are. And if we are both being honest, we never wanted this type of life. I can't say much on most of those issues but admittedly, the assassins are definitely a concern. However, regardless of any challenge, we will face it together." She pauses for a moment and then adds, "Could the solution be as simple as giving them a voice?"

"A voice to who?" He asks with a raised brow.

"The rebels"

"Okay, walk me through it please."

"I didn't grow up like you. I mean, we were okay with my parent's bookstore and community garden, but I can remember my Dad talking about how there were so many issues in the community going unheard. At that time, I don't think I fully understood what he was referring to."

"Raine respectfully, what's your point?"

"Why don't you appoint someone to be a representative for the rebels."

"It's not that easy my moon."

"If Malala Yousafzai can, so can you."

"Who?" Xolani says puzzled.

"Malala Yousafzai. Centuries ago, she was a human rights advocate for the education of women and children. At a time when girls were banned from attending school. She would often speak for those who couldn't or weren't being heard." Raine catches an unclear look from Xolani, "I'm sure if the rebels had a voice, a lot of the issues would go away."

"And how do I give them a voice?"

"You're the king right, make it happen," she says with a playful smile. Xolani cuts his eyes in her direction as her words linger in his mind.

"Thanks… We've tried negotiation talks before and have always met resistance. But I could try to have another meeting with the leaders of each community," Xolani states, "And possibly even a meeting with the rebels. Assuming they'll trust me enough to do so."

"See, I knew you'd think of something. You just needed the proper motivation."

"I just needed you," Xolani replies while he leans in for a kiss. Raine follows suit before Rashid bursts into the room with Marsella following closely behind.

"Why are you two always kissing when I'm near?" he jest,

"You're just lucky I guess," Xolani says, then asks, "How are things going with the Lumastar?"

"Well, your majesty," Marsella says, "the Lumastar's radiation levels have continued to increase, and based on the test we ran after you left, it appears that the Lumastar is going to go critical. The fallout from the blast radius will be unmeasurable."

"Also, sire," Rashid adds, "we are unable to tell when it will, well, Kaboom."

"And is that your scientific opinion Rashid? 'Kaboom'?" Raine says. Rashid replies with his face contorting to mock hers.

"Suggestions?" Xolani asks.

"We've looked into neutralizing the radiation but that too could cause a massive fallout," Marsella says.

"I have a plan but you're not going to like it," Rashid says with a boyish smile.

"This better not require having me jumping out of a perfectly good airplane again," Xolani replies.

"I can't say that won't happen, but hear me out," says Rashid, "Raine may have been on to something earlier when she said to take the Lumastar home. What if we take the Lumastar back to Malkum for him to return it back to its plane of existence?"

"Who's Malkum again?" asks Marsella.

"Long story, but Malkum is the fallen angel," Rashid says enthusiastically, "that shares a body with the lightning bird Kwane, the one who tried to kill us. But it wasn't his fault. He was under the control of Xolani's twin brother Xaden, whom I killed because he killed King Xerxes, the former King."

"Rashid," Raine nudges him.

"Right, but King Xerxes and Xaden were working together to get the Lumastar, to try and reverse the damage King Xerxes had done to the Mother Tree. But the Lumastar could only be brought to this plane through Malkum. He is probably the best person, creature... to know what to do about the Lumastar."

"Thanks for the unnecessary recap, Rashid," Xolani says, "But you make a good point. Perhaps taking the Lumastar back to Malkum is the best option."

"Agreed, but with respect your Highness, who should go?" Rashid asks. Xolani throws him a hard look before saying,

"The King's Five and I will go."

"Xolani," Rashid says, "As king, you can't go. There is too much at stake if you leave the throne. Plus, I don't really think you were one of Kwane's favorite people last time we were there."

"I believe you were the one it carried off, for a late-day snack?" Xolani jokes.

"Don't remind me," says Rashid.

"Raine," Xolani says, "you had a nice report with Malkum once we freed him."

"I'm not leaving Niya in her current condition, Xolani," she replies with folded arms. Xolani shakes his head slightly as he says,

"Raine, this is bigger than our family's issues. I don't want to…"

"Then don't." Raine snaps. Xolani pinches the bridge of his nose before saying,

"You are the logical choice."

"Lani, I am not going," Raine persists.

"You are," Xolani says, "with Haygena and Kaleo's support. You can be back before morning."

"Send them with Kasmine, Kacao, and Ramuth. Isn't that what the King's Five are for?" Raine says with a raised voice.

"You know I can't send all members of the King's Five for the same mission." He states.

"Fine, Gibbon was there," Raine retorts, "add him, or even Rashid here."

"Me?" Says Rashid with a gasp, "The last time I was there, the Kwane played with me like a razor dog's chew toy by clinching its disgustingly dirty talons in my shoulders, and dropping me several hundred feet." He rubs above his shoulders, "I still have scars by the way."

"I shouldn't need to explain but, Kasmine is the Security Chief and needs to remain here tonight for the ball," Xolani says as he stands, "Kacao and Ramuth have their duties and need to be here as well. And as far as Rashid and Gibbon are concerned, they will need to be liaisons at tonight's ball. These are people I can trust too..."

"You don't trust me?" Raine retorts.

"That's not what I meant," Xolani replies, "Why are you fighting me on this?"

"Lani, I'm not going," Raine says sternly.

"I'm done explaining." Xolani says, "Because this isn't up for debate Raine. You're going."

Rashid motions to Marsella as he begins to inch backward out of the room. He whispers, "I think we're going to go, while you both work this out."

"Stay!" Xolani commands, "There is nothing to work out. Raine is going with Haygena and Kaleo to return the Lumastar."

Raine looks at Xolani with eyes that water and says through clinched teeth, "As you wish your majesty," she then curtsies before heading towards the door. She turns slightly and without making direct eye contact with Xolani says, "Miss Lupita is back, I will take her with me, if the king doesn't mind. I need someone I can trust." And with a slam of the door, she exits.

Rashid and Marsella stand awkwardly, waiting for a break from the silence. Xolani returns to his seat and says in a low tone,

"I'm sure you two have things to prepare." Marsella and Rashid share a glance before Rashid motions for Marsella to go without him. She exits the room. Rashid watches her leave before saying,

"Lani, it's been a while since you and I have been able to just chat. Let's grab some java."

"I'd like that, my friend. But I need you to update Haygena and Kaleo about the Lumastar before they depart." Xolani raises from his chair and starts to exit. "And I need to go speak with Kasmine about tonight, excuse me."

Rashid with a slight shakiness to his voice says, "Lani, I understand that at your level, everything is urgent," "and I'm sure I'll never know the weight of a kingdom on my shoulders but perhaps you can take a moment to catch your breath?"

"Rashid," Xolani says in a low tone. "We have one of the most advanced nations in the world, but families still starve in our city's streets. My family's legacy is built on greed and corruption. I refuse to let that legacy go on any further."

"Lani, that's not your fault" Rashid says.

"But it is my responsibility to fix it. I ran from my responsibilities once and I cannot and will not do it again."

"No one's asking you to run Lani, A good king knows when to lead and when to follow." Xolani lowers his brow and says,

"You're giving me advice on being a king now?"

"Of course not. I'm just concerned about you. We've known each other for years and this is a side of you that honestly, I don't recognize."

"You think I'm turning into my father?"

"Actually, no," Rashid says with hesitation, "I was thinking of your brother." Xolani narrows his gaze and says,

"I think we are done here," and walks out. Rashid standing alone says,

"I guess we are."

Chapter 11:
All in her head

Xolani makes his way through the corridors of the Tree Palace. Servants and guards immediately move out of his way as he storms through the halls. Pivoting around each corner as though he is on the hunt. His body, poised to pounce on anyone getting in his way until he crashes into Lady Neyma and sends his papers flying through the air.

"Mother," he says unsurprised, "why are you always lurking in the halls and more importantly, why is it we are always running into each other?"

"I can go back to my little hut on the edge of the grounds if you prefer," she says jokingly. Xolani busy cramming his papers into their folders replies,

"No, no, that's not necessary"

"I'm glad," she says with a raised brow. She bends down to help him. "Is everything okay?"

"Yeah, just several things on my mind... How are the Ball arrangements going?"

"Good, the staff really stepped up but," Lady Neyma looks at her son and touches his hand softly, "you seem very distracted."

"I just have a lot on my mind," Xolani says as he stands, "Everyone acts like being King is easy and I am supposed to drop whatever I'm doing to cater to their needs."

"Well, yeah," says Lady Neyma. Xolani gives her a disapproving look. "What I mean is, you're the king, so naturally everyone brings their problems to you. But even if you weren't the king, your responsibilities would still be at odds. Being a friend, spouse, and parent each requires their own unique hats to wear. And unfortunately, we can't wear every hat at once. I mean we could but that would look silly."

"Funny."

"I thought so. Look Xolani, some days you are going to be a great king and others, a not-so-great father. A great father and a not-so-great husband on others. Remember what I used to tell you?"

"What?"

"We care because we can. We think because we should, and we do our best because we must. Do your best in each moment and you'll be fine," she says with a loving smile,

"If it was only that easy"

"I never said it was easy but it is doable," she says with a laugh. "But I must be off. I'm on my way to find Niya. I heard she has the most adorable little pet ever."

"Actually," Xolani says, "will you help me with something concerning Niya."

Lady Neyma replies, "Do tell." Xolani leans in closer to her ear before saying,

"With your gifts, we could..."

XOLANI STANDS IN FRONT of Niya's bedroom door and knocks. He hears her scurry about before she says,

"Come in."

Xolani stops in shock, trying to hide the horror of seeing what can only be described as the aftermath of a hurricane hitting her room. Clothes and shoes thrown about, furniture out of place, and stuffed animals of all kinds disemboweled or worse laying everywhere. Niya sitting in the eye of the storm, brushes Sissy's white and black fur.

"Um, we are going to ignore the state of your room for now." He says as he tip toes over a decapitated fluffy stuffed blue animal. "I have something I want to show you."

"Sure," Niya replies, "can Sissy come?"

"Sissy," Xolani says as a question, "now that wouldn't be short for something would it?"

"Nope, can she come?" Before Xolani has a chance to answer, Sissy leaps out of Niya's lap, scurries up his pant leg, around his shirt, begins sniffing his hair, and rests comfortably on his shoulder. Xolani grimaces but soon smiles as he sees the amusement in Niya's eyes.

"I guess she can come," he says, "but not on my shoulder." He grabs her gently and places her on the ground, where she stretches out her front black and white paws, then prances back to Niya.

"So where are we going?" Niya says enthusiastically as she pops up from the floor. Xolani simply says,

"You'll see."

"That's not fair" Niya says with a sassy tone.

"Who said anything about fair?" Xolani says as they exit the room. They make their way through the halls. Niya, holding Sissy in her arms, says,

"I know, we are finally going to visit Mommy's parents."

"I'm sorry," Xolani says with a tilt if his head, "why would you think that?"

"Keon and I were talking about Grandma and,"

"You know she likes you to call her Gram Gram," Xolani says.

"I know, but it sounds so silly."

"You may find it silly but that's how she wishes to call be addressed."

"Yes, sir"

"Wait, what were you and Keon discussing?"

"Nothing really," she says with a shrug, "just that, we've met your side, we were wondering when we'd meet Momma's side."

"I see," Xolani says with a smile, "In due time, I'm sure." They both continue to walk until they come to a long hallway with faded lavender walls that seem to be pulsating.

"I don't think I've been on this level," Niya says, "where are we?"

"This is or was the royal level where I was raised."

"The walls look so beautiful," she says with a reached-out hand. Xolani grabs her wrist before saying,

"These walls are directly connected to the mother tree and all her knowledge. Only the kings and queens of the past have been allowed to touch them."

Niya says, "Why can't I touch it?"

"I wish it were that simple. Our ancestors built this great palace inside the mother tree to be closer to the source, not realizing that the temptation for some was too great. So your great, great, great, great, great, great, great,"

"I get it."

"Granddad, King Xail Uwani IV, sealed off access to the network of roots that flow through the countryside to keep the knowledge from getting into the hands of people who may use it for their own personal gain."

"That doesn't seem right," questions Niya.

"What do you mean?"

"What about all the other people that want to do good and help others? How do they gain knowledge if we are keeping it for ourselves?"

"You're right. I haven't been part of this life for years, now that I am, I ask myself what have I done to help those in and out of the rings surrounding Nuhana. I guess I never thought to share what I've taken for granted. But I promise that will change. Here, let us continue walking to our destination."

"Which is?" Niya asks as she seems distracted by the walls before they begin to walk again. Xolani shifts his eyes forward and says,

"To see a guest."

A frown grows onto Niya's face. They continue onward in silence before Xolani says, "And I know you don't want to see her, but it may do you some good to finally face her."

"I don't want to see Qarinah," Niya says harshly as she stops, "That witch helped Xaden do whatever he wanted. She stood by while he... while he..." Tears roll down her face as the words get caught in her throat.

Xolani kneels to look Niya in the eyes and says,

"We've never really spoken about what happened. Would you want to talk about it now?"

"No," she says with harshness in her voice. Niya looks around and stares into the distance. Xolani remains silent, not sure what she is doing. "You can stop with the charade Gram Gram, I know we are still in my room."

The hallway starts to fade to reveal Niya's room and Lady Neyma standing in the corner where Niya was looking. Lady Neyma walks up apologetically and says,

"I'm sorry baby, we weren't trying to trick you,"

"Yes, you were," Niya says sharply.

"Okay, maybe a little," Lady Neyma replies, "but it was just to help." Xolani puts a hand on her shoulder before saying,

"We all are worried about you and just want to get you well."

Niya shrugs her shoulder and walks to her nightstand. She stares in the mirror as she strokes Sissy. "May I be alone?"

"My star, I" Xolani says before she cuts him off and says. "Please."

He and Lady Neyma turn and walk out closing the door behind them. They walk together for a moment in silence before Lady Neyma says,

"How did she do that?"

He replies, "What, seeing through your illusion? I have no clue."

"No one has ever seen through my gifts. She's the only telepath that I know of that's done that."

"Her gifts have grown way more powerful than I've ever thought. And I hate to say this, but we may have to watch her a little bit more closely, particularly with the ball tonight."

"Agreed."

―――⬤―――

BACK IN NIYA'S ROOM, she places Sissy on the floor as she continues to stare in the mirror.

"No one understands me," she says, "why can't I just be normal?"

"Who needs normal anyway?" an ominous voice says.

"Go away," Niya shouts, gripping her head, "I told you before, I don't want you here."

"Oh darling, it doesn't work like that," the voice says, "I'm here to stay."

Niya looks in the mirror. Terrified, she begins to close her eyes as a shadowy figure emerges behind her reflection, wrapping its dark shadowy hands around her shoulders.

Chapter 12:
What lays underneath

Niya opens her eyes to a white void of swirling, smokey nothingness. Looking around she yells,

"Hello!" But she only hears her own voice echoing back. She yells again, "Is anyone there?"

"Is anyone there?" A cold voice mimics her before laughing in the distance as it too fades away. The hair on her neck stands on end as Niya feels eyes watching her. She peers over her shoulder and asks,

"Who's there?"

"Niya?" She hears Xolani say. Her eyes dart over the empty void and asks,

"Daddy, is that you?"

"Follow my voice."

"I can't see you," she says as she eases forward, moving her hands through the dense fog.

"Help me Niya," the voice says as she continues to move slowly forward. Her hands trembling as she reaches out. "Help me," she hears as she inches forward. "Help me."

"Where are you?" She says with a hard swallow before tripping and tumbling down. Niya turns to see a body lying face down on the cold white ground, completely still as fog lays around it. Terrified, she reaches for the body.

"Daddy," she says with the sound of her heart's beat thrashing in her ear as she sees Xolani rotting and quickly decaying before her eyes. His mangled face, causes her to jump back and crawl away from the decaying monstrosity as it claws toward her.

"Niya, what have you done?" the twisted corpse rattles out. Unable to speak, Niya trembles with fright as she stumbles backward and stops, paralyzed. "How could you do this?"

"Da, Daddy, what happened?" She says as she cups her hands over her ears. "Wha, wha, what did I do?"

The corpse disjointedly stands to tower over Niya and says, "You did this to us."

Niya is speechless as she looks up into its empty sunken eyes.

"How could you Niya?" Raine's voice catches her attention, following it to see Raine standing over her, just as decrepit as Xolani.

"Mom, Mommy?" Niya mumbles out as she continues to look on in horror as now a similar version of Keon steps into her view. "Keon, I, I, how can this be? What happened?"

"You happened," they say in unison. "You destroyed our lives."

"No, I wouldn't, I couldn't." Niya says as she closes her eyes tight as if to somehow wake from this horrid nightmare.

"How could you?" They all say and keep repeating as Niya begins to shake her head back and forth, trying to wake herself. Then she notices the voices are gone. She slowly opens an eye to see they have vanished. She opens her other eye and sits up before standing slowly. She looks around the empty white void to see Xaden standing in the distance.

"You did this?" she says. But Xaden leans forward with his weight on his black cane, expressionless, as Niya shouts, "Answer me!"

Xaden struts forward before taking a seat in as it chair liquifies from the swirling mist. He taps the top of his cane three times and says,

"That wasn't your family just now, but you knew that, didn't you?" Niya's head slowly nods. "Why do you hide your greatness?" She tilts her head down to look toward the ground then with narrowed eyes she asks,

"What do you want?" Xaden places his hand on his chest, fining hurt emotions as he says,

"Oh come now, is that how you speak to a loved one?"

"I hate you for what you've done."

"That was ages ago, live and let live. Besides I'm not the monster you think I am, I promise."

"You're worse," Niya says.

"Ouch..."

"How are you even here? We killed you."

"You tried, but what can I say, it takes more than an axe to the back to kill me."

"This isn't real, it's a dream or nightmare," she says.

"Based on the nightmares I've been giving you lately, I would think you'd know the difference by now. Oh, what's the matter, you didn't know it was me in the back of your mind this whole time? Waiting, growing, driving you further and further out of your mind,... until I could take full control."

"I thought you couldn't control someone once you lost control to them."

"Under normal circumstances, yes, but you see child," Xaden stands, growing in size as he walks toward her. Almost towering over Niya as their surroundings grow dark, "Our connection was never severed or lost. I merely clung to you like a spider to its web. And what a marvelous web I've weaved," he says with glee.

"You can't do this, my parents will save me."

"Save you, from your own mind?" he says before menacingly laughing, "Don't be naive, you're too clever for that. Besides, your parents have been blind to the truth this whole time."

"I don't understand." Niya says.

A twisted smile emerges on Xaden face as he says, "All you really need to know, is that I would never, hurt, my own, daughter."

The void continues to grow darker. Its mysterious white fog swirls shift into grayish tone of emptiness. Niya eyes grow wide and says,

"You're crazy!"

"Deny all you like, but the truth is the truth." The void around them is almost pitch black as Niya steps back and says,
"You're lying and I don't believe you!" Xaden chuckles before saying,
"I don't need you to believe me." Everything is eclipse in black before Niya shuts her eyes and lets out a blood-curdling scream.

NIYA'S EYES OPEN AND she's back in her bedroom. She begins to stare at herself in the mirror. Tilts her head as she pushes her hair behind her ear and says,
"And now the fun begins."

Chapter 13:

What Are They

The sun shines bright while a sea of fluffy clouds flows beneath them. The Legacy's stealth design meets no resistance, while its powerful turbines purr with a quiet hum, almost unnoticeable to the crew inside. Haygena pilots the plane while Raine navigates. They converse about the mission as Kaleo and Miss Lupita sit closely behind and listens intently.

"Help me understand. This mythical lightning bird," Haygena says with a wrinkled brow.

"The Kwane," clarifies Raine.

"The Kwane is actually a man."

"The Kwane and Malkum are the same being-ish," Raine says.

"Right, and Malkum is the one that tried to kill you all last time?"

"The Kwane did. But to be fair, they were under Xaden's mind control."

"Oh, that makes sense," Haygena says with an eye roll, "you just said they are the same."

"I thought that as well," Kaleo adds in a hushed tone.

"They share a body," Raine says as Haygena smiles and just nods her head. "Look, Malkum is a fallen angel and so is the Kwane, sort of. The Kwane was one of the angels who tried to rise up against the creator. Malkum was, well... I'm not sure what he did, but he and the Kwane were punished with banishment from the heavenly plane. And also as punishment, they have to coexist in the same body... make sense? The only thing you both really need to know is that the Kwane, being a creature of the night, gets control of their body during the day and Malkum, being a man of light, gets control at night. Which is why we intend to arrive there a little after dusk, to avoid the Kwane and speak directly with Malkum," Raine says, then smiles. Haygena and Kaleo give each other a look before Haygena asks,

"Okay, so the plan is to simply give Malkum back the Lumastar, can't see anything going wrong with this."

"When Rashid, Lani, and I were finally able to speak with Malkum, he was helpful, a bit of a jerk, but helpful. I don't foresee any reason he wouldn't help this time. And yes, it should be as easy as going in, finding him, and giving it back."

Kaleo sits back with the temple of his head resting against his index finger, and asks,

"How will we find Malkum?"

"Ooh, I'm glad you asked," Raine answers excitedly as she jumps up and motions to follow her to the back of the plane, "last time the equipment with us was limited but this time I brought a whole gambit of things to try out. Nothing fancy. Mostly equipment to track heat signatures, seeing how the Kwane and Malkum give off a lot of heat."

"What about the lightning trees, don't they give off heat as well?"

"Correct," she replies while lifting the lid to a crate, "however, their heat signature is vastly different from Malkum's and or the Kwane's," she continues, not noticing Kaleo and Miss Lupita's attention is still focused on the contents of the crate. "So, we shouldn't have any issue… You two okay, what's," She pauses after looking in the crate to see Keon fast asleep and yells,

"Keon Daseme Raveness!" He jumps up, startled, as Raine continues, "Explain yourself, young man!" Keon sits up and rubs his arm as he keeps his head down and says meekly,

"I wanted to help."

"Keon, I told you to stay put. And now we are going to have to turn around just to take you back. I bet your father has the kingdom looking for you!"

"I told Niya."

"Niya knew and didn't stop you? What is wrong with you two?"

"No, I told her after we were in the air and begged her to shield me from your-"

"From my gifts, so I wouldn't feel your presence. And as we get further from her reach, her protection would fade slowly, and I wouldn't notice the change. I swear, you two. Just sit over there until we plot in a new course and take you back."

With flared nostrils, Raine storms back to the front. Kaleo looks at Keon and says,

"Your motives were noble young one." Kaleo places a hand on Keon's shoulder and motions him to have a seat. Keon follows and sits as Kaleo walks past and stands behind Raine and Haygena. Miss Lupita takes a seat next to Keon and comforts him with a pat on the leg.

"Of all the times to pull," Raine mumbles under her breath.

"We can't take him back," Haygena states. Raine turns to her and says,

"Excuse me?"

"We are coming up on the lightning forest," Haygena replies, "And we need to get the Lumastar to Malkum before, well, you know... He will have to stay on the Legacy."

"I agree," Kaleo says in a low tone, "returning him now could hurt more lives than it could help."

Raine takes in a deep breath and sighs loudly before saying,

"Point made. Haygena, please update Kasmine, so Xolani doesn't worry." Raine turns, pointing her finger at Keon, "This isn't over young man. You and your sister will be in trouble once we get back." Keon slumps his head, to stare at the floor of the plane.

A bleep from the consol is heard, catching Haygena's attention. She studies it from a moment before stating,

"There is a clearing coming up ahead. Near the base of the mountain."

"That's where we found him last time. There should be a cave opening with enough room to land the plane," says Raine as she fiddles with a piece of small equipment.

"I don't see a cave but what about that huge bungalow?" Haygena asks.

"What huge," Raine and Kaleo move to see as she continues, "Oh, THAT huge bungalow. Yes, land in that general area."

Haygena toggles a switch and then eases back on the yoke. They feel the plane shift as they begin their descent. Raine tells Keon to buckle himself in as Miss Lupita and Kaleo does the same. The plane lets out a gush of air as the landing gear contacts the rough dirt surrounding the mountain. Haygena once again flips a switch and they hear the levers of the hanger doors click and begin to lower as the brisk air of the pressurized cabin starts to leave them. With the exception of Keon, they all unbuckle themselves and move to the open door. Haygena opens a weapons locker along the wall. She quickly pulls out an axe with a chain for its handle and places in her back's holster. Kaleo lifts the lid on a black crate and takes out the Lumastar. He carries it over to a gray locker and gets out a black nap sac. He hesitates before turning and in a low voice he asks,

"Are we sure it's safe to put such a powerful...um being, into a bag?" Haygena shrugs as she replies,

"Rashid and Marcella said the bag is lined with a charcoal and lead mesh. Which should give us protection from the lumastar's radiation while we transport it".

Kaleo raises a brow as he looks at the bag unconvinced but then places the lumastar into the nap sack. Raine walks past and crouches down in front of Keon. She locks eyes with him and says,

"I need you to follow my directions exactly. Do you understand?" He nods slowly. "Good, I want you to sit in the chair your aunt was just in. You will be able to see us out of the cockpit. Stay low, do you remember our signal?"

He replies, "I'll feel an intense rush of emotions from you."

"Right, if you feel that," she says as she begins to point at the console, "I want you to hit that bright orange and that purple button together, okay?" He nods as she continues, "Hit those buttons and the plane will take you home."

She stands back up and gently touches his chin, "I'm proud of you Keon and you will be fine. Stay here and we will be back soon. No matter what, if you feel those intense emotions from me, don't hesitate, go." His innocent doe-like eyes tells his reluctance, but he says yes before Raine kisses him on the head. She grabs a metallic cylinder no bigger than a thick pencil from the weapons locker and leads the team out of the plane.

They move with caution toward the bungalow. The radiant lightning capsulated within the glass looking trees illuminate the scorched earth of the forest. The bungalow's vibrant colors and wild design stand out as they move forward. Raine begins to speak, but a familiar voice from up high says,

"I could smell your meat suits coming before you even landed humans." They look up towards the second floor and see a tall blond man standing on the edge looking back at them.

"Malkum? Is that you?" Raine asks.

"Who else would it be?"

"It's Raine."

"I know who you are," he says as he jumps down to land softly in front of them. "I may be eons old but I'm not that old. What is it that you want and why did you bring others here?"

"I'm sorry to bother you Malkum. We're hoping to get your help," she motions to Kaleo, who removes the Lumastar from his bag. "We aren't sure what's wrong, but the Lumastar is dying."

Malkum walks towards the flickering star and gently takes it from Kaleo.

"My poor friend," he whispers before turning back to Raine. "I told you all, this is a living creature that has the power to create a god and you've tried to kill it. Typical humans."

"It wasn't us," Haygena protests.

"It's never you. Now is it?"

"Malkum, we-" Raine tries to interject.

"From the time humanity was created you meat sacs have done nothing for this world! Genocide after genocide, war after war."

"Malkum please," Raine pleads.

"You pillage from the earth and return nothing."

"We want to return it," says Raine.

"Of course, now that it's too late, you want to fix it. You humans are unbelievable. You never learn do you?"

"Malkum," Raine says sternly, "throwing blame isn't going to help. We came to help the Lumastar."

Malkum shifts his focus from the Lumastar to Raine, examining her up and down. His eyes shift as he processes new thoughts. He takes a few steps before saying,

"I can send the Lumastar back to its natural plane of existence, but I cannot do it alone. I will need help from what you viruses call 'the old gods.'" Haygena's head tilts as her eyes narrow at Malkum before she says sharply,

"I've heard enough from this pompous windbag. You insult us and expect us to believe..."

"I don't expect your human pea brain to believe anything," Malkum snaps back. "I may be stuck in this realm for eternity, but I don't have to be stuck with you." He snaps his fingers and Haygena vanishes. Raine and Kaleo step back with mouths suddenly open. Kaleo's voice raises as he says,

"What did you do? Where is she?" Causing Malkum to slide back from the sheer force of Kaleo's voice. "I won't ask so nicely the next time," Kaleo says before moving into a more aggressive stance and taking in a deep breath.

"Do you really think you can hurt me skin wrapping?" Malkum asks with a smirk.

"There is nothing I can't do for her." The air thickens as their eyes lock, waiting to see who blinks first.

"Malkum enough," Raine says, breaking the tension. "where did you send Haygena?"

"She's likely a little disoriented but she's merely back on your ship." Malkum states. Kaleo eases his posture and stands with a disapproving grimace still on his face. "I can see there is a warrior behind those peaceful eyes. I like him."

"Malkum, what about the Lumastar? Will you send it back?" Raine asks. Malkum taps playfully on his chin. His blueish eyes twinkle as he takes a moment to answer.

"I can, but you won't like how." Raine and Kaleo glance at each other before he continues, "I will need pieces of the old gods."

Raine asks, "Pieces of the old gods?"

"Centuries before your last great war was recorded, you humans, regardless of the culture, worshipped a deity, or two, or three. You called them gods but they were actually more like fallen angels. From Ra to Zeus, they were all more or less angels stuck on earth. And I need you to get a piece of essence from at least five of them." He looks up at the sky to ponder for a moment before looking back down and continuing, "Yep, five should be enough, regardless of what god you find."

"I'm not understanding," Kaleo says, "you want us to go find gods, and ask them for a piece of their essence?"

"Humans, always so literal," Malkum says as he laughs to himself, "each god is different, and therefore so are their essences. Their essence could literally be anything. Just tell them I sent you and what we need it for. They will do the rest."

"You want us to go on a quest to find fallen angels?" Raine asks.

"I don't want you to, but, if you'd like me to return the Lumastar to its rightful plane of existence, then this is what you must do flesh coat." Raine's eyes narrow at Malkum's insult as he continues, "And personally, I wouldn't call them fallen angels to their faces. They've grown accustomed to being called gods."

"I'm sure," Raine says, "and how do we find these gods?"

"I'm feeling generous today, one-second." He grips the Lumastar tightly as he squats down and springs up to the second floor of his bungalow.

"I don't trust him." Kaleo says.

"As I said, he's a bit of a jerk but he's an honest jerk," Raine says before Malkum lands in front of them with a thud. Standing before saying,

"Some gods are spread out but others live together, so here."

He hands Raine a small, awkwardly shaped compass. "This compass will point to the one nearest you. I will keep the Lumastar until you get back. These gods are not as friendly as me and some of them flat-out do not like you skin bags. So use caution."

"Thanks for the warning," Kaleo says, "just out of curiosity, why do you have a compass to other angels, can't you just feel where each other are or something?"

Malkum glares at Kaleo before saying, "I created this compass with pieces of my essence, just for you. But if you don't like it, you can give it back."

Kaleo stands silently as Raine says,

"Thank you Malkum for your help. We appreciate it. Is there anything else we should know before we leave?"

"Since you ask, the Lumastar draws its energy from the source. That source is the light protecting this world from the dark. And since the Lumastar is connected to said source, if it goes, so does the light. And without light, darkness floods in. And based on the shape the Lumastar is currently in, I'd say you only have about 48 to maybe 52 hours to prevent this."

In a low tone Kaleo asks,

"Wait, what now?" And Raine adds,

"Malkum, that may have been a great thing to lead with."

"It didn't seem relevant at the time," Malkum says as he smiles.

"Right," Raine replies with a raised eye brow before continuing, "Is there anything else we may need to know?" Malkum with a quick, disgusted snort says,

"Not that I can think of, but if I do, I will let you know."

"Thanks," Kaleo says with a roll of his eyes. "We should go before Haygena comes barreling out of the jet." Raine gives him a nod in agreement and says goodbye to Malkum.

Raine and Kaleo take their leave to head back into the jet. Once inside, they find Miss Lupita caring for Haygena with Keon sitting close to them. Kaleo inches down in front of Haygena with a smile as he grabs her hand tenderly. Raine stops beside Kaleo and they bring Haygena, Miss Lupita, and Keon up to speed. Raine then makes her way to the cockpit as they strap in. She plots in a course before toggling the ignition switch. The engines rumble before falling into a quiet hum. Their bodies feel the weight of gravity pushing them down has the Legacy raises into the sky. Once above the lightning tree line, Raine pulls on the planes yoke and the engines roar before the jet soars into the clouds.

Chapter 14:
They Don't Say

The royal ballroom flows with elegance. Crystals refract moonlight from above. While candles align the walls, giving the large room a soft glow. Nobles, aristocrats, and dignitaries casually stand chatting, while enjoying the orchestrated music lightly floating through the air.

Gibbon with shoulders back, chest out and a gleam in his eyes, struts proudly through the crowd in his creamy rose-colored suit. The crowd's eyes shift in his direction as he makes his way down the gold-trimmed red carpet. His matching creme shoes reflect the bright red and gold of the carpet. He continues making his way to the throne, where Rashid stands ceremoniously at the far end of the room. Gibbon turns, once he reaches the opposite side of the throne, to face the crowd gathering around. He glances at Rashid, who nods in return. Gibbon turns his head to the orchestra conductor and gives her a subtle signal to change the music. The conductor motions to the orchestra. Causing soft music beautifully transitions into a more regal melody. Gibbon clears his throat before proclaiming loudly,

"It is my honor and privilege to present, his royal highness King Xolani Raveness, and his daughter Princess Niya."

The room brightens as the light from the candle's on the wall intensify. Xolani and Niya enter from the royal hall, causing whispers of excitement and intrigue to fill the grand room. Niya's dark brown hair cascades down in a single braid over her left shoulder. Held with a simple gold clip at the bottom of her hair, laying on her shimmering white jacket and matching white pants. A glorious white cape, with crimson red sparkles underneath, flows behind her as she walks gracefully. Holding Sissy in one hand, her other hand floats on Xolani's while he leads her down the golden cherry path.

Their hands leading, he steals a glance at his lovely daughter. Feeling the love from her father's gaze, Niya smiles. He continues to the throne as Niya glides off the path and rests within the crowd. He takes his seat and gives Gibbon a gesture to proceed. Gibbon gives two quick claps, causing the orchestra to change melodies again. Xolani sees Lady Neyma. He smiles coyly at her then notices a familiar friendly face standing next to her.

Xolani studies her round face and pointed chin. Struggling to remember where he knows her from as Gibbon begins to speak.

"From across the shores of the Atlantic Republic, Queen Sophina Barclay and her husband, Prince of Davenport, Erik Housner." The pair proudly strut down the carpet and bow to the king before making their way back into the crowd.

"From our sister land of Tiparthia, President Alexander Rodrigo." President Rodrigo finds his way back into the crowd after bowing to the king as Gibbon continues, "Traveling from the mountain vistas of Gatfuji, Prime Minister Yoshida Nakamura and First Lady Daiyu." They move forward in unison before bowing and returning to the crowd.

"Descending from across the far western regions of St. Kenyan Island, Queen Amara Violet Garcia" Queen Amara moves forward in a glamorous motorized chair. She tilts her head gracefully to the king and heads back into the crowd.

A group of fierce warriors makes their way through the crowd. Gibbon scrambles and stutters, until he manages to say,

"Introducing Queen Octavia of the Rompeiian Empire of Grétily and her guard." They march toward the throne in tight formation. Stopping on the Queen's command, they pound their chests together in one swift beat. She gives another order, and they swivel an about-face and march back off. Gibbon's eyes go wide before glancing over to Rashid, who glances back with a shrug.

Gibbon returns his gaze and continues to call a parade of leaders and nobles as Xolani fights to keep his focus. Not wanting to be there, his emotions overwhelm him even as he attempts to smile. His mind drawn to Raine and the mission he forced onto her. *"Was it right?"* He thinks, *"Will Malkum help them? What will Raine do if he decides not to return the Lumastar to its rightful plane? I hope Keon isn't being a handful. He is in so much trouble when he gets back..."*

Gibbon's voice grabs his attention,

"From the great borders of the Amerigo Continent, President Douglas Kumbak and First Lady Elizabeth."

Xolani is filled with disgust to see his old rival waddle down the carpet. Xolani pushes his feelings to the side as he thinks, *Maybe he's changed, maybe he's different now.* Kumbak in a white and red suit, stops before trotting his wife, in her long blue sequin dress, around for all to see. *"Nope, still the same."* Her long blond hair flows as she glides effortlessly in her ocean-blue gown. They continue walking and then bow to Xolani. Kumbak's fading blond hair flops down as he bows, barely able to bend over his own stomach. Kumbak lifts his head slightly to gaze at Xolani.

"I am happy to be in your presence, King Xolani," he says through his pinched mouth. Xolani keeping his true thought to himself and says,

"Thank you for coming President Kumbak." Xolani then motions for them to return to the crowd before saying, "If you please."

Kumbak and Lady Elizabeth slither off the carpet and disappear into the crowd. Gibbon continues announcing dignitary after dignitary, and politician after politician. Xolani smiles politely at each and every one. Once Gibbon finishes the remaining names, Xolani stands to say,

"Thank you all for coming. I am honored to be surrounded by such nobility. Please, let us start the evening off with a toast." Various servers begin weaving through the crowd carrying single trays with glasses of champagne. Xolani turns and Rashid hands him a partially full glass.

"'N man wat nooit sy foute herken nie, sal nooit vrede ken nie," he says facing the crowd, "which roughly translates to, a man who never recognizes his mistakes will never know peace... Said by the former king. My father, King Xerxes was a great, but prideful man who made several mistakes throughout his reign. But to be fair, so do all men and dare I say, even some women."

Xolani pauses as the crowd reacts with a roar of laughter. As they die down he continues, "And I'm sure I will make a mistake or two as well. However, my plan is to recognize and correct my own mistakes as well as those by my forefathers. To learn from our shared pasts and make a better day for all." He raises his glass high, causing the crowd to do the same as he continues, "So let us heal this world from the mistakes of all of our forefathers and together move forward in peace and prosperity."

Everyone takes a sip from their glass before Xolani shouts, "On with the ball!" And places his glass on the arm of his chair.

Gibbon motions to the conductor. She taps her podium a few times to set the rhythm. Causing them to play a lounge-style jazz piece. The music dancing through the air as conversations erupt throughout the room.

Xolani glances over the room to see Niya causally chatting with a server. Flashes of holding her as a baby sweep through his mind as he smiles. He snaps back as Gibbon walks up and whispers close,

"Sir, I hope I'm not out of line but it is your responsibility to move about the room and socialize. People may take offense if you don't."

"Right, right" Xolani replies as he stands, "Thank you for reminding me."

"You're welcome, Sire."

Xolani, with his arms folded behind his back, walks forward, scanning as he ponders who to talk to. He sees Lady Neyma and Marsella in his gaze, standing close and chatting. Without a thought, his body pivots in their direction. They both notice him and smile, inviting him over. He continues towards them.

"Xalen!" a loud voice shouts. Xolani stops and swivels to see Kombak standing proudly behind him. "It is an honor to see you again," Kombak says with a sense of mockery.

"It's Xolani now, President Kumbak. But you may call me King Xolani."

"Yes, of course, King Xolani, old habits you know." The words oozing from Kumbak's lips as he continues on, "You can't expect me to change so quickly after just learning my dear old friend had magically returned from the grave."

"I do expect that and I don't recall us being friends," Xolani says, "however, we are adults now and I'm sure we can be civil. If, for nothing else, the sake of diplomacy"

"Absolutely, I merely hope to build a bridge between our two peoples, is all." Xolani instinctively raises his brow. "It's true, look," Kumbak assures as he places a hand on Xolani's shoulder but removes it once he sees the disapproving glance from Xolani. "I mean no disrespect. I only mean to make a mins." Xolani can't help but react with a grimace before saying,

"President Kumbak, I appreciate the sentiment, however, I must see to all of my guests. If you don't mind, please excuse me." He goes to take his leave, but Kumbak quickly intercepts and says,

"Your majesty, do you remember punching me in the face?" Xolani thinks to himself with joy,

"*How could I ever forget? Blood ran down your nose, like water* and *you ran away crying.*" Then responds in a civil tone, "I hope you can forgive the mere actions of a foolish, impulsive child."

"No one deserves to be humiliated like that, particular in front of their peers. But I'm sure we both have grown past that unfortunate incident."

"We both were young. Right?" Xolani says.

"Right" Kumbak says, "I spent years hating you. But I'm sure we both can sweep our past dealings under the rug... especially if my country can start importing our goods into yours tax free." Xolani's eyes narrow as he says,

"Nuhana has a stick policy on taxing all imports at the same rate. No country may get a discount or handout." Kumbak sways away slight before saying,

"A handout, of course not. I merely suggest a small favor between old friends. And as a favor, I can make sure his highness if given,... very, special, treatment whenever he visits." Xolani steps forward, looking down at Kumbak and says,

"As a friend, I will say politely, my country and I don't deal in favors and as a friend I will also pretend this conversation never happened. Have a wonderful evening President Kumbak" Xolani goes to walk away but Kumbak cuts off his path and says,

"I was merely testing you Sire. You are true royalty. Please, if there is anything I or my country can do for you or Nuhana, please never hesitate to ask."

"Thank you President Kumbak," says Xolani, "now if you will excuse me. I must see to the other guests."

Kumbak bows to Xolani before walking away. Xolani turns slightly and greets the guest nearest to him. Then taking his time to mingling with guest after guest. The minutes drag by as he floats to each person, smiling politely and shaking hands as he was taught to do so long ago.

All the while, he tries his best to keep his growing worry about Raine and Keon from showing by focusing on each individual and the conversation at hand. His mind wanders continuously back to Haygena's message that Keon is safe and they're almost there.

"I should've gone with them, I wonder if Malkum will actually help them" he thinks.

"King Xolani," a voice says, interrupting his thoughts. "Are you okay?" Xolani snapping out of his trance to see Queen Amara's light brown eyes staring at him. He quickly says,

"My apologies Queen Amara, please, continue."

"I was saying it would be advantageous for our two countries to continue trade negotiations. The western region has always benefited from Nuhana's raw materials as much as Nuhana has benefited from our grain and sugar cane exports."

A server walks up with a champagne tray. He lowers it for Queen Amara to take a glass. Her white glove reflects of the gold bubbly beverage as she graciously places her fingers around the glass and takes it from the tray. Xolani can't help but notice how the champagne matches her golden tan dress as he takes a glass as well.

"Very true," Xolani replies as he notices the look of nervousness on the server's face as a slight bead of sweat rolls down his temple. He continues to speak, "Our countries have been great allies for generations, and I have no reason to see that stopping. However, if you would excuse me Queen Amara. I must attend to an urgent matter that has come to my attention."

"Of course," she says with widen eyes. Xolani quickly scans the room until seeing Gibbon and casually hurries toward him. Gibbon is laughing with a small group of guests. Xolani gently grabs Gibbon's arm gaining his attention. Xolani says with a smile to the group of guests,

"May I steal Gibbon for a moment?" They all bow gracefully to Xolani as he pulls Gibbon away and says softly,

"I need you to locate Kasmine and see if she or any other security members have noticed anything out of order tonight."

"Yes sir, is everything okay?"

"I'm not sure. Find Kasmine and have her report back to me."

"Of course, Your Highness." Gibbon scurries off while Xolani continues observing the room cautiously as he strolls.

Chapter 15:
It's not what you think

Xolani continues wandering around the room searching but not sure for what. He sees Marsella chatting with Rashid and can't fight the smile making its way across his face as he observes them.

He lingers a momentarily, as he watches their flirtatious interaction. A pat here, a soft laugh there, all reminding him of Raine. He soon continues walking through the grand room, casually smiling at each guest, careful to avoid raising suspicion as he tries to fight a 'gnawing feeling.

He toys with the notion of placing the champagne glass down but feels it adds to his calm demeanor. Xolani subtly observes the servers as they invisibly pick up and swap champaign glasses from around the room. Xolani sees Niya still chatting with the server from earlier. He moves to investigate but is stopped by Kasmine.

"Your Highness," Kasmine says as she salutes, "Kacao has the Tree Palace secured and Ramuth has the royal security patrolling the grounds. No one has reported anything out of order." Her body is stiff as a rod, the ideal soldier with her black hair and purple streaks pulled tightly back into a bun. Her uniform is crisp and surpasses regulations.

"Is everything okay, sir? Gibbon mentioned you had some sort of suspicion. Should I end the ball?"

"As much as I would love that, no, I'm sure it was nothing. I saw... Niya has been speaking with that server all night." With widening eyes she asks,

"Should I take him out, Sire?"

"What? No! Of course not," Xolani says before contemplating the request for a second, "well... no. I'd just like to know who he is."

"Johnathan Hender, we normally wouldn't have someone so young as a server but he was highly recommended by other staffers. And since his hiring, a few months ago he has shown nothing but pride for his work."

"He must be special to have been here a few months and already working a royal event," Xolani says. "And now, he seems to be taking up an interest in Niya," he says in a disapproving tone as they both observe the awkward flirtation between the two tweens.

"Should I arrest him, Sire?" Kasmine suggests.

"What?" he asks in a raised vocal tone before continuing to says, "No, why are you like that? They are just kids. Maybe detain him for a while but not arrest him."

She puts a hand on her ear before saying, "Red Group One, converge on Johnathan Hender."

"Cancel that order," Xolani says quickly and continues as she tells security to stand down, "I was joking." She looks at Xolani with a deadpanned expression and says in a voice devoid of emotion,

"It wasn't very funny Sire."

He rubs the temple of his head and says, "Kasmine, don't worry about Johnathan. If you haven't found anything out of place, I'm sure things are fine. Go back to monitoring the ball please."

"Yes, your Highness," Kasmine says, she starts to walk away but like lighting hitting his brain, the thought of Raine comes to his mind and he says,

"If you get any reports from Raine and her team, update me immediately."

"Yes, Sire," Kasmine says before turning and walking away. Xolani stands there for a moment not sure what to do with himself before seeing Lady Neyma alone on the balcony. He quickly finds his way through the crowd and gently taps her shoulder as he says,

"Isn't this your party?"

Lady Neyma smiles and says, "I know. I just wanted a moment alone." Xolani quickly lifts his hand apologetically as he says in a soothing tone,

"Oh, I'm sorry."

"I didn't mean it like that."

"I know," he says, "I probably should get back to the guests and let you have that moment." He starts to walk off but Lady Neyma says,

"I'm just so proud of the man you've become," Xolani turns to see a joyful tear in her eye as she continues, "I know this will sound weird but just seeing you up on the throne, in spite of all I've done." Xolani tilts his head and says,

"In spite of all you've done, I don't think I fully understand" She just smiles and says,

"Doesn't matter, I'm proud of the king you've become."

Xolani lowers his head as he rests on the balcony and says,

"I don't feel like a king. We party while people starve in the streets, something's off with Niya, plus, I let Raine leave in such a bad way."

"Heavy the head that wears the crown." Lady Neyma says.

"Absolutely,... sure you don't want it?" he jokes.

"Being in charge was never for me. I was more behind the scenes taking care of you, your brother, and your sister. But even that didn't turn out okay."

"We turned out okay," he says while adverting his eyes.

"I let your father run you off and brainwash your sister."

"The brainwashing was more so Xaden, but fair point," he says.

"Xaden... Well, to be honest,... he was never quite right." The air fills with the sound of chatter from the ball as Xolani contemplates what to say and then settles on,

"Things weren't easy for you. Dad trotted other women in front of you when I was a kid and once, he got rid of us, locked you away and threw away the key."

"That's not exactly how everything went down Xolani." Xolani moves back slightly as he raises a brow. Lady Neyma continues, "Your father really did love me, as I still love him. He just loved me in his own way is all. And yes, he did have a wandering eye but I could have left, however I chose to stay."

"Don't make excuses for him." Xolani mutters.

"I'm not," She states, "I'm simply taking accountability for my own actions, son."

"And I suppose it was your actions that locked you in that tiny little shack?" He replies sarcastically.

"Actually yes, there was no point in me staying in the castle and I couldn't go back home, so your father room for me on the royal property."

"How generous of him" Xolani says with folded arms.

"I know you don't want to hear it but through the years, he and I grew to have a better understanding of each other."

"The man tried to destroy Nuhana!"

"I didn't say he was perfect, but even in his flaws there was always grace."

They both stare off into the distance. Glowing tillandsia light up the night sky as the hang all over city buildings in the distance. Lady Neyma, takes a sip of her drink. They stand on the balcony taking in the starry night sky as the last words of their conversation linger into the air.

"What are you doing?" Niya's dark voice pierces the silence. She stands in the archway stroking Sissy.

"Niya," Xolani says relaxing his posture, "you scared us."

"Are you having a nice night honey?" Lady Neyma asks.

"I'm not your honey." Niya growls back.

"Niya!" Xolani snaps, "I'm not sure what's gotten into you, but you need to apologize right now!"

"It's all right," Lady Neyma says calmly, "I'm sure she's just tired. After all, she is up way past her bedtime."

Niya gazes fiercely at them before Xolani says sternly,

"I believe your gram-gram is right." He grabs her arm tightly, "You seem tired. It's time for you to call it a night and retire for the evening."

Niya pulls her arm away. "Fine," she says in a huff and proceeds to walk away. Following behind her, Xolani says,

"Don't you walk away from me." He reaches for her but is only able to grab air as Niya teleports just out of his reach. "Niya, this is unacceptable behavior, and you..."

Xolani is cut short, as Niya turns abruptly. She closes into Xolani's personal space as she says,

"You treat me like a child."

"Then don't act like one," Xolani says, "you are being rude and unbecoming of a princess."

"Sire with all due respect," Gibbon says sheepishly, "perhaps this matter should be handled..."

Gibbon gasps for air as he claws at his throat. His body levitates as he fights to breathe.

"Niya, are you..." Xolani says but pauses mid-sentence as he turns to see the desolate look in her eyes. Sissy's low growl from the ground grabs his attention.

"Niya," he says, "put Gibbon down." Xolani keeps his stoic stance as a chill runs through his body from Niya's cold stare. "Now," he says sternly. Kasmine and the Royal guard creep closer to the impending threat. Gibbon's body slowly goes limp as he rises higher.

"Niya!" Xolani shouts, his voice cutting through the silence of the spectators as they watch in horror. "You're hurting him. Put Gibbon down, now!"

"As you wish," Niya replies baring a devilish grin, flinging Gibbon's motionless body into a crowd of guards. Then with two swift movements, Niya kicks Kasmine's chest and sends her hurtling back. Niya lands to then take out several guards.

Sissy grows ferocious before leaping onto Xolani. He keeps the rapid beast at arm's length. Its slobbering teeth are inches from his face as he falls back. His back hits the ground hard but he manages to keep the tiny terror at bay. It fights to break free of Xolani's grasp but he keeps a tight grip. Rashid yanks a tablecloth from underneath a pile of dinnerware and snatches Sissy up into it with one swift swoop. The tablecloth moves violently as the demon dog claws to break free.

Xolani stands and sees Niya sprinting toward him. He stands ready as she leaps through the air. But he quickly feels a painful blow to his back as Niya teleports and strikes him from behind.

"Niya," he says as he recovers, "what is the meaning of this?" He feels her arm tighten around his neck as she whispers,

"I told you Xalen, your time is up."

"Xaden?" Xolani replies in an uncertain tone before glimpsing Kasmine aiming her pistol at Niya. "No!" he yells as the loud bang of the gun echoes through the room.

Chapter 16:

They walk among us

"Are we there yet?" Keon says loudly as the group sits restlessly inside the Legacy. His foot tapping on the planes floor with extreme boredom. Raine turns to Keon from the cockpit and says,

"Considering you shouldn't be here to begin with, I wouldn't worry about how long it's taking. Please don't ask again... besides, I'm surprised you didn't sneak one of those cartoon books onboard with you."

Keon pouts and says, "I wish I would have. Like the one about this really cool dragon that could fly really high and burn down whole cities and..."

Raine looks at Miss Lupita with a narrowed gaze. Miss Lupita rubs her neck and looks toward the ceiling pretending not to see Raine's stern look. "I think his name was Zaya. Are we going to see dragons Mommy?"

"Probably not son, however anything's possible I guess." Keon smiles before asking,

"Are we almost there?"

"Keon!" Raine says sternly, "What did I just say?"

Keon's eyes widen with an innocent glare before saying, "I didn't ask if we're there, I asked if we're almost there."

"Semantics Keon, really? We will arrive shortly" Raine replies before turning back around. Keon leans toward Miss Lupita and whispers,

"What's semantics?"

Miss Lupita gently pats his knee in response. Raine moves a few switches before casually asking Haygena in a very low tone, "How much longer?"

"How am I supposed to know?" she snaps back, "I thought this thing was going to take us to the closest angel, god, whatever they are! The needle keeps moving. Like we're chasing a ghost. How do we locate a god if they keep moving?"

"I only ask because you're the one currently piloting Haygena, no need to get mad."

"I'm not mad," she replies in a huff.

"Sure," Raine says as she begins to pick up a Com-d and continues, "I'm going to give Xolani an update." Silence fills the Legacy. She puts the Com-d back as the air becomes cold. A chill runs down her spine and the hairs on Raine's neck stand on end. The moisture from her breath catches her eyes as she instinctively takes in a deep breath and exhales.

"Haygena, you feel that?" She asks but a deep young voice echoes from the back of the jet replies,

"She can't hear you. None of them can."

Raine grabs her staff as she whips around in a combative stance. "Who are you and why are you here?" she demands before seeing a very light-skinned teenager with greasy black hair and thick eyeliner sitting on a cargo container near the wall, unbothered by her threat. His skinny frame can be seen through his dingy gray suit.

"When one searches for death, they often find it," he says in a menacing manner.

"What did you do to them?" She asks, pointing her staff towards him as she inches forward. He calmly says,

"Don't be rude. Nothing is wrong with them. No one sees me unless death is near."

"But we're not dying?" Raine says as she steps back.

"And yet, I am here." He says with a chill of arrogance as he admires his black polished fingers.

"We're just looking for gods," Raine explains, "Malkum said..."

"Malkum!" he shouts and jumps up, "Of course he'd send mortals to do his work. What is it he wants now?"

"Malkum is helping us." Raine says.

"Is he now?" He replies with a roll of his eyes.

"Yes, the Lumastar is dying and he's helping us return it to its proper plane. We just need to get pieces of essence from five different gods."

"Interesting," he says while stroking his smooth chin. "Guess he didn't say energy never dies but just goes somewhere else. Transferred through the cosmic sphere and revitalized elsewhere."

"But what would that mean for the earth and all of us?"

"Ashanti would see to it that the earth would be fine, as she always does, you humans though, probably not so much."

"Will you help us? You are a god after all, aren't you?"

He jumps to his feet, brushes his floppy hair out of his eyes with his hand, and says,

"I'm flattered, but technically no. As powerful as I am, I'm just a glorified transporter," Raine's eyebrows raise while he continues on, "I am the Orion of life, the Ajal of all, and Thanatos to most, but you may call me Anpu, the harbinger of death." He bows to Raine as the color drains from her cheeks as she whispers,

"Death."

"Oh, let's not be so formal. After all, I'm not here to collect any of you, at least not yet" he chuckles, "Anpu will be fine. After all, you sought me out and here I am." Words rush through Raine's mind, but she stands frozen as Anpu circles around her like a shark to its prey. "I guess Malkum didn't tell you that you'd find me first. Figures, he's always been one to leave out the details. So, how would you like to proceed?" Raine stands there for a moment before saying,

"Proceed? Proceed with what?"

Anpu rolls his eyes before jumping onto a crate and squatting to look Raine deep in the eyes.

"My dear child, what is it you desire?" he says with the words slithering out of his twisted mouth.

"I'm not sure I follow," she says with narrowed eyes and a slight tilt of her head, "are you giving me...wishes?"

"Oh God no, Malkum sent you after me for a reason, correct? And I am merely asking what that reason is?"

"Well, Malkum didn't send us after you, specifically."

"Flattery will get you nowhere darling," Anpu says with a raised brow.

"That's not what I meant," Raine replies quickly, "As I mentioned, we are looking for gods to ask them for a piece of their essence."

"You, and your motley crew just decided to chase down gods and ask them for, their essence, and expect us to give it to you?" he chuckles, "You humans, I swear are some of the simplest creatures alive. How did you think this conversation would go honestly?"

"Look," Raine says with authority, causing Anpu to sit and rests his head on his fist. "for some reason, you're toying with me. Please, help us, or leave." Anpu sits there with a giant smile before saying,

"You are fascinating. Exquisite even," he leaps off the crate and walks slowly as he locks eyes with her. "Of all my lives, I have never encountered such a ravishing creature."

"Um, thank, you," Raine replies with more confusion than disgust. "Malkum said, he needs pieces of essence from five other gods to send the Lumastar back to its original plane. Do you know what he meant?"

"Of course, I do," he says while never breaking eye contact. "In layman's terms, he's wanting my, our, power. Or at the very least, a piece of it, my mortal muse."

Raine takes a step back and says, "I think you have the wrong idea, little boy."

Anpu moves seductively to close the distance between them. Before saying,

"I am no child, my dear. I am eons old and merely look like this because it is what you want to see."

"You're saying that I want to see a pre-pubescent boy, hitting on me?" Anpu sighs and steps back. Then says,

"Of course not. Anyone who gazes upon death, which is I, sees one of two things. Either what brings them comfort or what they fear most."

"I don't feel comforted."

"I can change that, let's stare longingly into each other's eyes," he says with a flutter of his eyes. Raine, not amused, makes one swift move, and points her staff dead center in his chest, pushing him backwards. "Easy love, just being friendly," Anpu says with a smile.

"I don't have time for this," Raine replies, "and neither does the Lumastar. Either help us or leave."

"Temper, temper, just having a bit of fun. It's not often I can just have a conversation with you skin suits without someone begging or pleading for their life." Anpu reaches into his coat pocket and pulls out a tiny thimble. He holds it in between his index and thumb. Raine looks at it and then looks at Anpu. He then says, "I can see the skepticism in your eyes," before placing it in her hand. "But this is what you seek from me."

"A thimble," she says as she stares curiously at it.

"Open your eye and you will see the truth," he says slowly, "But be warned, taking a piece of gods can come with a price. And the rent will always come due." His voice echoes through the jet. Raine looks up and Anpu is no longer there. She turns around and looks in all directions for him until the sound of Haygena's voice repeats in her head.

"Raine. Raine. Raine!"

Raine blinks rapidly before realizing she's back in her seat and Haygena is yelling at her.

"Raine, you okay? It's like you froze for a second."

"I, uh, I'm not sure what happened," Raine says as she feels something on her index finger. She lifts her hand to see the thimble resting on it.

"This stupid compass has a new heading on it now. Should we keep following it?" Haygena asks. Raine lifts the thimble higher and says,

"Follow it, I have our first piece and that's our next."

Chapter 17:

The Plan

As Niya vanishes Xolani feels a piercing pain in his shoulder and collapses. The pain shoots through his shoulder while he lays on the floor. Kasmine runs to his side.

"Your majesty," she says apologetically, working to help him, "I didn't mean to. I was…"

"I know," Xolani says as he staggers up. "Where's Niya?"

"She disappeared Sire," Kasmine says. Rashid then says,

"She took that decrypted devil dog too."

Xolani looks around and catches a glimpse of Gibbon still lying on the floor with several guards around him. "Is Gibbon all right?" he yells across the room.

"He's breathing your majesty," a guard replies, "but hurt pretty bad."

"Get the medics up here now," he commands. The guard replies,

"Already on their way Sire" Xolani looks to the crowd of guests, with their various mouthes hanging open and hands toward their chest in shock. He holds his wound as he says,

"Thank you all for coming tonight, and my sincerest apologies. I believe it is evident that I have some urgent matters to attend to and must leave. However, my staff and guards will see to it that all of you make it safely to your transports. Again, thank you, and goodnight."

The guest's part as Xolani makes his way quickly through the crowd. Rashid, Lady Neyma, and Kasmine quickly follow behind him.

"Kasmine," Xolani commands, "gather Kacao, Ramuth, and some guards,"

"Xolani," Lady Neyma says, but Xolani continues, focused,

"And head to the detention level to keep an eye on Qarinah."

"Sire?" Kasmine questions, "Shouldn't we be looking for Niya?"

"There's no time to explain," he commands, "Niya isn't herself, and she will be going for Qarinah. Contain Niya without harming her."

Kasmine gives a quick nod and hurries off to carry out Xolani's order. Lady Neyma and Rashid continue to walk briskly, trying to keep up with Xolani's pace.

"Xolani" Lady Neyma says as they near an elevator. Xolani replies, "Not now Mother."

He brushes his bracelet against a flat black panel. An arrow pointing up appears above them and motors can be heard turning. As they wait for it to come Xolani turns to Rashid and says,

"Do me a favor old friend,"

"Xalen Augustus Uwani!" Lady Neyma shouts. Xolani gives a very angry look before simply saying,

"Yes."

"That wasn't Niya, was it?" She says concerned.

"Mother come with me," Xolani says, "Rashid check on Gibbon and then meet me down in the crypt." The elevator chimes as the doors slide open. Xolani and Lady Neyma step in before Rashid replies curiously,

"The crypt, what are you looking for down there?" Xolani inserts a key into a small wall plate inside the elevator and turns it clockwise. The elevator doors begin to close while Xolani replies,

"A dead man."

Chapter 18:
Buckle Up

"Something's not right," Kaleo says in his low tone as he grips the control column in front of him.

"What do you mean?" Haygena asks.

"I'm having to consistently-" warning alarms sound, cutting him off.

"I give you the controls for less than a second..." Haygena says, as she flips switches and grabs the controls in front of her.

"It's not my fault," Kaleo interrupts, "it's like something is forcing us in a different direction."

"Switching controls over to me," she shouts. Kaleo glances at Haygena from the corner of his eyes as she fights to control the plane. "Somethings not right," she mumbles.

"So, it's not just me then?" he jokes while flipping switches.

"Seatbelts," she says sternly, ignoring his comment to focus on flying.

"What's going on?" Raine says as she raises from her seat wiping sleep from her eyes.

"The controls aren't responding," Haygena says.

"Do we know why?" Raine says as she fights to stand.

"Working on it," replies Kaleo.

"Seatbelts now," Haygena says in a huff. Raine quickly yells to Miss Lupita to wake up as she reaches over Keon's shoulder. His droopy eyes slowly open while Raine tugs his shirt and calls his name. He wakes confused but quickly understands the situation. Raine refocuses toward the cockpit and says,

"Haygena, we're heading straight into the mountain."

"I know." Haygena snaps.

"We need to eject!" Raine screams.

"Altitude is too high," Haygena replies, "we could freeze to death, go hypoxic from lack of oxygen, or both."

"Our alternative is crashing into the mountainside," Raine says, "Hit the eject!" Haygena flips up a glass lid and slams her hand on a bright red button. Immediately the canopy flies off. Miss Lupita is thrust back into her seat as her chair blasts out of the ship, followed by Keon and Raine. The force pushes against their skin as they hurdle upward. A brief moment of stillness and calm finds them among the clouds before they begin to descend. The force of the wind rips across their faces before their parachutes deploy and slow their fall.

Raine frantically looks around to catch her bearings. She sees Miss Lupita and then Keon, passed out from the force but sees no sign of Kaleo or Haygena, until she locks eyes with a ball of fire erupting from the mountainside. She looks again, worried their seats didn't eject.

No sign of them anywhere in the sky. Maybe their trajectory shot them over the mountain? she asks herself. Or at least the other side. They can't be gone like that. They just can't be.

She looks away as tears push against her eyes. She breathes to focus her attention on Miss Lupita, who doesn't seem to have noticed the explosion. Then she shifts to see Keon awakening from his loss of consciousness.

His vision beginning to return before his eyes show the soul-shaking terror of being blasted out of the plane without notice. His limbs cascaded together as if there was a buildup of commands before he passed out, and now the shock hits him.

He catches Raine's motherly gaze and feels a warm sense of calm rush over him. He closes his eyes and thinks of what to do. I single thought hits him and his body begins to expand. The safety harness holding him to his parachute snaps one by one under pressure. The panicked calls of Raine and Miss Lupita are silent whispers compared to the wind rushing past his ears. His body grows until he is gargantuan, and lands with a thunderous earth-shaking three-point stance.

He quickly stands and catches Miss Lupita and Raine in his outstretched hands. He places them on the ground as he returns to his normal stature.

"Don't you ever do that again!" Raine yells at Keon as she release her harness and run to hug him tight, "How did you think to do such a thing?"

Keon mumbles into Raine's chest, reminding her to loosen her tight hold on him. He takes a breath and says,

"I saw it in one of the books Miss Lupita gave me."

"I bet it was the Astonishing Gigantor," Miss Lupita says in a loud voice and continues as if speaking to herself, "or maybe it was Bug-guy and the Stinger?"

"Um..., I don't remember his name," Keon says while scratching his head, "but he could grow and shrink like me. He even saved his friends when they were falling like we were."

"That's very nice my dear," Raine says cutting him off, "I can't wait for you to tell me more, but right now we need to find or build a shelter."

Miss Lupita slowly raises her hand. Raine gives a slight head shake before saying, "Yes?"

"Did you see..." she starts to say. Raine looks at Miss Lupita with saddened eyes. She quickly glances at Keon and looks back at her.

"Unfortunately, no," she says, "but they know how to protect themselves. Our mission, same as theirs, is to find these angels or rather," she puts her hands up and bends her fingers on both hands to emphasize the word, "gods."

Miss Lupita goes to speak but as her mouth opens her words fall empty when she sees smoke funneling off the mountain.

Raine can see the revelation in Miss Lupita's eyes, and keeping Keon's back to the mountain, she says,

"We need to figure out our next move and keep to the plan. Kaleo and Haygena would do the same. Did either of you happen to see a town or village during our descent?"

"I don't think so," Miss Lupita answers before saying, "but I did see a lake."

Keon asks, "Why are you looking for a village Mommy?"

"We're going to need supplies," she replies, "possibly warmer clothes, hiking gear, and if possible, some medical supplies would be nice." Keon nods his head with a smile as she continues, "I think you're right, Miss Lupita. I believe I saw that lake as well and I may have seen a house or two near it. The only question remaining is, which way?"

They think for a moment then Miss Lupita looks to Raine with a smile. Raine returns her gaze with a tightened face before the realization of what Miss Lupita is thinking hits her face and they both look to Keon. Who says,

"What?"

"Here's your chance my boy," Miss Lupita says, "grow and tell us what you can see near us."

"All right!" Keon shouts, "Can I Mommy?" With some hesitation Raine slowly says,

"Yes, but don't go too big like you did a moment ago. You may get lightheaded and faint."

Before she or Miss Lupita can utter another word, Keon says,

"Okay," and his body grows, doubling, tripling expeditiously in size, until a hazy blue lake resting at the base of the mountain comes into his view. "I see it," his booming voice says, causing Miss Lupita and Raine to cover their ears.

"Oops, I see it." Keon says in a whisper as he covers his mouth after noticing their actions, "The lake, I see it." He pauses for a moment and then says, "Smoke, I think, coming from a house, just on the other side of the lake."

"Excellent Keon," Raine yells up, "Do you happen to see a village or town?" He looks around for a second before saying,

"No, just the... I don't feel so..." Keon shuffles back and forth as he raises his gigantic hand to his face. Raine and Miss Lupita maneuver around his enormous feet as they shift back and forth.

"Keon," Raine yells, "Shrink back down!"

"What?" he yells back down as the world feels like it's spinning around him.

"Shrink back down!" Raine yells as she and Miss Lupita cover their ears yet again.

"Okay," Keon says with a slur of his words. He begins to slowly descend back to his normal size. But bright lights dance in his vision as his world grows black.

Chapter 19:
A Sibling Revelation

The elevator doors close and Xolani says, "How did you know Niya was Xaden?"

"A mother knows her children," Lady Neyma says, "no matter where they may hide."

"So, I guess I don't need to worry about telling you Xaden is back." She pauses for a moment and with a low voice she says,

"Actually, there is something I need to tell you."

She looks away as Xolani looks at her and says with a grimaced face, "What?"

Lady Neyma avoids his glare as she says,

"Xaden isn't who you think he is." Xolani's brow raises as she continues, "Xaden is a cloned copy of you." He narrows his gaze as she keeps her eyes focused on the floor and continues, "I've wanted to tell you ever since you've come back into my life, but I was afraid of making the same mistake twice."

"What mistake?"

"The night of you and Xaden's Scion Contention... I told him the truth. That he was merely a clone and had no claim to the throne," Lady Neyma said, with a weight of guilt in her voice. She stokes her arm slowly as she continues,

"I was trying to keep you from fighting one another, but he became enraged and wanted nothing more than prove he was the real son and true scion."

"I don't understand, why would you clone me?"

"When you and Xaden were born," she says with tears flowing down her eyes, "there were complications and we lost Xaden... We had you but, losing a child is... the grief was too much... I went behind your father's back and used you as a template. I combined my gifts with necro-magic to bring Xaden back... However, it didn't bring him back. It created something new. It pulled out the worst of you to create him."

"You can't be serious. You expect me to believe this? Father didn't get suspicious when a magical baby just appeared?" Xolani says.

"I carried this Xaden, just as I carried you," she pleads, "Your Father had no reason to suspect, until..." Lady Neyma's voice gets softer, "Until he started to grow faster. It was just easier to have the kingdom believe you were twins."

"And Father went along with this?" Xolani asks.

"He thought it would bring out the best in you both... That is until we started to see the darker tendencies in Xaden. I didn't want to see them at first but as you both grew older it became apparent. But Xaden's still my son and I only want the best for you both."

The elevator stops as the doors chime and open. As Xolani steps out, he says,

"So, why tell me now?"

"After you were exiled, and everyone thought Xaden was dead, I suggested to your Father that Xaden's mind could survive in the astroplane. He thought I had gone mad. So he banished me to that hut, said I was stricken with grief again and that he didn't want me to tamper with necro-magic again. But I tell you now because Xaden is misunderstood and I'm sure if I could only just talk to-"

"No," Xolani says, "we are past the point of talking. Once I remove him from Niya, his time is up." Xolani walks out of the elevator, leaving Lady Neyma there watching as the doors close.

Chapter 20:
The Cabin on the Lake

The sound of rolling laughter awakens Keon. Dim lighting breaks through his opening eyes. "Mommy?" he says in a fog of confusion.

"I'm here," Raine responds as she hurries to his side. "I'm here." Keon rubs his eyes to help clear his vision faster. He makes out rustic wooden walls with various types of gear and tools hanging all along the cabin. Miss Lupita takes a sip of her tea as she sits at a quaint table in the middle of the small room in front of a roaring fire.

"Where, where are we?" he asks.

"We are in the lovely home of Mr. Kijin. He has been entertaining us with a few stories. Where did you say we were again, Mr. Kijin?"

Keon peaks over her shoulders to see a man of short stature standing just behind her, whose smile was warmer than the bustling fire.

"We are at the base of the top of the world," Mr. Kijin replies. "Would you like some hot cocoa young man?" Mr. Kijin says, but Keon simply shakes his head no. "Or maybe some cider?" Keon smiles and politely says, "no, thank you." "Okay, but if you change your mind. You'll let me know?" Keon nods his head before sheepishly retreating into his mother's gaze.

"Now, what was this business about needing to get to the top of the mountain?" Mr. Kijin says.

Raine responds, "We mentioned our plane crashed and about the others that came with us but, what we didn't say," Miss Lupita clears her throat in an attempt to stop Raine, but Raine keeps speaking, "we are seeking out gods for pieces of their essence."

"Excuse me, you're seeking out whom and for pieces of what?" Mr. Kijin asks.

"Gods and a piece of their essence," Raine takes a moment to try to read Mr. Kijin's unfocused stare before saying, "you don't believe us?"

"I don't think it's for me to believe or not believe. I feel if you believe, that's all that matters. However, I must apologize for not saying earlier that I'm mostly sure your friends are okay."

"Mostly sure?" Miss Lupita says,

"The mountain is partially a facade, hiding the entrance to the land of gods."

"Are you a god, Mr. Kijin?" Keon asks with wide-eyed enthusiasm.

"I am simply a vessel, and I believe we all have a little touch of the creator in us. After all, we all are god-like in our own unique ways, if that makes sense?" Keon scratches his head and Mr. Kijin begins to speak again in a clarifying tone,

"Imagine the creator being an ocean, vast, wide, and deep. Sustaining life for all that live in and around it. Now imagine, you and I are cups filled with that ocean water. The water in our cup has the potential to do everything the ocean can, you just have to find your connection to the source."

"I've never thought of it that way," says Miss Lupita.

"Most don't unfortunately." Replies Mr. Kijin.

"So how long were you going to let us sit here and pretend we were crazy?" Raine asks.

"Only until it wasn't funny," Mr. Kijin says with a wink to Keon. "But if it makes you feel better, I'm sure one of the beings inside the mountain felt the compass pull and guided your friends in unharmed."

"I'm glad to hear Kaleo and Haygena may be safe, thank you." Raine says as she stands, "We appreciate your hospitality Mr. Kijin, but we must be off."

"I should warn you," he says, "getting to the mountain will be a challenge." The group looks at him bleakly as they all feel a chill come into the room. "The entrance to the land of the gods is guarded by awful Adroanzis. Horrible snake monsters. They are nasty, sneaky creatures born of Adro[1], the evil Water Snake God."

He moves to grab a fire poker and begins to stoke the embers before tossing another log on. "They live in rivers and lakes, lying in wait under rocks and any small crevice near the water for innocent humans to walk past. I do most of my foraging during the day because, if you walk at night, watch out! The creepy creatures will follow you home, or worse."

"Thank you for the warning, Mr. Kijin, but creepy snakes or not," Raine says, "we have to get to that mountain as soon as we can. Haygena and Kaleo could need our help for all we know."

"I felt you might say that," Mr. Kijin says, "so, if you must go, hold hands as you journey to the mountain and, whatever you do, don't turn around. If you so much as peep behind you, you've had it. Keep your eyes fixed ahead, no matter what is going on, and pretend nothing is happening. They will hiss, pull, and taunt you, but ignore them at all costs. They are powerless if you don't pay them attention. That's the only way to stay safe."

"Thanks," Raine says before glancing back at Keon. His eyes wide with fear. "We will be fine," she says as she places a gentle hand on Keon's cheek. "Like everything in life, just one footstep at a time."

Keon smiles lightly. Raine swiftly turns around as Mr. Kijin begins to speak,

"Once you've reached the mountain, look for the leaning stone and pass under it to find the gods you seek."

Miss Lupita says, "Maybe you should come with us, I'm sure we could use the help."

---

1. https://www.godchecker.com/african-mythology/ADRO/

"I would love to but... I must be honest. The moment I step out of this cabin, the Adroanzi will hunt me down, unmercifully. You see, they are made to protect the gate of the gods and also to keep me here."

"That's awful Mr. Kijin, but why?" Raine says.

"I think that may be a conversation for a different day. After all, I believe you all have the world to save."

Raine goes to speak but realizes they haven't told him the details of their mission. "Wait, how did you?"

Mr. Kijin's eyes twinkle briefly at Raine before he looks to Miss Lupita and asks, "Is there anything in here you might be able to morph into weapons?"

Miss Lupita's face can't hold back her surprised expression before she slowly scans the small room.

"I don't see any material in its raw form for me to manipulate but I do see one or two things Raine may be able to use."

Raine quickly scans the room and smiles big as she eyes the objects Miss Lupita was hinting at and says,

"You know what, I think you may be right."

Chapter 21:

Dead men don't sleep

Xolani exits the elevator and is greeted by the cold, damp, still air of the crypt. He walks down the dimly lit row that weaves through the roots of the mother tree. Xolani glances quickly at the statues of ancestors resting in the hollows of the roots. He reads the names of the queens, kings, and nobles as he passes by each vault. But slows momentarily once he sees the crypt of his father, King Xerxes Thaddeus Uwani.

He continues onward, passing an empty spot reserved for Lady Udella Neyma. Finally he stops at the vault of his brother, Xaden Lucius Uwani. He stares with a grimace at the statue of Xaden. His skin feels flush as he stares, memories flooding his mind, recalling all the horrible things Xaden had done to him and his family. He closes his eyes to slow his breathing and calm himself down.

As he begins focusing on his breath, a faint, ominous voice says, "Xalen," and he feels a tap on his shoulder that jars him back. He releases a blast of fire from his hands as he pivots in the direction of the voice. The crypt lights up. Rashid dodges quickly from the passing flame. He watches it burst into the far wall and fizzle out before Rashid says,

"Okay, no more Sire jokes," while brushing at the steam rising off his shoulder.

"I'm sorry," Xolani says, "I thought... nothing. Help me with this." Xolani walks to Xaden's vault and motions Rashid to do the same on the opposite side. "I need to see if his body is still in here." Rashid seems a little puzzled, but helps Xolani push the massive stone top off the vault. It lands with a thud as dust and dirt fly into the air. Both Xolani and Rashid begin coughing as they wave the debris out of their faces. Once the dust settles, they peek inside.

"I know you two are twins," Rashid says, "but without him being all crazy, laying there looking peaceful, I never realized how much you two looked alike."

"Geez, thanks...." Xolani replies with a smirk. "I'm actually surprised his body hasn't started rotting yet."

"The vault keeps his body preserved," Rashid says, "his body won't start noticeably breaking down for another year or so." Xolani shoots Rashid a look before Rashid says, "Sorry, I thought you didn't know." Xolani begins staring at his brother's remains, looking for some clue that he may have missed until Rashid says,

"Um, okay, are you going to tell me why we're down here, waking the dead?"

"Right before Niya vanished... she said she was Xaden." The air grows thicker as Rashid says,

"Xaden, your evil twin?"

"Don't call him that."

"Sorry, evil sibling" Xolani ignores Rashid's comment as Rashid continues, "I don't understand, I thought the axe lodged in his back killed him."

"I thought that too," Xolani says, "but maybe we were wrong. Or maybe Niya is having some sort of breakdown from the trauma of being under his mind control. I don't know. I just know I needed to make sure his body was still here."

"Why," Rashid asks, "I thought Qarinah would be the priority if Xaden was back."

"He'll need his body as much as he'll need her if that's really him."

"Kasmine and the remaining King's Five are with the other fifty guards in the detention cell. I'm not sure that's a smart move for her, him... whoever."

"Speaking of Kasmine," Xolani says, "I should check in with her." He raise his wrist close to his mouth and presses a few short times on the flat screen of his Comm-D watch. He then says, "Kasmine, report." A few seconds go by before a quick burst of static breaks through the silence and Kasmine's voice calmly says,

"King Xolani. Qarinah is secure in her cell with several guards posted on all entryways. I, Kacao, and Ramuth are standing outside her cell as we wait on further orders, Sir."

"Good, keep me updated on any new developments..." Xolani is cut off as screams of panic can be heard through his Comm-D watch. "Kasmine, what's going on?" he shouts, but she doesn't respond. More shouting and gunfire can be heard, until silence. "Kasmine, Kasmine report!" he yells, but silence is all that replies until a distorted voice comes through.

"Xalen," Niya's voice, twisted and dark, continues, "I told you... your time is up." Static from the watch echos off the thick walls of the crypt before Xolani cuts the feed. He turns to Rashid and says,

"They're coming..." But before Rashid can respond they stand frozen as a purple haze fills the room. It spirals and forms a deep dark purple circle, with Qarinah and Niya stepping through.

Niya still in her white suit and cape, stands close to Qarinah dressed in her prison finest. A dark gray jumpsuit with containment straps dangling from her arms and waist.

Xolani stands in disbelief as he faces Niya's cold stare as she strokes Sissy in her arms. Her youthful and innocent eyes are replaced with the long-forgotten evil gaze, reminiscent of Xaden's cruel intentions.

"Niya," Xolani says with heartbreak in his voice, "what are you doing?"

Qarinah steps forward with a twisted smile as she says in a raspy voice, "Niya isn't here. But our rightful king is."

"What are you talking about, you pompous old hag?" Rashid says.

"We're the same age idiot!" Qarinah snaps back.

"Yeah, but you don't look it." Rashid fires back. Qarinah fills with rage and screams before launching herself toward him. Niya's arm extends, stopping Qarinah before she can move too far. Niya moves forward before saying in a voice not her own,

"I think it's time the adults speak." Qarinah lowers her head and takes another step back. "We don't have to fight Xalen,"

"It's Xolani, Xaden," he says in response, "you have my daughter under your control, and you expect me not to fight?"

"I expect you to do what's best for your daughter," Niya's voice says, "She has tremendous potential, and it would be a shame if..." she sticks out her arm, exposing it to a small pebble that begins to hover up and floats toward it. The pebble spirals for a second before picking up speed. Slow, steady. It builds momentum before striking her arm. Blood slowly oozes out of the mark left by the pebble. "Something happened to her, know what I mean?"

"What is it you want Xaden?"

"To be the one true king" Xaden's evil smile shines through Niya's face as Xolani looks deep into her eyes to see the true villain and says,

"You can have the thrown, just give me my daughter back!"

"Um no" Xaden says. Causing Xolani to launch towards them. But he is cut off by Qarinah as Xaden's twisted smile shines through Niya's face. Qarinah and Xolani battle it out for mere seconds before Rashid and Xolani feel pressure building around them, a force keeps them from moving.

"As much as I would love to kill you, I need you alive," Xaden says as he moves to stand inches from Xolani, "at least for a little while. You see, I've had time to think and we are going to finish what was started so long ago." Xolani notices a purple hue beginning to cover Niya's face as it illuminates the room. "No worries brother, I'll be killing you-I mean, seeing you, real soon." Niya shoves Xolani as Qarinah delivers a push kick into Rashid's chest, sending both men falling through a portal behind them, landing in the Tree Palace's confinement cells. Rashid and Xolani recover quickly to see Niya and Qarinah waving goodbye as the portal closes.

"I really hate her," Rashid says.

"Me too, but she's not our main problem. We have to get out of these cells and figure out what's Xaden's next move."

"It's not obvious? He has to be after his body."

"I got that, but what else? That is, other than wanting to kill me?"

"He's really playing into the evil twin cliche, isn't he?" Rashid says with a smile. Xolani smiles out of a feeling of obligation rather than humor before saying,

"How do we save Niya?"

"What about our Comm-D to contact Kasmine?"

"Not from within the cell, remember? I can't even use my gifts in here."

"So we're stuck."

"Appears so for now, which means the only thing we can do is wait until Xaden is ready to finish whatever was started so long ago." A moment passes before Xolani and Rashid look at each other and say in unison,

"The Scion Contention!"

Chapter 22:

Rock, Paper, Scissors, Snakes!

"Remember!" Mr. Kijin says in the doorway of his cabin, "Keep walking forward, the Adroanzi can't harm you unless you look back." The group waves good bye to Mr. Kijin as they begin their long walk.

Under the cover of darkness, they move as the moon twinkle brightly in the reflection of the lake's surface. Raine notices the stars shining high above them, dancing to a beat only the universe can hear. And just below lies a gorgeous snow-covered mountain tops, painted perfectly by the moonlight. She takes it all in as they move quickly and quietly.

Keon in the middle, holds their hands as the words of Mr. Kijin, *"Keep walking forward. They can't harm you unless you look back."* Replay, like a song in his mind. He continues moving forward but with every shadow or unexplained noise, his heart stops, wondering if the Adroanzi are following them. The compulsion to look back, just for a second to see if they're there, pulls on him. But the reassurance of his mother's and Miss Lupita's hands holding his helps him stay facing forward.

The soft sand of the lake's shoreline cushioning their path, they move with stealth-like accuracy further and further away from the safety of the cabin. A cool night breeze gently hits them. But soon the feeling of eyes watching them and frequent rustling from the tree line puts them on alert.

They keep moving forward as Mr. Kijin instructed, but begin to hear a soft crescendo of lips smacking from behind. Miss Lupita feels a warm sensation as if someone is breathing on her neck. She continues to walk, trying to ignore the uneasy feeling, as her heart races. Then the subtle feeling of creepy fingers trail down her back. Fighting the urge to alert the others, she maintains the same grip on Keon's hand.

Without looking down, she notices an eerie presence slowly wrapping itself around her waist, gradually getting tighter. It sleethers up her waist to her torso and around her shoulders.

Miss Lupita works to steady her breathing to calm her pounding heart before whispering, "We must hurry."

Raine, catching herself from turning, responds, "Is everything all right?"

"Right as a screen door bottomed ship," Miss Lupita says with shallowed breath. "I'm fine, let's just keep..."

"Miss Lupita," Keon says as he feels her hand loosen. He turns his head.

Raine feels the tug of his hand as Keon slows his pace. She's mortified by the sight as she turns. A legion of Adroanzi slithers behind Miss Lupita, and several are wrapped around her.

"No!" Miss Lupita shouts, "Don't look!"

But it was too late. The Adroanzi's huge burning eyes narrow in on Keon and Raine. Saliva drips from their long fangs as their slimy tongues move from corner to corner on their scaly lips. Raine instinctively pulls Keon behind her. She touches the iron poker she attached to her belt before leaving Mr. Kijin's cabin. Her skin becomes iron as the Adroanzi slither quickly to their prey. They pounce into the air and come down like a swarm of wasps over them.

Raine swats Adroanzi after Adroanzi with the poker. Careful to not let any past her. She twists and turns, catching them as they fall, only to sling and hurl them back.

Miss Lupita struggles to move as the Adroanzi grow tighter around her. She stretches her hand out toward the water. Fish start fumbling onto the shore and morphing into King Cobras. Miss Lupita faintly says, "Help us, please." The King Cobras fan out to start attacking the Adroanzis.

Several King Cobras hurry over to bite the ones holding onto Miss Lupita. The Adroanzi shriek in agony as the King Cobras rip them off Miss Lupita and shakes them furiously.

Miss Lupita runs to Keon and Raine's aid, as they continue to swat the hideous creatures away. One leaps towards Keon, but flies past him as Keon shrinks to avoid it. Keon grabs its tail as he enlarges and twirls it round to combat several other Adroanzis coming his way.

"Look!" Miss Lupita yells as she points and runs to them. Raine quickly peaks behind her and sees the leaning rock. She turns back to Miss Lupita but is shocked to see, Anpu, standing in the distance. She softly utters the words,

"No," before yelling, "Keon, run to the leaning rock."

"Mom we're winning," he utters triumphantly.

"Keon!" Raine yells.

"But..."

"When I count to 3, I want you to run as fast as you can to the leaning rock."

"Mommy, I can't leave you!" he says with tears streaming.

"I'll be right behind you baby, but I need you to go."

"You both go," Miss Lupita chimes in, "I'll hold them off."

"Lupita, you can't, it must be me," Raine shouts,

"Don't make this harder than it needs to be," Miss Lupita shouts, "go."

"You don't understand," Raine pleads. Miss Lupita locks eyes with Keon and says,

"One..."

"Mommy, I..." Keon says while wiping a tear,

"Lupita!" Raine says.

"Two…" Miss Lupita continues,

"Keon go!" Raine shouts as her skin returns to normal and she fights through the tears. She grabs Keon's hand and looks to the leaning rock just around the bend of the lake. She hears Miss Lupita shout, "Three!"

Raine bursts from their spots, pulling Keon with her as they bolt toward the leaning rock. The terrifying sounds of the deathly shrieks and battle cries of Miss Lupita are slowly muffled by the wind rushing past their ears. They hear the hateful hissing of several Adroanzi on their heels.

Miss Lupita's scream cuts through the battle sounds and causes Raine to glance back. She sees Miss Lupita's body engulfed and overpowered by the Adroanzi as Anpu walks toward the massacre.

Raine shouts but no words come out. She sidesteps an Adroanzi that narrowly misses biting her heels.

She continues forward as she yells to Keon, "Faster Keon, we have to go faster!"

She holds his hand tight but feels her grip loosen as his hand gets larger. Soon she finds herself running with newfound passion as Keon has begun to surpass her. The pain of exhaustion hits her chest, but she can't stop. She must keep going. The pound of each step echoes through her tired body.

The leaning rock grows larger and gets closer faster than expected. Confusion hits her as she feels her body being lifted, no carried. She blinks and feels the rush of wind whooshing past her face. She looks at Keon, smiling as he runs with her in his arms at blazing speeds.

Raine looks to the leaning rock, that is closing in fast. But Keon isn't slowing down. She feels her heart pound through her chest as they close in on the solid wall underneath the leaning rock. *Oh no!* She thinks as Keon keeps running. She closes her eyes and braces for impact.

Chapter 23:
My Old Friend

"Are you done yet?" Niya says as she makes her way down a long metal ramp with Sissy strutting close behind. The dark chamber is barely lite but old tribal carvings can be made out along the walls. They make their way to Qarinah who is working over a table with Xaden's body covered with a white sheet and various concoctions in beakers all around.

"I don't want to rush this," Qarinah says, "it took me several years to return your spirit to your body last time."

"Sense you've done it before, I don't see what's taking so long."

"It's not that simple Xaden, my gifts allow me to mold objects into living creatures. But combining an object with arcane alchemy, ... I just need a little more time."

"Time is not what we have, Niya's mind is stronger than I anticipated. I need to leave her body before I put an end to her."

"You're going to kill her?" Qarinah ask with a raised voice.

"Is that a problem?"

"No, I mean I thought Xolani was the priority."

"You don't need to think. Just do what I say. Xolani is the priority but why not have a little fun in the process?"

"But she's only a child," Qarinah says concerned. Niya with narrowed eyes and flattened lips says,

"You're not going soft on me, are you?"

"Of course not. I just don't see the point of going out of our way to kill her if we don't have to," she replies.

"No loose ends," Niya says, "we will have to go after Raine and their other half-breed fugenie when my body is restored, and I'll take care of Xolani."

"You say Niya is stronger than you thought, wouldn't it be better to keep her around to exploit her gifts?"

"Perhaps?"

"We could use her to torment Xolani that much more," Qarinah adds.

"I do like the sound of that" Niya replies as she picks up Sissy and scratches under her chin.

"Princess Niya," a voice says from just inside the doorway behind them, "I've brought President Kumbak as requested."

"Excellent," Niya says after turning to see the man standing at attention, with Kombak eagerly waiting behind him. "Kumbak, you may come forward." Niya smiles then waves the soldier off and says, "You may return to your post." He bows and exits hastily. "Kumbak, it's been a long time." With a tilt of his head and scrunched brow, Kumbak says,

"It's only been a few hours since I saw you last, Princess. Are you feeling okay?"

"I'm wonderful," Niya says with a smile before buddying up beside Kumbak and continuing, "Listen, I'm going to need a favor from you."

"Me?" He replies with a raised brow.

"Yes, you are just the man I need to help nudge Xolani off the throne."

"Wait," Kumbak leans away slightly, "you want your father to abdicate the throne?"

"Of course not, I want him to die by my hands and I then take the throne." Kumbak hesitates and tilts his head before saying,

"Beside the fact you are a child, the council would never honor that. And I could never be a part of such a..." Niya places her finger over Kumbak's lips to silence him and says,

"All you need to do is persuade the council to change a rule or two within the Scion Contention and I will handle the rest."

"The Scion Contention is only used in situations of identical siblings. And last I heard, your father's twin Xaden died years ago."

"Qarinah, I think it's time we update Kumbak on the good news." Kumbak looks with a furled face, watches as Qarinah pulls back the drape covering Xaden's body. Kumbak's eyes grow wide before a slow sinister smile rolls across his lips. He then asks,

"So what is it you'd have me do and what is in it for me?" Niya smiles and says,

"Let's just say this will be a very lucrative deal. And all you will need to do is talk."

"Talk?"

"Yes," Niya replies as she pats Kumbak on the back and gently ushers him back up the ramp, " and oh, deliver a small message to a dear, dear friend of ours."

Chapter 24:

Numb

Keon stumbles to his knees from exhaustion and drops Raine. They both scramble to recover before standing. Raine looks back to see a stone wall. The rough texture tickles as she touches the stone. Not sure exactly how but they managed to go through it. She examines the wall for some sort of marking, to see where they may have entered but is unable to find one.

"Keon," she says as she turns to find him zooming back and forth. Barely able to see him as he moves. A vague outline remains as he moves.

"Keon," she says as he darts away in a blur. She pans around in his direction and takes in their new surroundings. Lush meadows flow into streams that empty into a vast lake.

"This is gorgeous," she murmurs before remembering they need to keep moving. She yells, "Keon, we need to go!"

Keon whips back and stands there for a moment and replies, "Mom! Did you see that?"

"I did and I'm excited about your new gift, but we need to keep moving."

They start to move but Keon stops suddenly and says, "Aren't we going to wait for Miss Lupita?"

Raine pauses, replaying the horror of Miss Lupita sacrificing herself for them. And even though she was used to loss in her life, fleeing with Xolani, leaving her life with her parents, she's had to learn to let things go in the moment and face the emotions later.

But seeing Anpu standing there made his words echo that much louder and truer,

"*The bill always comes due.*"

She pushes through the thoughts and goes to speak. But Keon's child eyes keep her frozen. How would she tell him they've lost his teacher and friend? No, family, Miss Lupita was like a grandmother to him.

The words hide from her lips as she searches for what to say.

"Miss Lupita..." holding back tears, she continues, "did what she thought was right, and held off the Adroanzi for us. She would, want, us to keep going."

"Momma, why do you look sad?" Keon asks, "She'll be here in a moment." Raine looks Keon in his shimmering green eyes and says, "She's not coming."

Keon's eyes begin to swell as he processes what was said. He shakes his head before scrubbing a hand over his face. Looking at the ground he says in a low tone.

"We have to save her." Raine kneels down to grab his chin and says,

"We have to stay on mission." But Keon's hands explode up and he shouts,

"We can't just leave her!"

Raine is almost knocked back but keeps her balance to stand and say, "I know it seems harsh but it's the right thing to do. We need to keep going, find the gods to get the pieces of their essence, maybe find the Legacy, and hopefully Haygena and Kaleo."

Keon sits on the ground and holds his knees to his chest as he sways back and forth. Raine kneels and rubs his back. Heat from Keon warms her hand until he becomes hot to the touch, and pulls her hand back.

"Keon are you feeling..." But before she finishes her sentence, he bursts off, leaving a trail of fire in his wake.

Chapter 25:
It Can't Be That

"How's your shoulder?" Rashid asks.

"Just a graze," Xolani says as he sits with legs crossed and eyes closed, trying to meditate, "I'm sure it looks worse than it feels."

A few moments drag by as Rashid stands with his arms folded, tapping his feet and says,

"So, you're just going to sit there like a stump on a log?" Xolani sighs and says,

"If you haven't noticed, I'm reflecting on our situation. Perhaps you should do the same."

"Reflect?" Rashid asks sarcastically, "Okay."

Rashid moves across the cell and plops down, almost knocking Xolani over as he crosses his legs to mimic Xolani. Rashid begins to chant before Xolani says,

"Rashid, enough"

"Hold on Sire, I'm reflecting," Rashid says in a huff. "I'm meditating on the fact we're stuck in this cell."

"Rashid," Xolani says calmly, "I'm not blind to our situation, but your attitude isn't helping."

Rashid takes in a deep breath before saying, "You're right. I just can't believe how easy it was for that hag, to literally kick us in here. How is that even possible?"

Xolani thinks for a moment before responding. "The better question is, how did Xaden escape death, again."

"You don't think he astro-projected into Niya, do you?" Rashid asks.

"Astro-projecting his mind to some random plane of existence is how he survived last time. This time however, he must have been able to keep his mind attached to Niya somehow, when he had control over her as he was dying. Unfortunately, I don't think that's our biggest problem."

"Then what is?" Rashid asks.

"The Scion Contention, where I have to fight him while he's in Niya's body," Xolani replies.

"We're just guessing he's going to challenge your right to the throne." Rashid says, "And even if we're right, he broke out the hag queen herself, Qarinah. You don't think she will create a body for Xaden again, do you?"

"Actually, she won't have to," Xolani says, "they didn't know we were down there. They came to the crypt for a reason."

"Can't Niya feel where people are?"

"No, Raine can. Niya hears people's thoughts, if she's listening. And that gives her an idea of a location. But she would never do that,"

"Xaden would," Rashid says.

"True... but we were too far down for her, him, to reach or sense us. They must have come down there for his body."

"I told you to cremate him before you put him down there."

Xolani rolls his eyes as he ignores Rashid's comment and continues, "As of right now, the only course of action we can do is wait."

"He's right you know," a youthful voice says. Rashid and Xolani sit in silence for a second as they look for the source of the voice. Johnathan Hender appears still wearing his black and white waiters uniform, in front of their cell. "Excuse me, your majesty. I'm still getting used to my gifts."

"You're the kid server from the ball tonight," Xolani says, "that was talking to Niya. Ron, John, Johnathan, right?"

"I'm not a kid, Sire," Johnathan replies, "and yes. My name is Johnathan, but everyone calls me Sheer."

140

"This probably isn't the best place for you ki..." Rashid says before correcting himself, "Sheer. You should get out of here while you can."

"Lady Neyma asked me to sneak down here since my gifts seem to keep me from Niya's influence."

"My mother told you to come here?" Xolani asks.

"Yes," Sheer replies, "she's keeping part of the palace under her illusion gift to protect the very few of us that Niya can't control."

"Niya can see through her gifts," Xolani says.

"Lady Neyma keeps us and the illusion moving away from Niya. But luckily Niya has the servants and guards moving mostly around the palace. From what I gather, she and some other weird-looking women are working on something."

"Something?" Rashid asks as he gives Xolani a smirk.

"I don't know," Sheer says apologetically, "they mostly stay locked in the old throne room, and I didn't want to get too close to them."

"Smart." Rashid says before continuing to blurt out, "But why take the risk to come down here then?"

Xolani shoots him a look of disapproval, then quickly says, "I think what he means is, what is so important that my mother would risk sending you down here?"

"Right," Sheer says, "Lady Neyma said to tell you that, some guy named Xaden wants to kill you."

"There's a revelation," Rashid mumbles as Sheer continues,

"But I guess, he knows he can't fight you outright. So he's keeping everyone from the ball to have them watch you two fight it out in some old ritual..." Sheer taps his foot as he thinks, "The ziom conference, the zenom..."

"The Scion Contention," Xolani says.

"Yes, that was it, the Scion Contention. Wait, how did you know that?"

"Long story," Xolani says, "it wouldn't be the first time Xaden and I have done this. I'm not sure what his game is. It's illegal to kill during the fight."

"So why bring it back," Rashid asks, "since he just wants to kill you?"

Sheer steps closer to the glass and says, "Lady Neyma said death during the battle is now legal. President Kombak persuaded the council to change the rules."

They all stand silent as the cold prison air wraps around them, heavy footsteps begin echoing through the hall, alerting them that someone is coming.

"I'll come back if I can," Sheer whispers quickly before his body vanishes. The steps get louder as they close in on Xolani and Rashid's cell.

"It certainly is a good day, isn't it?" Kumbak says through his twisted smirk. Xolani and Rashid, now at the back of the cell, rise quickly upon seeing who it is.

"Kumbak," Rashid and Xolani say in unison before Xolani continues, "what are you doing down here?" Kumbak smiles as he pretends to admire his pudgy little fingers and says,

"I'm only here, as a friend, to check in on another friend."

"There you go with that word, friend, again?" Xolani says with an unbelieving tone.

"See Xalen, that was always your problem," Kumbak replies, "your distrust."

"Right, it has nothing to do with you being a smuckle does it?" Rashid blurts out. Kumbak chucks and says,

"Rashid, I see much hasn't changed. Except for that brutish thug mentality has finally landed you where you belong." Rashid goes to speak but Xolani beats him to it saying,

"Kumbak, why are you down here?" Kumbak waits a moment before responding.

"I have a message for you, from a mutual, friend." Xolani doesn't look thrilled as Kumbak continues, "But this message is just for you. So, you'll have to come closer."

Kumbak motions with his finger to Xolani to come closer. Xolani hesitantly moves near and stops. "Oh, come now. You can get closer than that." Kumbak says. Xolani moves forward, millimeters from the glass. Kumbak leans forward to say in a whisper,

"Xaden wants you to know, your time is up Xolani and he will do to you what you did to him, in front of the world."

"Xaden's dead," Xolani says.

"We both know that's a lie and I will help him get his throne back."

"I thought I was a true royal?"

"Oh, you are, your majesty. But I want what's best for mine and your people. And I believe that happens to be Xaden, no matter what form he may come in."

Xolani stands tall and seemingly gets even closer to Kumbak's face as he says, "When I get out of here, I'm going to give you more than just a bloody nose."

"Promises," Kumbak says as he waddles off, continuing in the distance, "promises my friend, promises."

Xolani turns to Rashid and says,

"We need to get out of here." Rashid smiles wide and says,

"I'm way ahead of you. Hold still." Rashid moves quickly to Xolani, who says,

"Hold still for what?"

Chapter 26:
The Lost Boy

Pain radiants in her chest, intensifying as Raine pushes forward, trying her best to keep up with the flames left from Keon bursting off. But at her best, she is losing ground, and with every step, she falls more and more behind. The trail of flames grows cold as they begin to extinguish, leaving her as fast as Keon did. She finally stops, placing her hands on her waist, she leans back to fill her lungs with air.

Exhausted, Raine walks, unable to take in the surrounding beauty of the lush green grass beneath her feet or the blue sapphire sky above her. Her focus is on Keon. Her mind plays through various scenarios of him getting into trouble or worse.

Raine takes in a deep breath and exhales slowly. She repeats this to calm herself as she works to feel where Keon may be. She's stops again, quieting herself until she feels a nudge in her spirit.

"*Keon,*"

She says to herself. She walks slowly in the direction of her intuition. The faint sound of sniffling catches her attention.

She stops walking in order to pinpoint the sound's location. Closing her eyes, she focuses in and finds the sound floating on the breeze as the wind pushes past her ears and through her hair.

Raine moves with stealthy urgency as she follows the soft sobbing to a shallow cave along the base of the mountain. She whispers,

"Keon, is that you?" After a few sniffles, Keon replies,

"No."

She moves in, letting her eyes adjust to the dark. She finds him sitting on the dirt floor, with his head tucked in his knees. Raine gently touches his shoulder before saying,

"I know it's not easy, but we have to keep going."

Keon nudges his shoulder away from her touch and says,

"How could we just leave her?" Keon turns to her with tears streaming down his face. Raine grabs him tight and says,

"She held them off so we could complete the mission. And it's only right we keep going so her sacrifice isn't in vain."

"But how do you know she's gone?" Keon blurts out before Raine interrupts and says,

"I just know, and we need to keep moving."

"But Mommy, can we just," Keon says, but his voice trails off as Raine hears a soft growl coming from further in the cave. She straightens slightly to position herself better and listens. She hears the growl getting closer as Keon continues on. She places a finger over her mouth and whispers,

"Shhhhh" She takes Keon's hand and raises slowly, pulling Keon up with her. She steps backward as she watches the growing shadow moving toward them.

Teeth begin to shine over a horrifying rumble of igniting flames. Raine pushes Keon behind her as she says,

"Run." Keon stands motionless as the flames grow larger and Raine shouts, "Run!" as she turns and pushes him forward. Immense heat follows them as they make their way out and jump to the side before a bellowing fireball launches from the cave, leaving a trail of scorched earth in its path as it dissipates.

"Come on," Raine says as she pulls Keon and begins to run. They start to run through a field of plush, open grass before an enormous shadow rolls over them. A gigantic golden scaled dragon drops thunderously in their path.

They come to a halt as it snarls at them. Keon's eyes go wide with excitement. Its enormous dark wings fold back as its emerald green eyes lock in on them. Its sharp white teeth peek through its scaly mouth. Keon stares at the winged beast's large claws as it slowly inches toward them. An amber glow begins to grow as the pitch-black dragon's mouth ignites. It inhales and Raine shouts,

"Move!" She reaches for the poker she took from Mr. Kijin's cabin but it's not on her belt. She quickly pats herself down and feels a lump in her pocket. *My staff, it's still here.* She thinks and pushes Keon hard to the side as she pulls it out. It expands almost immediately as she pulls it out. Her skin shifts from her hand to her head and feet. Covering her whole body in a metallic silver. The staff springs out and elongates before Raine bursts forward and jabs it into the dragon's foot.

It roars so loudly that the sky seems to shake, dispersing fire into the heavens. It looks back down to find Raine standing, ready for a fight. It swats her, missing as she flips over its huge paws.

As she lands, a sudden hard pain hits her side as the dragon's tail makes contact and whacks her several yards away. It pounces to catch her off guard, but Raine recovers quickly and runs toward it. The dragon spews a stream of fire, engulfing her.

Raine emerges with a leap as fire flows off her metallic frame. She comes down hard on the dragon, smacking her staff on its nose.

It whelps in agony, stomping backwards while shaking its head furiously. Steam barrels from its nostrils before the dragon begins to charge toward her again.

Raine stands her ground but Keon darts in front of her, grabbing the dragon's attention as he runs past. The dragon starts to pursue him. Wind rips through Keon's hair as he glances back to see the winged beast soaring behind him. He keeps running, feeling the rush of the world passing him by. Blazing through the grassy fields and cutting over water, he runs with such velocity that he nearly forgets a dragon is chasing him until the heat of a misplaced fire ball hurtles past his side.

Keon refocuses and quickly u-turns and runs directly toward his pursuer. He launches himself above it and lands on its nose before running over it and back the other way.

The dragon fumbles but recovers quickly, turning to continue the chase. Keon has a good lead before reaching Raine and stopping.

"It's right behind me," He pants. Raine replies.

"It's okay, we'll take it together. Stand ready." They both assume fighting stances as the dragon flies furiously their way.

"Stop!" a voluptuous woman shouts as she appears just moments before they can move. The dragon soars up, missing them by inches, and lands back in front of them. The woman then pets it softly on the cheek before saying gently,

"That's enough now, Leonyx, I'm sure you gave our guest an awful fright."

"Thank you," Raine says. But the woman continues to stoke the dragon's cheeks. Raine then continues with, "This is my son Keon and I'm..."

"I know who you both are, Raine," she says before turning to face them. She brushes off her elegantly flowing, green, mossy dress and runs her fingers around her ear, pushing her breezy-mixed blue hair back as she continues, "What I don't know, is why you and your friends have decided to impede and disrupt the harmony of our lands."

"That wasn't our intent, Ms...." Raine says as she takes a step forward,

"I am Ashanti," she replies,

"Oh," Raine says, "Ashanti... thee Ashanti. Mother of earth Ashanti?"

Ashanti smiles and Raine's face lights up as she continues, "We could use your help, please. We are needing to collect the essence of several gods to return the Lumastar back to its realm and restore balance."

"Ah yes, your friends mentioned something to that effect," Ashanti says with a big grin. Keon and Raine's faces light up as they both shout Haygena's and Kaleo's names. Ashanti continues, "Yes, your friends also mentioned you were sent here by Malkum. If I were you, I wouldn't go around here saying his name. Not all of us have forgiven him."

"Forgiven him?" Raine asks but quickly says, "Doesn't matter. Would you mind taking us to our friends?"

Ashanti smiles and bows gracefully as she says, "Of course, right this way. I believe they are still speaking with some of the other gods," she leads them to the back of Leonyx and motions for them to climb up.

Raine's eyes widen as she stares at the huge beast that is now purring like a kitten. She turns to look down at Keon but finds him already on top of the enormous pet.

"Come on Mommy!" Keon shouts from up top. "It's not that high up here." Raine exhales loudly and says,

"It's not the height I'm working about, It just tried to eat us." Ashanti says,

"Leonyx meant no harm, promise." She then motions up as she says, "If you'd please." Raine looks skeptical but decides to climb up. Ashanti follows behind her and says,

"Leonyx will take us to them and to the other gods. Won't you Leonyx?" Leonyx's wings expand and begin to flap. Leonyx gallops forward, gaining speed, and soon the wind catches beneath her wings. They all face the sun as they glide with ease into the sky.

Chapter 27:

You Can't Be Serious

Xolani sits in the corner brooding while Rashid paces back and forth.

"Will you stop?" Xolani says.

"Sorry, I really thought that would work," Rashid replies.

"Don't worry, we'll come up with something else. Just please, stop pacing before you create a trench." Rashid stops but begins tapping the sides of his pants. "Rashid!"

"Right, sorry. I get fidgety when I'm nervous."

"Your nervous, I'm the one that has to fight," Xolani says as he rests his head on his arm.

"Remember the last time you were in a cell?" Rashid asks.

"Yeah, only the fight was before being in the cell and you weren't in it," Xolani says as he begins to remember. He tilts his head downward, sees the gold trim shimmer on his red sash, and jumps up to say,

"Kle a louvri nenpòt pòt!"

"What?" Rashid says.

"Kle a louvri nenpòt pòt!" Xolani shouts again before continuing to say, "The key to open any door. We've had a key this whole time!" Rashid's eyes light up as Xolani unties the sash from around his waist. Xolani stands for a moment looking at the sash before Rashid says,

"You know how to use it?"

"Not a clue, I've never had to use it before." Xolani replies. He walks over to the transparent cell doors and waves the sash around. Up, down, side to side but nothing happens. Xolani thinks for a moment and says with authority as he holds the sash to the cell doors,

"Kle a louvri nenpòt pòt," the gold stitching begins to glow before the cell doors open. Xolani motions to Rashid to follow. They leave the cell only to hear guards marching toward their location.

"déjà vu," Rashid says, as Xolani replies,

"Yeah, but this time, I don't think we have a way out."

Kasmine, Kacao, and Ramuth round the corner with expressionless surprise to see them out of their cells. They pull out their shock sticks out of their holsters and charge toward Rashid and Xolani.

"Guess it's time to fight," Rashid says.

"We can't hurt them," Xolani replies, "they are under Xaden's control."

Rashid nods in agreement before Kasmine swings and nearly hits him. Rashid grabs her wrist and forces her toward the wall. She throws her foot against the wall and thrusts herself and Rashid backward. Rashid stumbles, almost hitting Xolani. Xolani sees him and bends over, allowing Rashid to tumble over his back before Xolani gives Kasmine a swift kick to her back, knocking her down. Rashid quickly emerges with a right hook to Kacao's chin, knocking him unconscious.

Immense pain jolts through Rashid's body as a shock stick hits his back. Xolani knocks the shock stick loose from Ramuth's hand, she then lunges toward him. Xolani sidesteps to avoid her attack and throws out his arm, close-lining her in the process. She lands hard as her head lands with a loud thud. She rubs the back of her head as she starts to rise and says,

"What, what happened?" Xolani lends a hand to Rashid to help raise him up before saying,

"You were under mind control, but you're free." She looks at Xolani and says,

"Your Majesty," and gets down on one knee, "I am so sorry. I did not know what I was doing. I could see but couldn't stop myself from,"

Xolani raises his hand to silence her and says, "It's all right, we know." He grabs her by the arm and pulls her up. "We are going to need..."

Blood trickles slowly out the corner of her mouth. Xolani catches Ramuth as she falls. They look down to see a large father shaped dagger lodged in her back. He lays her down softly as he and Rashid look down the hall to see Qarinah standing with a satisfied grin.

"What have you done hag!" Rashid yells.

"Flattery will get you nowhere," she replies.

"She didn't have to die Qarinah," Xolani says as he stands.

"Unfortunately," Qarinah says as she moves forward, "Her fate was sealed when you decided to leave your cell. Now come with me before more have to die."

"We're not going anywhere with you," Rashid barks, "you nasty gopher-mite."

"After all these years it's cute you're still infatuated with me but it's growing tiresome," Qarinah says, "and since we don't need you, the killing can continue with you. Xolani, follow me or your boyfriend dies."

Xolani begins to move before Rashid stops him and says, "She's bluffing." But then a dagger whizzes through the air and pierces his thigh. Rashid screams from the sharp pain penetrating his leg. He grabs his thigh falling to the ground and says, "Oh, I hate you so much."

"Call my bluff again and see where the next dagger goes," Qarinah says.

"All right," Xolani says, "I'll go. But he needs medical attention, as do the rest of these guards."

Qarinah tilts her head, as if to examine Rashid's wounds and says, "I don't believe I hit any arteries, he'll live. Just put some pressure on it until we, I mean I, return." She motions to Xolani to come forward before saying, "Oh, Rashid. Be a good boy and crawl back into your cell for me." Rashid looks at her. She returns his gaze before he struggles to stand and hobbles back into the cell. "good boy."

She presses a button on the wall, resetting all the cells. The sound of metal gears turning sharply into place echos through the halls. She looks at Xolani and says,

"Let's go. Xaden has a surprise waiting for you."

Chapter 28:

Don't Forget A Gift

It all seems like a dream, fluffy clouds float past Raine and Keon's heads. The gentle kiss of the sun warms their cheeks as the wind glides through their hair.

Leonyx soars freely before making her decent. They all tighten their thighs and grab hold as best they can while she folds in her wings and dive bombs toward the ground. Raine closes her eyes as Keon screams with delight. Leonyx extends her wings in the last moments to soar above the tree line. With her newfound momentum she climbs back into the sky as if aiming for the sun. Raine tilts her head to shield her eyes. She hunkers over Keon to keep him from falling back as they hold on tight. Leonyx floats in the sky as she glides gracefully before plopping down to land.

Raine hurries down Leonyx's back and says, "Let's not ever do that again."

Ashanti gracefully slides down with a smile while Keon shouts, "Can we go again please?"

Raine looks up at him with a disapproving frown as Ashanti says,

"I'm sure Leonyx would be happy to take you all up again later. After all, we will have to find our way back down."

"Down?" Raine ask as she realizes she is standing on the edge of a very large platform. Her skin becomes pale as she peers over the side and inches back from the ledge. "Please tell me you have an elevator?"

Ashanti smiles and says, "Where would the fun in that be? However, I believe we have more pressing business to attend to." Keon makes a sad face before finally hopping off Leonyx. Ashanti pets Leonyx and says, "Thank you" before turning and motions for Keon and Raine to follow, saying,

"This way"

They are both awestricken as they proceed to follow her to an enormous pantheon. Its marble-like columns seemed to go beyond the stars, with its gigantic doorway that even a dragon three times Leonyx's size could easily fly through.

Haygena's familiar voice can be heard arguing with someone. Keon bolts ahead with his newfound speed as Raine trails behind.

She hurries into the pantheon and is taken back by its enormous beauty and size. Long blueish gray columns stretch from the floor to the moving ceiling. Raine gasps as she watches the ceiling swirl and move with various shades of white and blues.

"Gorgeous, isn't it?" Ashanti says as she walks up beside her, "Ptah was gracious enough to make it for us all, shortly after we arrived here. He truly outdid himself."

Raine looks to Ashanti with a slightly blank expression before Ashanti says,

"It's okay, most humans don't know who Ptah is, on account, he isn't a god of worship. He's a god of creativity and creation. And seeing most mortals don't value creativity, he often gets overlooked... Pity."

"Raine!" Haygena shouts excitedly. Raine turns in time to catch a hug from her as Haygena asks, "Where's Miss Lupita?"

Raine's eyes tear up, but before she can reply a sneaky voice says,

"We get it, you all are happy to see each other. Can we get on with it?"

Raine looks over to see three enormous beings seated on golden thrones before them.

"I have better things to do than sit here and converse with fleshies." He continues as he places his head on his hand. His long spider leg-like fingers stretch, covering the side of his face.

"No one is asking you to stay here Ogun." Takhor, the god of justice says. His booming, deep voice vibrates through Raine's body. He sits poised against the back of his chair with his chest held high and chiseled chin resting on his hand.

"Yes, I agree," says Mami Wata with her strong angelic voice, "You may leave at your own convenience Ogun."

Ogun folds his arms and pouts in his chair. Before Takhor says,

"However, in his own way, he may have a point. We do need to move on. I believe Haygena was pleading their case."

"Takhor, as we mentioned," Haygena says as she motions to her and Kaleo, "the Lumastar is dying and to restore it, we are respectfully requesting a piece of essence from each of you to take back to Malkum."

"Malkum!" Mami Wata, the goddess of transformation, huffs, "That no good vallakie can't possibly be trusted. How do we know he didn't con you into coming for his own purposes of using our life essence to make us weaker, while making himself stronger?"

"Malkum is a lot of things," Takhor says as he leans forward, "but even he knows the cost of too much power."

Ogun laughs, "You are a bigger fool than I thought Takhor, if you'd believe anything Malkum says."

"Says Malkum's old lieutenant," Mami Wata jokes. Her shimmering sea blue gown flows with the current of her laughter. Ogun gives her a brief look before saying,

"Whatever, you know it's a bad idea to trust him again. Plus, Takhor is being unusually quiet at this point."

"Listening," Takhor replies, "I wouldn't want to jump to any rash conclusions, would I?" They all take a moment before Takhor looks at Keon and asks, "Little one, why are you here?"

"Me?" Keon asks before looking at Raine. She motions for him to continue. Keon looks back to Takhor and says, "I'm here to help sir."

Ogun laughs loudly at the notion of Keon helping.

"Ogun!" Mami Wata shouts.

"My apologies," he says with clear disdain, "but, how is it, they come to our domain, asking of us our essence without the thought of giving us something in return? I think, if they want our essence, then we merely should receive compensation."

Mami Wata leans toward Ogun and says, "What is it that you could possibly want?"

"A fight with the boy!" Ogun says joyfully.

"Absolutely not!" Raine shouts.

"Such emotion for such a minor transaction," Ogun says.

"Minor," Raine shouts, "he is my son! Not some sort of play-thing for your amusement."

"How dare you raise your voice at a god!" Ogun shouts. Raine continues and says,

"A god doesn't bargain the fate of the world on their own selfish whims."

Before Raine can utter another word, Ogun leaps from his throne in a puff of smoke, reappearing inches from Raine's face. His long tall frame towers over her as he says,

"You speak as if we are equals meat suit. I could peel your skin from your bones while your son watches."

"Enough!" Takhor yells. His voice booming as it echoes in the sudden silence. "Ogun, stop the theatrics and return to your seat."

Ogun puffs out of sight before materializing comfortably back in his seat.

"That will not happen again," Takhor continues, "these mortals came here to save the earth. Which must I remind you is our home too. And if it were to vanish, so could we."

"Yes," Mami Wata chimes in, "very true."

Kaleo steps forward and bows as he speaks in a low tone, "Respectfully, may we have your essence?"

Mami Wata looks to Takhor who's stroking his chin. Ashanti walks forward. Resting a hand on Kaleo's shoulder before saying,

"I will lend my essence as well."

Kaleo smiles politely before standing. The room grows quiet as an awkwardness fills the air. Ogun sits looking toward the ceiling as all eyes have gravitated to him. Takhor says,

"Now you are the one overly quiet, Ogun." Ogun folds his arms as if not hearing Takhor's words. "Ogun!" Takhor shouts, "This child has shown more maturity than you today."

"Then take a piece of his essence!" Ogun shouts back before standing, "We are gods! Why do we cater to these gas bags."

"Enough Ogun!" Takhor shouts. Ogun sits back down slowly as he strokes his chin and says,

"These mortals need to prove they're worth. If they do, then we give them our essence," everyone begins to smile until Ogun continues, "and what better way to prove you're worth, then to see, if you meat sacks can defeat me in combat."

"You can't be serious?" Ashanti says, "You know you have the advantage."

"Why would I make the offer if I didn't?"

"Takhor, this can't be fair?" Ashanti asks. Takhor sits back and thinks for a moment before saying,

"Ogun makes a valid point."

"Ha" Ogun says loudly as Takhor ignores him and continues, "They need to prove their intention." Ogun then turns to Raine and the others and says, "my followers would always bring me gifts before asking anything of me. And since you brought nothing, I see it only fitting that you give me the gift of a spectacular fight. Do you accept?"

"Takhor," Ashanti says, "you know as well as I, Ogun doesn't really care about proving anything. He only wants to fight."

Haygena adds, "Ogun, is the god of war. We would be foolish to fight him unprovoked."

"Correct," Kaleo says, "he has eons of experience. How would this be a fair fight?"

"Whoever said fights were fair?" Ogun says, "That is the beauty of a good fight. However, this is about proving your worth, no matter what others think," He sticks his tongue out at Ashanti before continuing, "I am willing to limit myself to just the potential most mortals display... Do we have a deal?"

"This is not Keon's fight," Raine says, "pick someone else for your sick games".

"How about," Ogun says with a smile, "the four of you, versus me, and if one of you win, we give you our essence. But when I win... I still give you a piece of my essence. How's that?"

They all look at each other before coming to an agreement. Raine stands tall and says,

"Let's fight."

Chapter 29:

Sibling Rivalry

Footsteps echo their movement as Qarinah and Xolani make their way down a long stone corridor. Xolani focuses on the large wall ahead as the repetitive sound of their shoes are replaced by the sounds of an enormous crowd's commotion growing louder with each step. A familiar voice is blasted through the stadium's intercoms.

"My dear, noble people," Xolani quickly recognizes Kumbak's weasel voice. "I know I am not native to this beautiful land but I love this country as if it were my own. And it would beseech me to not tell you what I know now as the truth... In his short reign, your reluctant king has constantly let the good people of Nuhana down. Lack of economic growth, food shortages, and let's not mention the domestic terrorist he is allowing to roam ramped through your city streets, harming good, fair, and honest citizens such as yourselves."

"What is Kumbak doing, Qarinah?" Xolani demands.

"Isn't it obvious?" she replies with a twisted smile, "Warming up the crowd for your big entrance."

"He's fabricating the truth," Xolani shouts.

They hear Kumbak prattle on. Qarinah moves in closer and runs her finger over Xolani's chest.

"I've never noticed but you're kind of cute when you're angry."

"Get your hands off me," he says through gritted teeth.

"Fine," she says with a smile, as she steps back, "your loss."

A loud burst of cheers cuts through their conversation. Light pierces through the hall as the wall begins to rise.

Xolani instinctively covers his face while his eyes adjust to the illuminated situation, with one eye slowly opening and the other following. Dust is sucked in and swirls in the light as the walls rise.

"What is this?" he asks,

"Come now, I think we both know what's about to happen," Qarinah says with evil intent.

"Enlighten me."

"This is where you'll fight your last fight, Xalen, and get what you finally deserve."

"Rashid's right, you are a hag," Xolani says. Qarinah uses her elbow to deliver a shift blow to his stomach. Xolani falls to his knees, gasping for air. She bends down, pulls his head back, and whispers,

"This is all for you, and don't get any bright ideas like not fighting or trying not to win. Because if I get a hint of you not acting accordingly, I will slowly, painfully and disgustingly, end Niya. And all while you watch." She violently lets go of his head, "So play nice with your brother and lose gracefully so the whole world can see just how pathetic you truly are, your majesty," she punches him hard in the gut before patting him on the back.

"You can threaten me all you like," Xolani coughs out, "But if you touch a hair on her body, I swear there will be no rock you can slither under. No place for you to find peace because, I, will end you."

"Enough!" Xaden shouts from behind them. Xolani turns to see Xaden, in an all-white suit, standing prominently behind them.

"You've done enough Qarinah, and Niya is waiting," he commands. Qarinah tilts her head and walks away, back down the corridor.

Xolani staggers to stand on the stone stadium floor but rises to his feet. They both walk forward until they are face to face. Xaden says,

"Good day, brother"

Xolani grimaces as the two lock eyes. He tightens his lips so his thoughts of anger don't spill out. He breathes in slowly, feeling the cool air fill his lungs before saying,

"Where's Niya?"

"I wouldn't worry about her," Xaden replies, "after all, she's not the one in danger right now."

"This has gone on for far too long Xaden. Stop hiding behind a little girl, you coward!"

Xaden lets a twisted smile slither along his face as he says, "Isn't that the kettle calling the pot black?"

"Proof?" Kumbak blasts through the intercom, catching their attention as he continues.

"That's my queue," Xaden says and walks to the rising wall as Kumbak's voice continues.

"He leads us to believe there was only one heir to the throne of Nuhana, when in fact there is another..."

Xaden looks back and says,

"Oh, and don't worry about Niya, no harm will come to her. Unless you run... again." He turns to strut forward into the light and the crowd explodes with cheers. Kumbak says triumphantly,

"Xaden Uwani."

Xolani stands just before the light meets the dark and looks into the blinding light. He takes a moment to gather his thoughts and as he steps into the blinding light, he knows Xaden will not give him a fair fight and whether he wins or loses, he most protect Niya and all of Nuhana.

Chapter 30:

We have to go

The sun stands high in the sky as its rays flow down over everyone. They stand in a wide-open valley, as the lush grass dances with the gentle breeze.

"I thought we were going to fight?" Haygena says.

"Patience, fierce warrior," Ogun says, "we will get to it." He smiles as he lifts his head to catch the warm sunlight on his face.

"Ogun," says Mami Wata, "get on with it."

He looks at her from the corner of her eyes before gleefully saying,

"If we are to fight, we must do it right." The group looks puzzled as he continues, "We need a sight fit for a god to fight in. How about…" With a wave of his hand the beautiful valley changes to a desolate desert. "No, this isn't it. How about… Rome's great colosseum?"

Instantly, the sand begins to shift and morph into a glorious arena of Roman architecture, with large tall columns and massive seating.

"No, no, no," Ogun continues, "this will not do. How about…"

The columns vanish before all their eyes as an erupting volcano grows in the distance. A beach spreads beneath their feet as an ocean flows toward them, crashing several yards away.

"Ogun!" Takhor shouts to gain his attention. "Enough, your dramatics bore us and test my patience. We need to move on. Pick a location now!"

Ogun grinds his teeth before exhaling loudly.

"Perfection cannot be rushed Takhor. This needs to be right." Ogun turns and taps a finger to his chin, before looking at Keon and asking,

"Where would you like to fight, little one?"

"I'm not little... sir," Keon replies. He thinks for a moment before excitedly saying, "the moon!"

"Interesting," Ogun says to himself, "I hadn't thought of taking this fight elsewhere, very good."

The sun's radiant glow begins to fade as a dark gray illuminates the scene. Star light pricks through the blackened sky, twinkling in the distance. The vista, filled with shades of gray mountains and wide open moon creators. However, Raine, Keon, Haygena, and Kaleo begin to float in agony off the rocky gray terrain. Clawing at their necks as they gasp for air.

"Look," Ashanti says as she points, "they are floating away."

"They need air," Mami Wata adds.

"Fascinating" Ogun states.

"Well," Takhor says as he motions to Ogun to give them air.

"Oh right," Ogun says before snapping his fingers giving them instant relief before they plummet back to the dusty harsh ground.

"Th-th-thank you," Raine sputters out. "Were you trying to kill us before we even had a chance to beat you?"

"How absurd," Ogun says in repulsion, "to suggest I would need to stoop to such a level to beat mortals." His annoying fake laugh fills the air.

"Right," Raine says as she and the others find their way back onto their feet.

"Are we going to stand here or are we going to fight?" says Haygena.

Ogun looks at her from the corner of his eye before swirling his arms in a circular motion. Yards from them, raised thrones begin to shift up from the gray surface. Four in a row with three small ones in front of them. Mami Wata, Takhor, and Ashanti take their seats above the others, while Raine, Haygena, Kaleo, and Keon look at Ogun.

"I will take you one at a time," says Ogun, "All your natural abilities are allowed and you may choose any weapon to combat with me. I, on the other hand, will only use gifts accessible to humans and of course my double-edged battle axes."

Ogun reaches both his hands behind his back to pull out two massive round-edged axes. They seem to gleam as he swirls them proudly.

Haygena, not phased by Ogun's tactics asks, "And how do we know when the battle is over?"

"Each match is over when I have gotten you to submit or I have landed a fatal strike." They all look at each other before Ogun continues, "It won't kill you. At worst, it will cause a brief moment of un-consciousness."

"How kind of you," Raine says, "and you lose once one of us has done the same you as well, correct?"

"Yes," Ogun replies with a slight smirk, "that is correct. But I wouldn't expect that to happen... Now, let us select weapons. What do you choose?"

Haygena steps forward and says, "My chain whip axe."

Ogun smiles as he says, "Very well." A stiff chain materializes into Haygena's clenched fist. The chain becomes the handle as two axe blades grow opposite of each other. "Next?" Ogun asks.

Kaleo looks to the gods observing before turning and speaking softly,

"A sling blade"

"Interesting choice," Mami Wata says as Takhor adds,

"Yes, it is."

A swirl of dust and rock begins to form in front of Kaleo, tightly elongating as it spirals up, until the dust explodes with a light boom, revealing a staff taller than Kaleo with a double-edged hooked blade at its end. Kaleo grabs it from the air and admires its craftsmanship.

Ogun looks toward Raine but before he utters a word, she shakes her head, reaches into her pocket, and pulls out her small metal cylinder.

"My staff is all I will need." She squeezes it, causing it to expand in length before she slams one side to the ground.

"Very well," Ogun says, then turns to Keon and says, "And you?"

Keon looks down, then back up.

"Kaleo has taught me how to use many weapons," he says softly, "and I thought I should ask for my sling bow with some arrows. But then, I thought of Miss Lupita and what she would do." Keon's eyes begin to water as he fights the tears and continues,

"She would often tell me that everything we need in life is within... So, respectfully Mr. Ogun, sir. I won't need a weapon."

"Remarkable," Ashanti says.

"Indeed," Takhor adds. Ogun towers over Keon with a repulsed look. His eyes are half-cocked as he says,

"You think you can best me child with nothing but your wits."

The air riddles with tension as Keon doesn't reply. He stares up at Ogun, as if analyzing him before smiling innocently and replying,

"Sir, could you back up a few feet? Your breath smells."

A roar of laughter explodes from the other gods as Ashanti whispers,

"I've been wanting to say that to him for centuries."

Ogun whips his head in her direction before re-engaging and pointing an axe in Keon's direction.

"How about you make me, little one," he says with a snarl. "You can be the first that falls under my might."

Raine pulls Keon back by his arm but he quickly worms free of her grasp and says,

"You're willing to fight for what we need and so am I. I got this Mommy."

"Keon," Raine says, "at least choose a defensive weapon, son."

"Keon," Kaleo says softly, "perhaps this isn't your fight yet?"

"No," Keon says sternly, "let me fight, please?"

They all share glances before Raine smiles slowly and nods her head. Ogun licks his lips and whispers,

"Excellent," before motioning for them to take their seats.

Kaleo looks to Haygena and they touch hands briefly before they find their seats next to Raine.

Keon and Ogun square up. Neither flinch or move.

Ogun swirls his double-bladed axe around swiftly before letting the handle land on his shoulder.

"Are you ready, little one?" he asks.

Keon takes a defensive stance. Ogun mocks Keon as he mimics his movements. Suddenly, a burst of dust erupts where Keon was standing and the crowd is left confused. In a blink, Keon is now standing in Ogun's place with a trail of ridges leading to Ogun, who lies flat on his back yards away.

He pops up, and wipes his chin.

"Cheap shot boy," Ogun says, "It won't happen again."

"I thought you were ready," Keon retorts, "I can move slower?"

"Insignificant little..." Ogun says before Takhor shouts,

"Seems like young Keon may be too much for you in your old age Ogun."

He looks sternly at Takhor with disdain as the other gods laugh. Ogun focuses back on Keon and walks toward him.

"Try that again."

Keon smiles as he says, "Okay," and in a flash, he runs at full force toward Ogun, leaving a trail of dust behind him. The world barely moves as Keon gains ground on Ogun. Keon jumps and aims for Ogun's nose as the momentum carries him forward. Ogun smirks and sidesteps, catching Keon off guard as he swings his giant axe at Keon.

Keon shrinks before the blade nears him. He lands with a hard thud while growing back to normal size. But quickly feels weightless as Ogun picks him up from behind and slams him into the dirt. An audible gasp comes from the crowd as they see the final moments of the assault.

"Keon!" Raine shouts.

Ogun grabs Keon and pulls him up by his throat. Keon struggles for a moment before his body mass increases in size. In moments he is towering over Ogun, who has let go and stares up at Keon with his usual smirk.

"Size is not relevant in a fight little one," Ogun says. Climbing Keon quickly, like a child on a tree, Ogun manages to avoid Keon's massive arms and violently maneuvers up Keon's body as Keon tries to knock him off.

But Ogun finds rest at the base of Keon's neck as he wraps his legs around Keon's throat and squeezes with all his might.

Keon gasps as he claws and tries to pull Ogun's legs apart. The more he fights, the tighter Ogun's grasp seems to be as it becomes harder and harder for him to breathe.

"Do you yield boy?" Ogun asks. But Keon shakes his head as he continues to pull at Ogun. "Do you yield!" He asks again.

Keon fights to stay on his feet as he stumbles forward and backward, until finally, he jerks himself backward. He uses all his might to fall onto Ogun. They tumble backward with an enormous boom, shaking the ground.

The fresh air frees Keon's lungs as the pressure of Ogun's legs are finally released. However, Ogun quickly twists to wrap Keon in a headlock.

Keon shrinks out of Ogun's grasp to re-emerge with a mighty kick to Ogun's stomach. The powerful blow sends Ogun fumbling through the gray-colored dirt.

Keon notices Ogun's axes as he gazes toward Ogun's trail. Ogun rises slowly with a sinister smile resting on his face.

"My turn," he says before blasting forward. But before Keon can react, he feels a litany of punches ransacking his young body. Keon does his best to move, dodge, and block the assault but every step causes more pain. Every block leaves him vulnerable to impending agony. And every dodge leads him into a different violent impact.

The crowd, with the exception of the other gods, are unable to follow the fight and desperately turn their heads to follow the bursting sound of fighting clashes and groans coming from all around them.

"What's happening?" Raine asks, "Where did they go?"

"They are moving faster than your eyes can process," says Mami Wata

"But how do we follow what we can't see?" Raine asks.

"With intuition my dear," Ashanti says, "but I don't think you will need to worry about that now."

Keon's body appears as it falls lifeless through the air and lands a few feet in front of them. Raine runs off the stands to Keon as he lies there, not moving.

"You monster," she shouts while embracing Keon closely.

"What did you think would happen?" Ogun retorts, "I said this would be a fight to the killing stork."

"He's a child!" Haygena yells.

"Who you allowed to fight!" Ogun yells back, "He's not dead, just like I said. Who's next?"

"Me!" Haygena and Kaleo say together before looking at one another and then returning their glare back to Ogun.

"This just got interesting." He says, "How about I battle you both?"

"No," Raine says in a carefully controlled tone as she gently releases Keon. she stands, drawing in slow steady breaths and says, "my turn."

Chapter 31:
The Scion Contention

Shielding his eyes from the blinding light, Xolani steps forward. An onslaught of boos penetrates his ears while his eyes struggle to adjust.

"Even now," Kumbak proclaims, "he acts as if he could care less of what you think of him."

Xolani squints to take in his new surroundings. A vast subterranean stadium of spectators, the royal staffers, dignitaries, politicians and royals from the ball, all yelling as they look down at him. He catches a glimpse of Xaden poised in the middle of the arena.

"How can you just stand there Xolani," Kumbak asks, "without greeting this wonderful crowd?"

Xolani turns to see Kumbak in a balcony high above the crowd, standing at a podium as he speaks,

"You promised the people change but have given them the same rule as your father. It's time Nuhana gets a better class of ruler... Xaden!"

The crowd erupts in applause, causing Xaden to smirk before addressing the crowd,

"Dear people of Nuhana. I know my rumored legacy is not a great one, but I vow to be a better king than my brother, my father, and my father's father. I will be honored to be your servant king." He turns dramatically to look at Xolani, "But first I must finish what was started so long ago... I invoke my right to the Scion Contention."

Whispers and commotion begin to stir as the crowds talk to themselves.

"The last Scion Contention," Kumbak proclaims, "we lost these very heirs. One presumed dead and the other ran, like a coward in the night."

"Kumbak!" Xolani shouts before noticing Qarinah behind Kumbak, holding tightly to an emotionless Niya. He chokes on his words before clearing his throat and saying, "If I remember correctly, for the Scion Contention, am I not allowed a month of training to prepare?"

"Under normal circumstances," Kumbak replies with disdain, "yes. However, the law states, that if a contention is unfinished it may presume to the death."

Various gasps and slight cheers can be heard from the audience as Xolani steps forward. A sudden pull on his shoulder stops him as he turns.

"Don't be afraid, I will make this quick.", Says Xaden

Xolani shrugs his shoulder back, knocking Xaden's hand loose. He moves to, close the gap between them and says,

"The only thing stopping me from killing you is your beloved hag holding Niya."

A quiet lull falls over the stadium as tension radiates through the air. Silence grows as all eyes stare with anticipation.

"Well," Kumbak's voice breaks through, "I don't know about all of you but I'm ready. Let the Scion Contention begin!"

Xolani crouches down into a fighting stance as Xaden does the same. They move in unison as they step backward around one another. Each, cautious of the other, analyzing a place to strike, a spot of weakness in their forms, and any angle that may hurt the other.

Then Xaden bursts forward with a punch toward Xolani's face. Xolani quickly blocks, then counters with a swift uppercut to Xaden's gut. Xaden whizzes as he steps back, protecting his stomach. But he soon feels immense pain from a shattering blow to his jaw and ribs. He's knocked off balance as a gust of wind from Xolani's out-stretched hands sends him tumbling backward.

Xolani pursues, catapulting himself high into the air, bringing the full force of his knee down as he lands. Xaden twists out of the way, recovers, and gives two swift kicks to Xolani's side.

Xaden continues his advance with a fury of high and low kicks. Xolani is off-balanced but nimbly regains his footing before blocking the onslaught. He withstands the pounding pressure of each kick but notices the shifting dirt beneath him as his body is forced back.

He waits for an opening and grabs Xaden's leg. Xolani lifts him and hurdles him back through the air. A small purple ring behind Xaden circles open and engulfs him, before closing. Only to quickly open near the side of Xolani. Xaden launches out of the new hole with a veracious kick.

Xolani sees the attack from his peripheral. The breeze of Xaden's kick crosses his face as he sidesteps out of the way. Xaden lands gracefully and opens a portal beneath Xolani. Xolani loses his footing and drops through. Xaden closes it and looks up. Gasps and screams erupt from the crowd as they follow Xaden's eyeliner to see Xolani falling from a purple hole in the stadium's earthy ceiling.

His limbs move helplessly as his body falls through the air. The sound of his heart pounds in his ears, only to be outdone by the loud sound of the wind rushing past. The wind whips against his face as the speed of the free fall increases. Xolani's adrenaline pumping as his senses come alive.

Anticipating his final moments, he twists his body to face the ground. An intense tightening grips his chest as the ground grows closer. Xolani moves his arms into a circle pattern. Causing the dirt floor to begin moving in a circular shape as it rises, forming a smooth slide-like surface. Xolani's body drops into it and slides to the ground. He takes in a long deep breath as he stands, then shouts confidently,

"You're going to have to do more than drop me out of the sky."

"Then I guess I'll try a little harder," says Xaden as he pulls a jagged-tipped dagger from underneath the back of his jacket.

Xolani stands his ground, anticipating an attack. Xaden moves and Xolani launches several rock fragments from the slide, to hurtle them at Xaden. Xaden zigs through the rocky assault before lounging at Xolani. Xolani braces with a block it's too late, Xaden swiftly opens and moves through a portal to resurface behind Xolani. Xaden nicks the back of Xolani's leg with his dagger. Xolani clutches the back of his leg, holding his free hand up in defense. Xolani feels off-balanced as he tries to focus. But soon Xolani's jaw clacks as the sudden impact of Xaden's fists hits him. A gasp of air escapes him as he hunches over to clutch his belly in pain after Xaden lands another mighty blow to his stomach.

Dropping to his knee, Xolani fights to breathe. Struggling to stand he feels the hurt radiate throughout his body. His fists flicker and pulsate. Until they once again glow like embers and ignite. Xolani slowly stands tall with flickering orange and red rage glowing off his fist before taking a defensive stance.

"Try that again," Xolani taunts.

"Absolutely," Xaden retorts.

The vibrant hues lessen as Xolani's hands, once wrapped in flames, become a simple, bright, glowing amber. Xaden dashes forward with a combination of kicks. Each advance is illuminated by Xolani's glowing counters.

The force of each kick radiates through Xolani's body. His feet anchor down as his arms begin to get heavy. He sidesteps, avoiding a knee sweep by Xaden.

Xaden pounces forward onto his prey, catching Xolani off balance. Xaden tackles him to the ground. They violently tussle for a moment before Xaden is engulfed in flames from a blast of fire from Xolani.

Xaden rolls away in agony as he screams.

Xolani stands and extends his hands to douse Xaden with blasts of water. Towering over him, Xolani keeps his hand extended and says,

"I have more than enough reason to kill you, but this does not need to end in death, do you surrender?"

Xaden, with his suit singed and smokey, coughs as he slowly replies,

"Have you forgotten what I have?" Xolani slowly lowers his arm. Xaden gets up and says, "Good boy. You will never win, because I will always be one step ahead."

Xolani's hand starts to glow. But then explosions from above ignite all around, catching their attention.

Chapter 32:

Next Challenger

Ogun stands proudly as he says, "You've seen what I can do and yet you still want to continue?"

"Shut up and fight," Raine says before reaching into her pocket to take out her staff. It elongates as she twirls it and moves into a fighter stance. She then motions with her hand for Ogun to come.

"Oh, I like you," he says with his usual twisted smile.

"Let's see if you feel the same afterward," Raine replies.

Raine darts off while twisting her staff forward. Ogun swings his mighty axe causing Raine to slide inches from its blades. She turns to feel the full force of the pummel from Ogun's axe to her sternum.

Air leaves her chest, forcing her back. Blunt pain radiates through her chest while she finds her footing. Light shines off Ogun's blade and catches her attention. She moves slightly before it nears her face, cutting a shred of her hair.

She gives Ogun a swift kick to the side of his ribs and shoulder. She advances, continuing a barrage of blazing hits to his torso with her staff. Ogun drops his axes in the assault before blocking and avoiding her swings.

Raine twists and turns to land a hit on her target but her emotions have gotten the better of her. With each violent strike, frustration grows, until Ogun sees his chance and grabs hold of her staff. He takes it under his arm, catching her off guard and freezing Raine in her tracks.

Ogun sends a push kick to the center of her chest. Pain radiates again through her chest as she is launched back by the blow.

The force leaves her heaving in agony as she works to catch her breath. Holding her staff, Ogun makes his way quickly over to Raine as she's on all fours and gives a powerful blow to her side with the staff.

She gives an emotional cry as the impact sends her rolling over to her back.

"Your mistake was starting this fight in anger," Ogun says as he stands over her.

"And yours is talking too much!" She replies. And in one swift motion, Raine twists her body to swipe his legs, knocking Ogun's off balance. She quickly snatches her staff and points it at his neck.

"Do you yield?" Raine asks as she towers over Ogun. He laughs before she shouts, "Do you yield?"

"No," Ogun replies. But before Raine can react, the cold chilling pressure from Ogun's axe is pressed against her neck as his arm is tightly wrapped around her. Raine whizzes out,

"How did you?" Ogun leans in and whispers in her ear,

"Are ready to say goodbye to your son."

"Ogun!" Takhor's voice booms, "Enough! Let her go." Everyone is stunned as he continues, "The mortals have won."

Without releasing Raine, Ogun shouts, "What do you mean they've won?"

"You used divine abilities in the fight."

"I have done no such thing!" Ogun proclaims.

"You dare call me a liar, Ogun!" Takhor says, "Have you forgotten who I am… That was divine physical transference you used."

"What's divine physical, um whatever?" Keon asks as he continues to lay on the ground in pain.

Ashanti leans down next to him and says softly, "It's when our essence is in more than one place at a time. It's a way of being omnipresent, so to speak."

"Oh," Keon replies before Ogun blurts out as he releases Raine,

"It doesn't matter Takhor, and you know it! You just want me to lose!"

Takhor raises an eyebrow before saying, "I am justice and equality. You dare imply I would do anything but be fair?"

Before Ogun can speak, Raine says, "So he lost?"

"Yes," Takhor and Mami Wata say simultaneously.

"I have not lost anything," Ogun retorts, "you stopped the fight."

"Enough!" Takhor commands, "You broke your own rules and I grow weary of this game. It is time to pay the humans what we owe."

"I will do no such thing," Ogun pouts. "If they want my essence, they can take it!"

"Is this how a god behaves, Ogun?" says Kaleo, "Because, this seems how a conniving angel would act."

Ogun slowly turns his head toward Kaleo, with eyes like daggers as he says, "What did you call me?"

Kaleo stands tall and says in a low rumbling voice, "You heard me."

"Say it again," Ogun says through his teeth. The air grows cold as a chill runs through the crowd. Kaleo takes a step forward through the thickening air and says,

"You are no god of war, only an entitled trickster."

Ogun extends his hand to call his axe. It flies through the air but Kaleo twists his sling blade to knock the axe off its trajectory and into the dirt. He continues forward with a fierce slice at Ogun, cleanly splitting a piece of Ogun's shirt. Kaleo leaps to attack, slicing up, down, side to side, only to come up short as Ogun swivels and dodges each swing of the blade.

Kaleo tries for his legs but Ogun steps back to dodge the move before feeling a stiff blow from the blunt force hitting him in the sternum. Ogun rubs his chest and laughs.

Kaleo swings again but Ogun grabs the staff of the sling blade with the back of his leg and brings it to the hilt, giving Kaleo a return blow to his chest. The sling blade falls as Kaleo releases it under the fury of blows Ogun unleashes.

Ogun quickly feels pressure around his neck as the chain from Haygena's axe whips around it. He claws at the chain desperately as Haygena pulls tightly. She takes the chain into one hand and extends her open hand to release several concussion blasts to Ogun's back. He drops to a knee as he continues to pull at his neck.

"Haygena," Kaleo softly shouts, "move." She quickly whips the chain from Ogun's neck and flips out of the way as a high-pitched wail crescendos from Kaleo. He yells with such force the ground starts to crumble and peel back. Ogun fights to stay in his position. He hunkers down to protect himself from the blast. But Kaleo keeps the onslaught coming.

Everyone covers their ears as the sound reverberates throughout their bodies. Kaleo continues to scream until he needs a breath. He inhales and Ogun sees his moment. He bolts in a zig-zag pattern toward Kaleo and punches him in the stomach. Kaleo gasps as he crumbles forward.

Haygena's axe whizzes through the air before Ogun catches it, pulling her forward and giving her a right hook to the jaw. She flies back as Raine sprints up to send three swift blows to Ogun's body with her staff, hitting the back of his knee, his side, and then his shoulder.

He barely reacts to each blow before grabbing her by the throat and hoisting her into the air. But as her legs swivel in the air, she suddenly fumbles back to the ground as Ogun yells in anguish from Kaleo's blade, now wedged into his back.

It pokes through Ogun's chest as he stumbles forward while struggling to pull it out from its lodged position between his shoulder blades. Kaleo kicks Ogun's right leg as Haygena kicks the other. Causing Ogun to fall to his knees. Haygena wraps her chain whip around his neck and pulls tightly.

Kaleo yanks the long blade from Ogun's back and points the tip to Ogun's face. Raine stands near and commands,

"Do you yield?"

Ogun smiles and replies, "You think you've bested me mortals?"

"Give us what you owe," Raine states.

"Fine," he retorts with disdain. They release him. Ogun stands as his wounds heal before their very eyes.

He brushes himself off before pointing his finger toward Keon, who is lying still at the bottom of the raised bleachers.

His finger begins to glow. Keon moans slightly before slowly rising.

Ogun turns to Raine and presents a small purple button before saying,

"I will expect to get this back," she nods in agreement before he turns to face the other gods and says,

"Am I the only one who owes something?"

The gods make their way to the ground and Mami Wata says to Raine,

"Open your hand, my dear." Raine extends her hand and Mami Wata places a small hair clip in Raine's palm. Raine takes a second to watch its pale blue shine shimmer as she moves her hand.

Takhor steps forward to give Raine a bronze key. He drops it into her hand as he smiles at her before turning and walking back. Ashanti moves up and leans softly into Raine, gently placing a kiss on her cheek. A light golden glow radiates from Raine's cheek. Ashanti hands her a small amber stone and steps back. The glow fades and Raine says,

"Thank you all. I'm sure this will be more than enough to heal the Lumastar."

"Great, well, off you go," says Ogun, "The sooner you leave, the faster I get my essence back. I feel naked without it."

Takhor replies,

"No need for the visual Ogun.

"Mommy," Keon says, "how do we get back? I thought the jet crashed."

Haygena steps close and says,

"Legacy is fine."

"I saw it crash," Raine says.

"An illusion to deter unwanted attention." Mami Wata says.

"But where is it?" Keon asks.

"It's back in our haven little one," Takhor says before turning, "speaking of, Ogun, take us back."

Ogun raises an eyebrow and folds his arm in disapproval. Everyone looks at him as he pretends to ignore them until finally, he says,

"Fine!" and snaps his fingers. The moon dissolves around them to reveal lush fields of grass and a huge mountain landscape, with trickling rivers flowing around them.

A swift shadow flies past before Leonyx plops down and begins to lick Keon's cheek. He giggles as Leonyx's rough tongue tickles him. Keon nuzzles up to her and embraces the enormous pet.

They all begin to walk as they notice the river starting to bubble before them. Mami Wata kneels close to the water. The water continues to bubble as it takes the shape of a tiny water-like pixie.

Mami Wata leans close as the water pixie flutters over to Mami Wata's ear. It speaks frantically as Mami Wata listens intently. She nods and mumbles acknowledging statements before the water pixie dashes off with a splash back into the river.

Mami Wata stands with a long face before turning to Raine and saying,

"Your family needs your help."

"What do you mean?" Raine asks.

"Afeena heard from the Mother Tree."

"The Mother Tree," Keon says, "but it's all the way back in Nuhana."

"The Mother Tree's network is vast child... and she told Afeena to find you. Xolani and Niya will need you... something about Xaden being back," Mami Wata says.

They gasp as they process the possibility of Xaden's return. Raine thinks for a moment but before she can speak, Kaleo places a gentle hand on her shoulder and says softly,

"Haygena and I can take the essences to Malkum, while you and Keon go back to Nuhana."

Haygena chimes in, "Let us keep going and we can catch up once we've given everything to Malkum." Feeling Keon's hand embracing hers, Raine looks down.

"Mommy, they need our help, we should go."

"Even if I wanted to, we only have one jet. How can we get there?"

"It's never the how you should worry about," Ashanti says as she smiles and looks at Leonyx. Raine and Keon look at the lovable beast and Raine says,

"No, absolutely not!"

Leonyx looks at Raine as if smiling and extends her wings wide on the ground as she lowers her head. Raine fights the urge to look down at Keon, feeling his joyous smile burning a hole through her.

"It will be fun Raine," Haygena says. Raine replies,

"Yeah, fun, are you two sure you'll be fine?"

"Definitely," Haygena says, "we will make our way to the jet and head back to Malkum, once you're on your way."

Raine makes a disapproving grimace before starting to climb onto the Leonyx's huge back. Keon finds his place quickly as he launches himself up. Raine then says to Ashanti,

"Wait, how do we tell Leonyx where to go?" But Leonyx takes off, causing Raine's head to jerk back as Ashanti yells,

"She's telepathic, just hold on!"

They all watch them soar into the air as Raine's scream fades into the sky.

Chapter 33:

Yin & Yang

Paralyzing screams from the crowd mix in with sounds of crashing debris hitting various spots within the stadium.

"What have you done?" Xolani shouts at Xaden as he pulls him up by his collar.

"This wasn't me," Xaden yells.

They look up to see hundreds of rebels rappelling down. Xolani releases his grip on Xaden and they both take the offensive.

They are surrounded. Xolani gives Xaden a smirk and extends his arms to blast streams of fire out of his hands. Xaden catches the stream of fire with an open portal. And within seconds thousands of portals, no bigger than a pinprick, open all around the rebels as shower-like streams of fire burst through.

Rebels scream as they hurry to pat out the flames. Xolani twists his hands and begins sending flashes of water through Xaden's portals.

The pinprick holes open wider to release buckets of pouring water, dousing the rebels and forcing them to their knees. They begin to rise but Xolani and Xaden attack furiously.

Working together they deliver a storm of kicks and punches, leaving the rebels immobile. Until they hear a voice shout,

"Stop!"

They look up in the direction of the voice to see Kombak with his hands flung high in the air as guns are pointed at him, Niya, and Qarinah.

Xolani starts to react but feels Xaden's hand pull him back. He looks at Xaden and sees he's staring into the crowd.

Rebels have taken shelter in the crowd. With guns pointed at the people in the stadium. Xolani unclenches his fist as he notices a woman walking toward them.

She walks with wide strides, making her way onto the stadium floor. She stops to stand inches before Xolani and Xaden. She looks Xolani directly in his eyes before switching her place and making eye contact with Xaden. She then turns to the crowd and shouts,

"We, the people of Nuhana, are tired of this monarchy fighting over our fate. For centuries we have allowed kings & queens to benefit from our hard labor. They constantly fight amongst themselves in the lap of luxury while our people starve in the streets. It is time Nuhana takes a stand and proclaims its independence from tyrannical rulers, like these."

Several rebel soldiers run up with guns to surround Xaden and Xolani as she continues.

"These two bicker over who will profit off of our suffering, but I say no more."

"You have it all wrong, I want to help," Xolani tries to say before being knocked to his knee by a nearby soldier.

"Lies!" she shouts as she nears him. "Your family has had generations to help Nuhana. But you have done nothing."

Another solider hits Xaden in the face with the butt of his gun. Xaden smiles wiping the fresh blood off his lip says,

"You'll have to do better than that. In fact, why don't you practice on your friend here." Xaden points to the lone woman but the solider doesn't move. "I said, practice on her!"

They laugh at him as she moves closer to Xaden and says,

"He heard you but you should know, my gifts render all near me powerless. I'm surprised dear dead daddy didn't tell you boys about me. He used me to come up with his gene dampener technology... But allow me to introduce myself. My name is Beta and your family will pay for all it has done."

She bursts forward sending several swift blows to Xaden's chest and neck, causing him to fall, unconscious. Beta pivots and moves toward Xolani. He dodges her first attack but shooting pain fills his head as he feels the blunt force of a gun hit his temple. He falls to the ground and Beta sends a devastating kick to his side and a powerful blow to his neck. As everything fades to black Xolani hears a solider over him say to Beta,

"He has Alpha's sash."

Chapter 34:
Reunited-ish

The wind muffles Raine's screams as Leonyx soars through the clouds. Keon laughs freely as Leonyx glides high in the sky before starting to circle and gently descend down.

"Oh, thank the Creator," Raine proclaims as she keeps her face buried in the back of Leonyx, "it feels like she's landing."

Keon's face lights up as he peers over Leonyx's wing to see the beautiful double rings protecting Nuhana. His smile widens as he notices the people pointing and gawking at Leonyx as she soars high above them.

"Mommy look!" he shouts. Raine replies without moving,

"I'll look when we land."

"But Mommy," Keon persists before she finally raises her head a bit to see the Mother Tree partially blown open. She rises even more as Leonyx circles closer to see a gaping hole at the base of the Royal Place within the Mother Tree.

"What happened Mommy?" Keon asks but Raine has no words and barely utters,

"I don't know my agave, but we will find out."

Leonyx glides swiftly to the gigantic hole, passing over the exposed devastation before rolling up and then swooping down into the hole, where she extends her wings to hover and land gracefully.

Keon hops off while Raine is already kissing the ground. Leonyx begins to growl as Nuhana soldiers with shock sticks run to defend against the beast. Leonyx swings her tail, knocking several through the air before she swivels and swipes her large paw at others advancing forward.

"The Queen! We must protect her!" a soldier shouts as Raine and Keon are revealed from behind Leonyx.

"No, stop!" Raine yells, but the soldiers are filled with fear and continue to attack Leonyx. A soldier hits her with a shock stick. Leonyx lets out a painful cry.

"I said stop," Raine shouts as she knocks over a soldier and takes the shock stick from him. She uses it and shocks several others advancing against Leonyx. Raine twirls the shock stick before stopping it inches from a soldier's face and says,

"Stop!"

All of the soldiers follow her command as they back up cautiously with their shock sticks still raised. Leonyx growls while eying her enemies and is startled at the gentle touch of Keon. She knocks him down as she swings her head in his direction, ready to attack. She sees what she's done and instantly her eyes widen as her demeanor softens. She nudges his feet before he makes his way back up.

"It's okay, Leonyx," he says as he pats her nose. "I know you didn't mean it." She pushes her head softly into his chest as he hugs her face. Raine moves forward and says,

"She's no threat. Lower your weapons." Hesitantly, they all begin to drop their defensive stances and place their shock sticks back into their holsters.

"What happened here and where is Xolani?" They all look back and forth at each other, waiting for someone to speak up first. "Well," she says impatiently.

They all stand in silence until one lone soldier steps forward and says,

"Respectfully, my Queen, we wouldn't want to misinform you. It may be best if you speak with Kasmine."

"Then take me to her," Raine commands. But as they turn to leave, Kasmine, Gibbon, and Rashid, who is moving with a slight limp, walk into the largely demolished arena and stand in bewilderment.

"By John Henry's hammer," Rashid says with his mouth open wide, "the report was true. It's a dragon."

"I can't believe what I'm seeing," Gibbon says before Raine walks to intercept them as they approach Leonyx.

"What happened here?" She asks but they continue to stare at Leonyx as she lays down in front of them. "Kasmine!"

"Right!" she replies as she turns to Raine and says, "The rebels stormed the arena and took Xolani and Xaden hostage."

"How is that even possible?" Raine says with nostrils flared. Leonyx snaps quickly at Rashid, who pulls his hand back from trying to pet her and says,

"We're not sure yet. After he let go of his control of Niya we,"

"What do you mean he let go of control of Niya?" Raine shouts furiously, "Where is she?"

"She is safe, Your Highness," Kasmine says, "She is in her room with armed guards as we speak."

"I need to see her," Raine says as she storms off to Niya's room, "fill me in on everything."

They follow quickly behind her before a lone solider says,

"Um, your Highness," they all stop and turn toward her as she continues humbly, "what should we do about, the um?..." She motions toward Leonyx. Raine looks to the soldiers before glancing over to Leonyx and saying,

"If I were you, I wouldn't make her mad."

"Yes ma'am," she replies as she looks back to Leonyx. She and the other soldiers are left standing there as Raine walks off with Gibbon, Kasmine, Rashid, and Keon following behind her.

Chapter 35:

Wake Up

Xolani rises to a pounding headache but notices his leg is healed. "Finally," Xaden's annoyed voice catches his attention, "you're awake."

Xolani ignores him as he holds his head and says, "Where did they take us?"

"How would I know?" Xaden replies. Xolani looks at their new surroundings as Xaden continues, "We seem to be in some sort of hanger. With guards posted along the outer walls. Every so often one of them responds to the radios on their shoulders but they're posted too far apart for me to hear their conversations clearly."

"Can you create a portal out of here?" Xolani says.

"Why didn't I think of that?" Xaden says sarcastically, "Of course not. I've tried but I'm still not able to feel my gifts. That winch must still be near."

"That, or they also have the dampening technology father built off of her gifts."

"Either way, we must figure a way out."

"Now why would you want to leave so soon?" Beta says as she carries a chair behind her. They turn in her direction before she places the chair down and takes a seat. "You both must have questions."

"Why did you take us?" Xolani asked. Beta leans back in her seat and says,

"How else would I get your undivided attention."

"This is a waste of time!" Xaden shouts, "Let us go before I make you." She glances Xaden over and smirks before folding her arms and saying,

"You are in no position to negotiate, little man."

"Little man!" Xaden says furiously, "I will..."

Beta sends a push kick to Xaden's chest in one swift motion, sending him tumbling backward into the dirt. He coughs as he struggles to catch his breath. Xolani looks into Beta's hard brown eyes and says,

"You have our attention, what do you want?" She sits back down slowly as she keeps her gaze on Xolani. She takes her time as she pats some nonexistent dirt off her leg before raising her arm and waving a guard over. They drag two large black bags with them and place them beside her, then return to their position as she says,

"We found your spies trying to infiltrate our organization."

Xolani yells, "Those weren't spies, they were representatives trying to set up a meeting of peace with you."

"They did mention something like that before they died." Beta says. Xolani's lips purse before he says through gritted teeth,

"I ask again, what is it you want?"

"Equality, your Highness," she whispers as if it's a secret no one should hear. "The people of Nuhana are tired of being oppressed."

"The crown is working to repair the damage my father has done."

"Is it now?" she questions mockingly before connecting a mighty blow to Xolani's jaw. She continues as she kicks his stomach. "You think your father is the only one with blood on his hands!" Xolani wheezes as she continues, "Your whole monarchy is filled with nothing but greedy serpents and dictating psychopaths. Why should we believe you are any different?"

Xolani's restrained hands are raised as he tries to protect himself before panting out, "You're right. You are right. My family line has not lived up to the values we've tried to set forth." He motions back towards Xaden still catching his breath, "Prime example, but I am not my family."

"We shall see," Beta says before looking to the nearest guards. She stands and commands, "Get him up and follow me."

Chapter 36:

Give them the room

"We lost Ramouth," Raine ask as they continue down the purple halls, "the Rebels took advantage of a situation caused by Xaden and we still don't know how he returned."

"That is correct, your Highness," Kasmine states. "but, once everyone came out of their trance several of our guards were able to safely secure the princess away from Qarinah, and apprehending her. However, we haven't been able to get her to talk."

"Then you know what you need to be doing don't you?" Raine says in a commanding tone. Kasmine nods her head and breaks off from the group to carry out Raine's order. They walk for a moment before Rashid says,

"Raine, can we slow down for a second and talk?"

"Whatever it is, can wait." Raine replies without stopping. Rashid closes the the distance between them and grabs her arm, turning her around. Fire blazes in her eyes as she glares at Rashid. Gibbon and Keon step back to avoid getting caught in the inferno. "Rashid, remove your hand," Raine commands. Rashid lets her go and says,

"Raine, you..."

"Gibbon," She says, cutting him off to continue, "please take Keon to Lady Neyma."

"But Mommy," Keon protests but quickly regrets letting the words escape as Raine's intense stare finds its new target. He steps behind Gibbon, who then says,

"Yes, my Queen," and places a hand on Keon's back before saying softly, "Come on, my young sir."

Raine notices a slight limp in Gibbon's walk as she watches them go down the hall and turn away. She then looks at Rashid. He inhales deeply and says,

"I'm glad you sent Keon away. He doesn't need to see her yet."

"Rashid, time is short. Say what's on your mind."

"I understand how important it is for you to check on Niya," he says as he chooses his words carefully, "but getting Xolani back perhaps should be the first priority."

"I don't think you understand Rashid," Raine fires back. "My family is my priority and at this moment, Niya needs her mother. I'm sure Xolani can handle himself."

"I know, you're still mad at him, but at a time like this, it's important that Nuhana has its king. After all, I just..." Rashid says, before Raine says,

"Perhaps you should be meeting with the King's Five to create a plan to retrieve the king then."

Rashid starts to speak but is silenced by Raine's steadfast demeanor and only replies,

"Yes," and walks off. Raine stands alone for a brief second before continuing to Niya's room.

Raine walks with urgency through the halls. She turns the final corner to see two guards posted in front of Niya's door. Raine shouts,

"What is the meaning of this?" as she closes in. The guards snap to attention before one replies,

"Lady Neyma commanded guards be posted outside Princess Niya's room at all times... your Highness."

Raine pauses in front of them briefly.

The guards quickly part to open space for Raine as she walks past them and into Niya's room.

RAINE FINDS NIYA SITTING on the corner of her bed petting Sissy, oblivious to Raine's entry. She taps on the doorframe to announce her presence. Niya looks and lights up as she sees it's her mother.

She hops off the bed, almost tossing Sissy onto the floor as she sprints into her mother's arms. Niya is unable to control her tears as they cascade onto Raine's shirt. Sobs fill the room as they embrace. Raine holds her tightly and softly says,

"There, there, I'm here." Raine feels Niya's arm tighten around her. She gently strokes her hair. "I know there is nothing I can say to take away the pain Niya. But I vow to you, we will end him, once and for all."

Raine fails to hold back her own tears but as she feels the pain in her daughter's hug. They continue to stay wrapped in a loving embrace until Raine forces herself to slowly pull away and says,

"They took your father and I need to go help him."

"I know," Niya says somberly.

"Wait," Raine says in surprise, "How do you..." Niya stays silent as her head hangs low and replies,

"I'm still connected to him."

"Oh baby," Raine utters out as she embraces Niya again. But quickly releases and asks, "Wait, so can he..."

"No," Niya says unsurely, "or at least I don't think so. It's not like before. Before I constantly heard his influence. This time, I don't hear him directly."

"I don't understand," Raine says, "where you connected to him this whole time?"

"Yes but, it was kind of like," Niya says before pausing to think, "being locked in a glass room, where I could see and hear everything, without control. Now, it's reversed almost, where I can see and hear everything happening to him."

"Are you able to control Xaden?"

"No," she replies harshly, "and I don't want to. I just want him dead and out of my head forever!"

Raine's arms draw back to her core as they stand in silence while Niya's words linger in the air. Niya's eyes begin to glaze, then tears flow down her face as she says, "I just want to go back home Mommy." Raine takes Niya by the hand and says,

"I see you, Niya. And I hear you. I need to step away to meet with Rashid and Kasmine about getting your father back. And once we have our family together again, we are going home. I promise."

Chapter 37:

Keep thinking

"You can't be serious?" Rashid yells, slamming his hands on a round table filled with various council members.

"Sir," one of them says before continuing, "that may be our only option."

"To bomb the citizens of Nuhana is never an option!" Rashid fires back, "You must have lost your gooju-berry-loving minds. Not only could that kill the king, but could cause countless casualties."

"Perhaps you can propose an alternative solution," Kumbak says as he sits in a dark corner. Rashid turns with wide eyes to see Kumbak sitting behind him. Rashid says,

"Your diplomatic immunity may help during your impending trial Kumbak but you have no right or authority here. Get out."

Kumbak rises up slowly before getting closer to Rashid's face and saying with a smirk,

"The rebels have your king. It would be wise to entertain any and all plans. You can't let those rebels dictate how you run your country. They are no better than street merchants."

Rashid rears back and punches Kumbak square in the nose. Kumbak stumbles back and falls as he hands fly to his face in protection. He stands over Kumbak who is crying out in pain on the floor, holding his broken and bleeding nose, as he says,

"My mother was a street merchant, you pompous windbag. Now get out of here before I really get mad."

Kumbak scrambles off the floor and makes his way to the exit. He meets Raine as she enters the doorway. He sinks down in her presence before saying,

"Lady Raine, I didn't know you had returned. I was just leaving."

Raine looks at him in disgust and punches him in the jaw. He swivels at the force of her punch and lands hard against the wall, before falling to the floor. Raine calls out,

"Guards!"

Two royal soldiers quickly enter and she says, "Place him in a holding cell until his trial."

They quickly scramble to pick up the heavy individual. Kumbak then says as he is being dragged out of the room,

"Wait, you can't do this. I am the President of Amerigo!"

The council members stand as Raine's focus is back on them. She motions for them to have a seat as she walks over to an empty chair next to Rashid. She pulls it out and takes a seat before asking,

"What's the plan?"

The council members look nervously at one another before everyone's gaze falls on Rashid. He inhales deeply before saying,

"We haven't found a viable plan yet but we are working on it."

"Unacceptable," Raine says as she throws up her hand. A council member tries to speak but she continues over him, "This is important for Nuhana, and your king has been taken. Does that mean nothing?"

"Raine," Rashid says softly before correcting himself, "Lady Raine, the council is working on it. It is better for us to take longer to create a sufficient plan, than to barge in and not having proper intel."

"While you are debating and scheming, he could be suffering or worse," she fires back. Rashid takes a breath, looks toward the council members and says,

"Give us the room." The members are hesitant and look to Raine, who shouts,

"You heard him, out!" The members scurry quickly as they make their way out. Rashid waits until the last member is out before saying,

"Raine, I couldn't possibly know what you are feeling but we need to have a cool head about this."

"This wouldn't have happened if he hadn't sent me on that quest."

"You don't know that."

"I do know that. I knew something wasn't right with Niya and I could have helped her, which would have stopped Xaden before he even started."

"Maybe so," Rashid says, "but we can't dwell on that now. We need to find out where he is being held. Any luck with the hag in the cell?"

"I haven't checked in with Kasmine yet. I figured I'd come here first after checking on Niya."

"How is she?" he asks.

"Vengeful, but who isn't at this point? But you were right earlier, I just needed to check on her, you know?"

"Ya, I know. What now?"

"Well, I have an idea. However, I'd like to check in on Kasmine first." Rashid nods his head in agreement before backing away from the table. Raine starts to rise as well before saying, "You know, you are starting to sound like him."

"Well, one of us has to I guess," Rashid replies as they exit the room.

Chapter 38:
The Hag

Raine and Rashid walk down the hall of the detention cells. They both look puzzled as they see Kasmine standing beside Lady Neyma, whose face is twisting and contorting with concentration.

"What's going on?" Rashid says loudly before being shushed by Kasmine. They move in closer and Kasmine whispers,

"After having no luck interrogating Qarinah, I felt more unconventional methods may be in order." She quickly glanced at Qarinah and then back to Raine and Rashid before continuing, "So I asked Lady Neyma if she could alter Qarinah's reality, to make her think she has escaped... In hopes Qarinah would lead us to Xaden or even better the rebels and King Xolani."

"Brilliant, Kasmine," Rashid whispers excitedly. Raine stands with her arms folded and asks,

"Has Qarinah said anything yet?" Kasmine shakes her head no before stating,

"Lady Neyma has had her in this state for about twenty minutes and she hasn't spoken either."

"Because I am focusing," Lady Neyma says with irritation in her voice, "she is mentally stronger than anticipated. And chattering around me is not helping." Rashid whispers,

"Sorry," as he and Raine inch back. They all watch as stress and frustration grow on Lady Neyma's face. She moves her hands in a slow pushing manner. Until her hands suddenly drop and they watch Qarinah fall to the ground in her cell.

"Is she okay?" Kasmine asks. Lady Neyma turns and replies,

"She will be fine. Her resistance to my illusion gift was strong. Xaden must have trained her well."

"Did you find Xolani's location?" Raine asks. Lady Neyma smiles and says,

"I believe so. Or at the very least I may have a starting point of where we can look."

"*You're wrong.*" A voice says in all of their heads. They all look puzzled before Raine asks out loud.

"Niya?"

"*Yes, I'm sorry for intruding in your minds but I needed to know what she knew.*"

"Niya, what did you do?" Rashid asks.

"*Only what was needed. I placed a mental wall around her mind and let you see what you wanted to see until I found the information I needed.*"

"Niya, why?" Raine says.

"*He deserves to pay,*" Niya says.

"Baby, I know you're hurting but," Raine says.

"*No, he must pay for everything he's done!*" Niya shouts. Causing them all to grip their heads, and fall to their knees as Niya's voice pierces their ears. They soon begin to loosen their grips.

"*Are you going to help?*" Niya says as her voice grows more ominous. They all stay silent for a moment before Lady Neyma asks,

"Help you with what dear?" Silence remains as they stand waiting for Niya's reply. Until she finally says,

"*He was right, I have to save myself!*"

"Niya!" Raine shouts but no response. They all stand there processing what Niya meant before Rashid says,

"She's not thinking of going anywhere near that monster, is she?" He looks to Lady Neyma and hesitates slightly before continuing, "I mean, after what he's done to the people of Nuhana and to her."

"I think that's why she's going," Kasmine states. Raine then says,

"Of course it is. She wants revenge and I don't blame her."

"I don't think it's just revenge she's after," Kasmine adds, "she wants to kill Xaden."

"Would it be such a bad thing?" Rashid says under his breath before catching a hateful glare from Lady Neyma, who says,

"He's still my son."

"And she's my daughter," Raine says, "he must die but it will be by my hands, not hers." Raine begins to walk as they all follow behind.

"Raine you can't be seriously thinking of-" Lady Neyma says before Raine cuts her off and says explosively,

"Of what! Killing him? You are absolutely right I am! We've dealt with him once and he somehow managed to weasel his way back to life. But I promise you, your son better pray he's dead, before I get to him." Lady Neyma mouth hangs open as Raine continues, "Because the only mercy I will give him, is not having his mother witness it... Stay here and watch over Keon. Kasmine, get Kacao and keep my family and this palace secure. We will give Rumouth a proper burial once we return." Kasmine nods respectfully as Raine adds, "Rashid, follow me."

Lady Neyma stands alone as they walk away. Rashid, asks,

"How are we going to find him and beat Niya there?"

"I'm sure Niya has teleported to his location with her gifts already but I have an idea how we may be able to find him and get there.

"NO! ABSOLUTELY NOT!" Rashid protests as they stand around Leonyx in the arena. "You don't even know where she went or where they are."

"You're right," Raine says, "I can feel Xolani. It's very faint but I can feel him and perhaps our friend her can help fill in the gaps." She pets Leonyx with a wide smile.

"Raine, I don't know about this." Rashid says. Raine quickly replies,

"We don't have time for one of your hissy fits Rashid,"

"I'll try not to take offensive to that." He says with a tilt of his head.

"This is our only lead to find Xolani and Xaden." Raine pleads.

"You know, I still have the claw marks from the last flight I took with a wild animal... So no."

"Leonyx is our best chance," Raine says, "if I can do it, so can you."

Rashid curses under his breath before reluctantly saying,

"All right."

Raine gets closer to Leonyx and says,

"If I think of someone, could you fly us to them?" Leonyx nods her head in understanding. "Thank you, girl. Hop on."

Raine sits up front as Rashid climbs onto Leonyx's back. Raine and Rashid both hunker down before Rashid asks,

"Shouldn't we at least have some guards come with us? And this thing is safe, right?"

"Define safe," Raine replies. Her voice trails off as Leonyx leaps into the air and climbs high into the sky, fading into the distance.

Chapter 39:

A Whole New World

Xolani shuffles blindly, unable to see. Light peaking through pinholes of a sack on his head gives no indication of where he's going. A firm hand reminds him to keep moving as it shoves him forward. He trips over his feet but is able to keep his balance. They walk a little further until Xolani feels a slight tug on his restraints, indicating to stop. The light of the day blinds him as the sack gets yanked off his head.

He squints hard to look through the pain. Forcing his eyes open as he begins to take in the serene vista before him. An alcove of vegetation and life bustle all around him. Fruits hang from the trees, with all types of berries resting in the bushes below. The sound of kids frolicking and playing catches his attention and turns to see a vast community hidden by the outer tree line.

"Are we near the outer ring?" he asks. Beta looks at him and says,

"We can't just give you our location, now can we?"

"I guess not," he says, "what is this place and why did you bring me here?" Beta takes a moment and looks at the two guards standing next to Xolani and says,

"Retrieve the truth seer."

"But..." one tries to say. Beta gives a stern look and they both turn and scurry away. She goes behind Xolani and takes off his restraints.

"Thank you," he says as he rubs his wrist, "Are you sure that was wise?"

"I'm a big girl and can take care of myself," she replies with a smile, "besides, I have my lucky taser on me if you get out of hand." She pats her side, indicating the taser's location.

"Noted," Xolani says, "but you still haven't answered my questions. What is this place and why did you bring me here?"

"We call this place The Grove," Beta says as she starts to walk. Xolani follows beside her. "I brought you to meet a friend of mine. Plus, I want to show you that the people of Nuhana can survive without you and your regime." She lifts her arm and plucks some low-hanging fruit, "We have food." She takes a small bite as she points to a nearby stream and says, "We have fresh water." They continue on before she says, "And we work together so the individual can thrive."

"Then why the rebellion?"

"We have family, friends, loved ones that are dedicated to a system that overtaxes and under delivers. A system that constantly forces its people to mine its resources for that system's own selfish gains while the people are barely tossed the leftover scraps."

Xolani crosses into her path and stops, meeting her cold gaze and says,

"Bombing cargo shipments, stealing from diplomats, and killing peaceful messengers will not solve that. We need diplomacy, not acts of terror."

"Diplomacy is a big word that means nothing to those starving and being mistreated," Beta says, "action is what gets results. How else do you get people to care about a problem that isn't theirs? Everything we have done, we have done for the people of Nuhana."

"Violence only begets more violence," he retorts.

"It's easy for a man of power to judge the actions of those with none."

"I once gave up my power for love," he says, "but trust me, I love Nuhana and I will do everything in my power to make it better for all its people."

"You expect us to trust you after the generations of mistreatment?"

"If you don't trust me, then why bring me here?"

"My brother trusted you," Beta says with soberness to her voice.

"Who's your brother?" Xolani asks with a puzzled look. Beta smirks and glances down while saying,

"The very man you got that sash around your waist from."

"Alpha," Xolani says with wide eyes.

"Yes Alpha. He, with the help of others saved me from your father's experimentation. But while saving me, Alpha was captured. And his last words to me as they dragged him off were, Trust the prince."

"I remember meeting him that night but how do you know he wasn't referring to my brother?"

"Have you met your brother?" Beta asks.

"Good point," Xolani says.

"Your brother is a virus that has a talent for reinfecting the body. But you, on the other hand, may be what we need and it seems my son has taken a liking to you."

"Son?"

"Jonathan Hender," Xolani is taken back by the name and says,

"Sheer, I wouldn't have pegged him for a spy."

"He's not a spy," Say Beta as she turns her body slightly, "he's discovering his own path." Xolani raises an eye brow and replies,

"In the royal palace, where he is reporting back information to you?"

"No," Beta says softly, "he is simply a boy, who has conversations with his mother about his job, that's it. He doesn't even know I'm the leader of the rebels."

"So why even mention him?"

"Because he often tells me about how well you treat the staff and that you are actually trying to invoke change but politics seem to get in your way." Xolani feels flush with anger but softens his tone as he says,

"Then why are you fighting? You are the ones causing most of Nuhana's issues."

"I can see you are a good man Xolani but you are blind to what is really happening here. People would be dying in the streets of starvation if it wasn't for The Grove. Your council denies us basic human rights. No one in Nuhana is allowed to grow a garden within the inner ring. The majority of the fruits from our labor goes to your monarchy."

"That was a law put in place generations ago to prevent harmful practices from hurting the population."

"Then why not create courses to teach the people how to farm instead of restricting it altogether?"

"I can't say why it was restricted," Xolani says, "but we can work together to change that."

"I want to believe you," Beta says, "However, history proves those in power often corrupt it."

"Isn't that the kettle calling the pot black?" Xolani replies. Beta looks at him with confusion and says,

"I don't follow."

"It's an outdated expression. It just means you're trying to call me out on the same issue you have."

"We are not the same. I lead my people with honor and to the best of my abilities."

"That we have in common. Look, I would never ask anyone to do what I'm not willing to do myself. And just like you, I am doing my best to lead our people, hopefully, to a peaceful resolution. Can you say the same Beta?"

"Your kind doesn't listen to words, only to money and violence," Beta fires back. Xolani takes a moment before saying,

"You have me at your mercy, so it's easy to believe my words aren't genuine. But if given the option, if given the chance to end the violence and get our people what they need permanently, why not take it?"

Beta stands still in her resolve as she muddles over his words, "Beta, I've made my share of mistakes but the one that still haunts me to this day was caused by a legacy I thought I could run from years ago... My father planned to execute me," Xolani says slowly, "but as a result of my escape, my father... killed Alpha, and said it was me."

A long pause fills the air as the ambient noise around them rises to the front. Beta looks through the tree branches above her to glimpse at the peaking sky between the leaves and says,

"Why are you telling me this?"

"Even though I know it's not directly my fault your brother was killed, I believe it is time to make right what others have turned so wrong."

Beta thinks for a moment and then says,

"On some level, I already knew he was gone. But I didn't want to give up hope of seeing him again." Xolani moves close and says,

"Hope is a powerful thing. In the right hands, it can heal a nation. In the wrong ones, it can destroy one. Your brother's death is a tragic legacy of loss left over by my father. Let us work together and rebuild a better Nuhana. One where we all can thrive."

Beta tilts her head and looks at Xolani intensely before extending her hand. He begins to extend his hand before an old familiar voice shouts from across the groove,

"Xalen!"

They both turn to see an older gentleman run toward them. He stops inches from Xolani and sweeps him up in an enormous bear hug. "It's good to see you again, where's LaRaina?"

"She's not here," Xolani manages to say as the air is squeezed out of him. "I can't breathe." His lungs feel the relief as he drops back down to the ground.

"I see you remember Teh," Beta says, "He is why I brought you here."

"What does Raine's father have to do with this?" Xolani asks intensely.

"My gift can feel people's true intentions," Teh says with a big smile on his face. "And it lets her know if she can kill you or not." Xolani feels the painful sting of Teh's hand slapping him on his back.

"Wait," Xolani says curiously as he looks to Beta, "I thought your gifts nullify others around you?" She raises an eyebrow before saying,

"They do, but, I control my gift, not the other way around." She then looks to Teh and says, "Well?"

He looks at her and says,

"Same as the day I met him. Like most, he has the potential for great good and great evil but he leans more to the great good side. He'll be a great ruler if he chooses to be," then winks at Xolani who returns a confused look back. Beta steps toward Xolani, looks him deep in the eyes, and says,

"Do you choose to be?"

"I would like to think so," Xolani says humbly, "I only wish to serve the people and make this place better for all."

An awkward tension begins to build as they stare intensely at one another until Teh steps and asks,

"So, when will I get to see LaRaina and those beautiful grands of mine? I've seen them on the monitors and can't wait to meet them."

"The kids would be happy to meet you too, and she goes by Raine now," Xolani says. Teh frowns and says,

"Not very covert is it?" he laughs as Xolani says,

"A subtle change but effective enough. How's Dhavi?"

"She's ornery as ever," he laughs, "but good, keeping me busy."

"As much as I love a reunion," Beta interjects, "was there something else you needed Teh?"

"Just to meet my grand-babies," Teh says with a huge smile as he stares at Xolani. Xolani, taking the hint, says,

"There is no excuse. We will bring the kids to you at our first convenience."

"Don't give me that fancy talk," Teh says sternly, "you bring me those kids." But before Xolani speaks, Beta says,

"As touching as this moment is, one last thing. Your brother, what are you planning to do with Xaden?"

Xolani looks deep within before he speaks and finally says,

"I will always choose peace if given the option but I feel that is no longer a choice he chooses to give." A rebel soldier runs over to Beta, holding up a comm device, shouting,

"We're under attack!"

"By who?" Beta shouts back.

"Some girl! She popped in, out of nowhere, and started tearing up the compound looking for Xaden. What do we do?"

"Stop her!" Beta shouts back as she grabs Xolani by the arm and pulls him toward the soldier. "We need to get back to the dentition hangers!"

Xolani follows quickly behind Beta as she runs from the Grove, but not before he waves goodbye to Teh and says,

"I will come back."

Chapter 40:

Save Yourself

The yells of panic grow closer as Beta and Xolani sprint over slain bodies of rebels lying unconscious in the halls. Xolani follows Beta as she navigates her way back to the hangar where she left Xaden.

Gunfire echoes through the shouting, putting Xolani into a higher gear. Following the sounds of battle, he pushes past Beta as the thought of who it maybe pops into his head.

"Niya!" he yells but is barely able to hear his own voice through the battle noise. He rounds a corner that opens to the hanger. He comes to a dead stop with Beta nearly toppling over him as she comes to a halt as well. The hanger doors are twisted open, barely hanging on. They take in the carnage of bodies and destruction all around as a few soldiers are left shooting at Niya.

Muzzles flash with bursts of light but grind to a halt and fall inches in front of Niya. She walks toward them, like a lion ready to pounce. Niya raises her hand and flicks her wrist, sending the rebels flying into the walls, revealing what she's after.

Xaden cowering behind the rebels with his hands shielding his face. Exposed, he tries to weasel away. But Niya clenches her fist and Xaden, with a terrified expression, is frozen in place.

"Niya!" Xolani screams. She barely reacts to his call. Xaden's body begins to slowly lift up, his feet drag along the floor as Niya pulls him closer with her mind. "Niya, let us handle this!"

"No!" Niya's voice echoes through the hanger, "He deserves to die!"

"Yes," Xolani says as he moves closer, "yes he does, but that is not a weight that needs to be on you baby." Niya ignores him as her hands simulate choking. Xaden's life begins to fade as he struggles to breathe.

"Stop her," Xolani says to Beta.

"I couldn't if I wanted to, my gifts aren't working on her." Beta walks closer to Niya, who seems to be getting weaker as Beta gets near. "Put him down!" Beta shouts. Xaden drops suddenly and Niya turns her full attention on Beta. They lock eyes before Niya's eyes shift quickly, sending Beta flying through the air and into the hanger wall.

"Niya, no!" Xolani yells, "You are going too far."

"I haven't gone far enough father," Niya yells, "he's still breathing."

"Niya, you don't need to do this." Xolani pleads as he moves forward. But Niya places her hand up, with her palm facing him, freezing Xolani in his place.

"You don't understand," Niya says, "how could you? To have him in your head, day after day, driving you crazy. The things he's said, the things he's done... I must finish this!"

"Niya don't!" Xolani pleads as she turns around to face Xaden. He's managed to slither a few feet away but Niya drags him back with an outstretched reach of her hand. He flips onto his back with a twist of her wrist.

"I want to see you suffer," she says. Xaden begins to fight for air as he claws at his throat to breathe. Niya's smile grows wicked before she suddenly screams out in agony. Her body contorts and twists as electricity runs through it.

Xolani follows the stream of electricity crackling to its source. Beta, barely able to raise her head, lays on the floor, firing her taser at Niya. Xolani instinctively lunges forward into a powerful stance to save his daughter, launching his fist forward and pulling them back in one sharp fluid motion. The floor cracks in front of Beta and lifts up to block the flow of electricity.

Xolani runs to Niya as she falls, limp. He slides, catching her in his arms, and cradles her.

"I've failed you," he whispers as he places his forehead gently onto hers. He felt the soft beating of her heart on his chest before picking her up. Xolani carries her to Beta and says,

"Watch her." Beta, puzzled, looks at Niya then at him, and then back to her. She points the taser at Niya and holds it ready. Xolani turns to Xaden, who has managed to inch his way to the hanger door. "You wanted a Scion Contention, this is it. Get up!"

Xaden stops slowly before rising back to his feet and saying, "How can I fight you King Xolani, in this state?"

"Shut up," Xolani says, "and fight!"

He leaps forward, blasting bursts of flames in Xaden's direction. Xaden quickly opens a portal, and the flames vanish into it. Then Xaden launches the portal toward him. Xolani swivels right to dodge but feels the full force of Xaden's fist jabbing into his jaw. Xolani instantly spins in the other direction. Xaden doesn't let up as he delivers a fury of combinations to Xolani's face and body. Pain radiates from each blow as Xaden pounds into Xolani.

"You should have let me go, Xalen," Xaden says with a laugh. "Pity you won't be here when I make my way through the rest of your family."

"Enough!" Xolani screams unleashing a gust of wind that pushes Xaden back. Xolani swiftly stomps on the side of Xaden's knee. Then lays down a hard sharp cross, square on Xaden's cheek.

Xolani watches Xaden as he falls face-first to the floor.

Niya begins to wake and Beta steadies her taser. Niya speaks softly,

"I need to hold him." Puzzled, Beta just looks at her as Niya repeats again, "I need, to hold him," while she lifts her hand to her head in concentration.

Xolani picks Xaden up by the collar and with his free hand begins to create a vacuum of circling air above. He proceeds to direct the vacuum of air toward Xaden's mouth. Xaden struggles to keep his mouth closed as the air begins to leave his body.

Enraged, Xolani continues until Xaden's lifeless body hangs limp in Xolani's hand. He lowers his hand form over Xaden's body as he lets it drop to the ground. Xolani breathes heavily as he stands over him, working to regain his peace.

"Daddy," he hears Niya call out softly, breaking him out of his trance. He goes over to embrace her but a crash through the ceiling gains their attention.

Xolani dives toward Niya and Beta, avoiding the falling debris as Leonyx and the party crash to the floor. She unleashes a mighty roar only to see the threat neutralized.

"A dragon?" Xolani says. He, Beta, and Niya each make their way onto their feet.

"It can't be," Beta says, "Dragons aren't real."

"Xolani!" Raine shouts as she hops off Leonyx, "Niya, are you both okay?" She runs to them, followed by Rashid.

"A little banged up but fine otherwise," Xolani replies, "How did you, where did you get a dragon?"

"Long story," Raine says, "We thought, I thought, you were in trouble."

Xolani looks to Beta, who smiles slightly back at him and says, "I think we are good here."

"But Xaden," Raine says, "He's back?"

Beta and Xolani look toward the pile of rubble before Xolani says. "He was."

Raine asks,

"He was?"

"His body," Xolani says, "is under that rubble, destroyed."

"Lani," Raine whispers.

"I know, but it needed to be done," Xolani says, "but I'm not sure if I was able to work fast enough to stop his mind from leaving as well."

"I did," Niya says softly. They all look at Niya. She looks at Raine and Xolani both with bitter eyes and says, "That monster needed to suffer and I needed to make sure he never hurt anyone again. So I kept his mind where it needed to be until there was nowhere else to go."

A slow tear begins to run down Niya's cheek. Raine embraces her as Xolani follows and places his arms around them. They continue to hold each other tightly until Xolani releases his grasp and steps back. He wipes the tears from his eyes and clears his throat.

"Rashid, um, how is everything going at the palace?"

"A rescue mission was being mounted but I guess there's no need for that now? Lady Neyma is watching Keon and Kasmine is making sure the Tree Palace is secure. Kacao is overseeing repairs."

Rashid suddenly becomes hyper-aware of Beta and says, "But maybe I shouldn't just say palace business in front of random strangers. Your majesty, who's this?"

"Beta," she interjects, "but I'm sure I know more of what goes on in that place than you do."

"Excuse me?" Rashid says and then Xolani answers,

"She is the leader of the Rebels and apparently, Sheer is her son."

"Uh," Rashid says before it sinks in and says, "Uh. Wow, didn't see that one."

"It's all right," Xolani says, "our policies have not been helping Nuhana and that needs to change." He looks at Beta and says, "I won't speak for Beta but I only want the best for this land and all its people. From now on, I want you and a few others of your choosing to sit on the royal council to make sure the voices of all people are heard."

Beta thinks for a moment before speaking, "Your proposal is a great gesture, however, things won't truly change until we take the power out of those who wield it for their own means."

"I'm listening," Xolani says.

"I would be honored to be on this council but anyone with power can be corrupted by it, including myself. I suggest term limits and once a person has served two terms, no matter the position, they cannot be re-elected or placed back in any similar position."

"What if they are for the people and are doing a good job serving?" Rashid asks.

"No one is incorruptible. And the longer they have that power, the easier it becomes."

Xolani is slow to speak and ponders over her suggestion and says,

"Beta, I agree with you, and I will begin to set this policy into motion, but I would like to go a step further. I once unofficially renounced my title before but, that was the decision of a boy running from responsibility. You said term limits should apply to every title, well that includes mine."

Raine and Rashid stand with brows raised as they listen, "Rashid and I will work to get this into place and remove the monarchy to let the people truly rule the land."

"Lani you can't" Rashid says as Raine smiles wide.

"I can and we will me friend." Xolani says, putting a hand on Rashid's shoulder. "The people need to rule, not a monarchy disconnected from the people. And once we return, we all will usher in a new Nuhana."

Xolani extends his hand and Beta quickly extends hers in return and they shake.

Xolani notices that Raine and Niya have been standing quietly behind them and says to Raine,

"We should get Niya back, I'm sure she needs some rest," as he places his hand on her shoulder gently.

"Hold on," Beta says, "what about what she did to this place and my people?"

"I hope we can excuse the act of a child, as long as we send a crew to provide medical help and repairs, that is if you'd like to share your location now. Fair?" Xolani says.

"Fair," Beta replies. They start to walk toward Leonyx before Xolani asks, "How did the mission go? Where are Haygena and Kaleo?"

"Again, long story," Raine says, "actually though, I haven't checked in with Haygena or Kaleo since we separated," she looks to Beta and asks, "Do you have a high-frequency transmitter here?"

Beta smiles and replies, "Doesn't everybody?" They follow Beta as she leads them to a small panel near the entrance of the hanger and removes an insert to expose a highly advanced radio system. Xolani asks,

"Um, where did you get that?"

"Some questions are better not to ask your Highness," Beta says as she turns it on and directs Raine to the controls. Raine says thank you and begins tuning into the right frequency. She picks up the connected mic and says,

"Haygena? Kaleo? This is Raine. What's your status?" The sound of static feels the air as no response is heard. Raine tries again, "Kaleo? Haygena? Are you there, over?" Static continues. Raine places the mic down and says to the group,

"I'm not sure what's happening, they should have..."

A terrifying voice begins to speak and says,

"They are predisposed at the moment but I will tell them you called."

Standing confused for a second, Raine utters into the mic,

"Malkum?"

"Very, very good meat sack," he says, "I would like to thank you and your crew for getting everything I needed, bye."

The mic goes cold as static plays through the air again. Raine turns back to the group and says, "The gods were right, we shouldn't have trusted him."

"Gods?" Rashid and Beta say.

"No time to explain," Raine says, "I don't know what he's planning but we need to get back to the lightning forest and fast."

"Agreed," Xolani says, "I don't think we all will fit on your interesting choice of a pet here. We'll have to get back to the tree place to get one of the Night Hawks."

"I can do it, Daddy," Niya says, "I can get us there." They all look at Niya, who is still shaking from the events previous, as she stands up courageously.

"I know you can," Raine says, "but you've been through so much and you need your rest."

"Your Mother is right, my star," Xolani adds, "if you really want to help us, teleport us back to the Mother Tree and we can take a Night Hawk to help Haygena and Kaleo face who knows what from Malkum. But we need to go, now."

Niya gazes back and forth at all of them before saying,

"I need everyone to touch me."

"Wait," Raine says, "we may need Leonyx."

They look at the gentle beast, who shuffles over to them and lays her head softly on Niya's leg. Niya then says,

"Okay, are we ready?"

They look around to notice Beta isn't holding onto Niya. Xolani asks,

"Beta, we could use your gifts."

Beta smiles and says, "I'm sure, but I don't think this is my fight. Besides, I need to check on my people and clean up this mess."

He looks back to Niya and asks, "Do you remember the lightning forest?"

"I remember it all," she says before closing her eyes. In an instant, they vanish and Beta is left standing there alone.

Chapter 41:

Gangs all here

The hanger dissolves in an instance with the vivid lightning forest appearing in its place. Trees of glass containing lightning coursing through them. No grass, just scorched earth all around.

"Niya!" Xolani says with flared nostrils, "You were supposed to take us to the Tree Palace?" Niya says,

"We need to save Aunt Haygena and Kaleo"

"We do not." Raine points to Niya before motioning to Herself, Xolani and Rashid, "We are the one going forward. You are teleporting yourself back to the the Mother Tree, now!"

She looks at her mother, wanting to protest but knows not to keep pushing at this moment. She simply says, "Yes ma'am. I love you." And runs to hug her. They embrace as Raine says,

"I love you too, now go."

Xolani says, "I love you, Sweetie." Niya smiles and says I love you back. Then she looks to Rashid, who says,

"I know kid, go."

Niya vanishes before their eyes. Rashid then says,

"This seems oddly familiar," Raine replies,

"Except for the huge dragon with us." Xolani adds,

"Honestly, I'd trade that dragon for the Legacy, to grab a weapon or two. By chance did either of you stop by the armory before you left?"

Raine replies as she taps her pocket, "I have my telescopic staff but that's it outside of my gifts."

Rashid adds, "Well, I just have my keen wit and some batons attached to my back."

"Okay," Xolani says, "we'll have to make those work. Any thoughts on what we do next?"

"Leave?" Rashid says. Xolani gives a disapproving look and replies,

"Thoughts that will help the situation."

"Actually," Raine says, they look at her, "since you two were here, Malkum's built an elaborate bungalow where his cave was. Perhaps Xolani and I approach from the front to investigate, while you swing around and come from the side."

"I like that, but no," Rashid says.

"What is with you, Rashid?" Raine asks.

"Have you two forgotten the last time we were here," Rashid says defensively, "that thing hooked its claws in me and took me on a not-so-scenic tour at 500 feet in the air."

"Rashid," Xolani says.

"I still have the claw marks."

"Rashid!" Raine shouts.

"Yeah," Rashid replies.

"So, what's your plan?"

"I thought you'd never ask," Rashid says while smiling and looking at Leonyx, causing Xolani and Raine to roll their eyes before listening to what he suggests.

———◆———

XOLANI HUNCHES CAREFULLY behind a lightning tree as he shields his eyes from the blinding light it emits. He does his best to spy on Malkum. As Malkum starts with the bronze key, he carefully places the god's pieces of essence, one by one, in a tight circle around the Lumastar.

"Where could Haygena and Kaleo be?" Xolani thinks to himself as he searches the area with his eyes. He gazes over the compound to finally see them tied and gagged beneath an overhang of the bungalow. But just as he finds them Malkum announces loudly,

"I smell you human," and places the thimble on the ground. "The lightning trees cannot hide you. So you might as well come out, Xolani."

Xolani stands tall as he comes from behind a lightning tree and approaches Malkum.

"What are you doing, Malkum?" he asks, but Malkum doesn't reply. He keeps his focus on placing the amber stone down next.

"Did you know," Malkum says slowly, "that when I and the other angels were cast out, there was no hearing? No getting to state our case of why we did what we did? Just cold, harsh judgment, punishment, and then banishment? Can you imagine how that felt?"

Xolani takes a moment before saying,

"I can't. But is that why you wanted the essences from the other angels, so you can go back?"

"Oh no, no, no," Malkum says with a slight joy to his voice. He rises up after placing the hair clip down, "This isn't some feeble attempt to go home. This is about freedom."

Xolani stands quietly for a moment as he notices Raine sneaking over to Haygena and Kaleo. She begins to untie their ropes as he says to Malkum, "Freedom, what do you mean?"

"Of course you don't know," Malkum says, "but I will humor you as you keep trying to stall me for whatever feeble plan you and your team have concocted." Malkum places the last piece of essence, the purple button, on the ground, completing the circle. He stands next to the Lumastar before continuing, "You know that I have this pesky demon attached to my charming personality. And I mean to rectify that."

"So you just want to free yourself from the demon?" Xolani asks.

"No!" Malkum explodes, "I want justice! I was sentenced to this, this hell, with no parole, and no release date! I spend my nights hearing this thing roll around in my head, while during the day, I get locked away in its mind as it scourers the lightning forest with such beastly savagery. Do you know what that's like? Eons on this plane with this thing? And as long as we are connected, I can never, ever leave."

"Malkum, we would've tried to help you if," Xolani tries to say before Malkum cuts him off and says,

"Help me? What can a mortal do that I cannot?"

"Get those pieces of essence for starters," Xolani retorts.

"Enough!" Malkum says before extending his hand into the air. The pieces of essence start to glow and then slowly rise off the ground. "I need the pieces to heal the Lumastar and amplify its power, because, not only will I finally be free, but I will truly be a god among men on this pitiful plane."

"Not on my watch!" Rashid yells as he tosses a baton, hitting Malkum in the back of the head before it boomerangs back into his hand. Malkum exhales in agitation before saying,

"You bone bags will regret that." The Lumastar begins to flash before shooting pulses of light through the pieces of essence. The light radiates inward and covers Malkum. He glows with this bright yellow energy and begins to laugh evilly. The glow intensifies as the pieces of essence dem and fade away.

A concussion burst hits him in both shoulders, knocking him off balance. He looks back in the direction they originated from and sees Haygena standing with Kaleo and Raine ready to fight. He looks back to Xolani, who is also taking a fighting stance.

"You really think you have a chance against a god?"

"You're no god," Xolani says, "just a disgraced being that thinks it's above everyone else."

Malkum snarls at Xolani before extending his arms and firing a stream of light in Xolani's direction. Xolani feels the heat of the blast as he twists out of its path. He briefly looks at the wake of destruction left by the blast. Xolani looks back at Malkum but catches a glimpse of Kaleo. Who's Polynesian tattoos glow, as he takes in a deep breath. Xolani quickly dives out of the way before covering his ears.

Kaleo begins to perform a Haka, hitting on his forearms intimidatingly before letting out a furious yell. A supersonic sound erupts from him as he continues to scream a primal chant toward Malkum. The earth erodes and crumbles as Kaleo screams. Malkum works to keep his balance. His knees buckle under the weight of Kaleo's scream and falls to one knee.

Kaleo advances, keeping Malkum pinned to the ground. But then something starts to fight and claw its way out of Malkum's back, breaking its way through the glowing energy. Dirty white claws emerge first as they burst through. Rashid is frozen as he watches its long beak rise out next. It climbs out of Malkum and shoots up into the night sky. Rashid screams out,

"Leonyx!"

The massive beast stumps forward from behind the mountain and shouts up into the night sky, in pursuit of the Kwane. Animalistic battle cries cover the landscape as Kaleo continues to subdue Malkum. But as he chats the Kwane swoops down and sinks its talons into Haygena's shoulders and takes her high into the air, with Leonyx closely behind them. Her agony from the sky rains down droplets in her pain, catching Kaleo's attention and causing him to stop his assault on Malkum. Malkum takes full advantage of this moment. And within the blink of an eye, he moves with three swift steps to gain ground on Kaleo, and sends a powerful blow to Kaleo's chest, forcing him to fly back through the dirt. Raine extends her staff to absorb its metal properties before twirling it and slamming it towards Malkum's head.

But he hears her coming and grabs the staff from above and uses it to fling Raine in the other direction. She tumbles with her staff through the dirt before finding her footing and taking a defensive stance.

Xolani fires several bursts of water toward Malkum. One fizzles out on Malkum's back before he turns and dodges the rest.

"Pitiful," Malkum says. Tiny light orbs bubble out from all around Malkum and float around him, then suddenly, they disperse throughout the air. Xolani twists and turns to dodge but is hit and instantly feels the jarring pain of electricity course through his body.

Raine sees Xolani get hit and shouts,

"Lani!" This gains Rashid's attention as he swats the last orb to the ground with his baton.

"I'm okay," Xolani says as he struggles to stand and collapses to his knees. Raine starts to move toward him but he quickly puts his hand up and says, "Stop Malkum."

She looks to Malkum, then to Rashid, and says,

"Toss me your batons."

Rashid pitches his batons to Raine. She drops her staff to catch them and absorbs their properties. Her skin quickly shifts into a hardened rubber state. She dashes over to Malkum hitting him in a fury of coordinated strikes.

She hits his side hard, then attacks his left knee, causing him to buckle and fall. She strikes hard to his shoulder and lands a blow to his cheek, making Malkum swivel face-first into the dirt.

"Look out!" Rashid yells. But it's too late. Loose rope slithers up her leg and around her body, holding her in place. She struggles to free herself as the ropes get tighter, causing her to drop Rashid's batons.

"We trusted you!" Raine says as she struggles to free herself. Malkum smirks and says,

"That was your fault."

But before Malkum can continue, a low mumbling gains their attention. It grows louder as it becomes clearer. Kaleo pushes himself up to stand. Chanting, Kaleo begins his Haka again.

"You again?" Malkum says. Kaleo only gets more ferocious in his movements Malkum's full attention is on him as Kaleo screams,

"Now!"

Raine tackles Rashid before a wave of sound knocks Malkum unbalanced. Seizing the moment, Xolani raises his hand to lift the earth beneath Malkum, flinging the mound of dirt high and sending Malkum way into the air. He pulls the dirt mound from under him and swirls it above Malkum. The mound pushes against Malkum. With the weight of the mound pushing him faster and faster until he slams back into the earth.

A huge cloud of dirt covers the area. Xolani fans the dirt out of his face and asks,

"Is everyone all right?"

Sporadically they all reply yes. Then Kaleo says in a lower tone,

"We need to go after Haygena, that thing took off with her."

"Yes, for her and Leonyx" Raine says. Xolani adds,

"Kaleo and Rashid, go and..."

Rumbling beneath their feet stops them before Malkum erupts through the dirt, causing them to be propelled out of the way as he yells,

"Enough!"

He towers over them and says,

"You mortals are so infuriating! You should be wiped out of existence!"

"You're not so lovable yourself, creep," Rashid says. Malkum tilts his head and says,

"You will be the first, insect." Malkum extends his hand toward Rashid. It begins to flicker but as Malkum is about to fire a blast, a loud yell is heard in the distance. "What now?" They all turn to see Haygena soaring through the air on Leonyx's back.

"That's my lady!" Kaleo says triumphantly. Malkum launches three bursts of energy at her. Leonyx maneuvers around them with ease and then fires a stream of fire with several concussion bursts from Haygena, back at Malkum. Malkum dodges the fire but is quickly hit and stumbles as the concussion burst hits his shoulders, and then his chest. Haygena directs Leonyx to fly in a circle as she continues to blast Malkum from above.

Kaleo sees the opening and screams at Malkum, keeping him locked down. But then a bright burst of light radiates from Malkum, blinding everyone momentarily. Haygena and Leonyx crash nearby. Xolani rubs his eyes as he tries to regain his sight.

Malkum stands confidently as he says,

"You are only delaying your defeat. Bow down now, and I will show you mercy."

Xolani, getting his sight back, stands tall. Raine, Rashid, and Kaleo follow suit. Haygena limps over to Kaleo with Leonyx by their side. Malkum stares at each of them and says,

"This is the way you want to die? So be it," and he charges forward. Xolani sprints into action with Kaleo, Raine, Rashid, Haygena, and Leonyx behind them. They run full speed toward Malkum as he closes in. They nearly collide when a streak of lightning crashes down in their paths. Mami Wata, Takhor, Ogun, and Ashanti appear before them, stopping them in their tracks.

Chapter 42:

In the final moments

"I was wondering when you'd show up," Malkum says to Ashanti, Ogun, and Takhor, who have appeared and stand regally before them. Raine, Kaleo, Rashid, Haygena, and Xolani stand in awe.

"You have broken the universal laws, Malkum," Takhor says with a deep booming voice, "unless you release and return the power now, you will be taken beyond."

"Oh please," Malkum scuffs, "I am now the most powerful being, here and beyond. There is nothing any of you pathetic angels can do about it!" Malkum laughs. But Takhor stands unamused.

"You are right," he says, "you have absorbed pieces of our essence, which is forbidden, and forbidden for good reason. No one entity can hold that much power, without the ultimate sacrifice. You seem to have forgotten that." He points just over Malkum's shoulder.

With terrified eyes, Malkum looks over his shoulder to see a smiling Anpu beside him. Anpu places a hand on Malkum's shoulder and says,

"It's time to go," Malkum pushes Anpu's hand off him and says,

"Don't you dare touch me. You all pretend to be gods while I have achieved it! Do you think you can just come here and tell me what to do? This is my realm now and I dare any of you to try and stop me!"

An axe manifest in Ogun hand as he moves forward to challenge Malkum, but stops when Anpu raises his hand. Anpu walks casually in front of Malkum. Anpu looks him straight in the eyes and says,

"The bill always comes due. And you have forgotten the only thing binding you to this world was your demon." Deathly screams and howls echo behind Malkum as a portal begins to open. Anpu continues, "Your penance here wasn't a curse or punishment, it was to help you learn and grow. But you became bitter and resentful, creating a harsh life for yourself while your counterparts built a utopia." Decrypted hands claw their way out of the portal as the howls and screams intensify, "You chose to revel in your misery, and then steal what wasn't yours. However, your greatest offense is living below your potential and destroying yourself and any chance you ever had of truly living."

Malkum feels the pull of the portal tugging him backward. He fights with all his might but slowly begins to drift back. He falls to the ground and claws in an attempt to pull himself forward.

The firm grip of elongated hands clasp onto Malkum's ankles. They climb up his legs as they pull him closer and closer to the portal. He yells,

"You can't do this! I won't go!"

"But we can and you will," Anpu says calmly. Malkum continues to fight his losing battle, disappearing into the black abyss of the portal before it vanishes as quickly as it came.

Silence overtakes them for a moment before Rashid asks,

"Um not sure what happened but, did you just... is he...?"

"That is not for you to worry about. Just know," Anpu says to Rashid before winking at Raine, "The bill always comes due."

Raine walks over to Anpu and says,

"If I may ask you Anpu, I saw you just before a friend... family member sacrificed herself for me and my son. Is she..."

Anpu interrupts her and says,

"Maybe you should ask her, yourself." He points to where the portal was and a new one slowly materializes. Miss Lupita steps through. Raine runs over to hug her and they share a long embrace before Raine says,

"I thought you died."

"Naw," Miss Lupita says, "I've just been chatting with Yosé, I mean, Anpu."

She waves at Anpu. Raine looks puzzled and asks,

"Yosé? I don't understand. Is Anpu the boy you met in Port Ambit?" But before Miss Lupita or Anpu can respond, Ogun says loudly,

"As touching as this reunion is, there is still a bigger matter at hand."

"Yes," Takhor says, "the Lumastar needs to be returned."

"In the fight with Malkum," Xolani says, "I honestly forgot about the Lumastar." They scan the area for its location until they find it hovering a few yards away. Its familiar yellow tent has been replaced with a pulsing red-ish orange glow.

"Are you able to return it to its natural plane?" Xolani asks.

"Only with the pieces of our essence," Ashanti says, "and it will take too long to regain our essence back."

"Respectfully," Rashid says, "Miss?"

"Ashanti," she replies.

"Ms. Ashanti, how long is too long? Are we talking a few minutes or a few hours?" Haygena jabs him with her elbow, "What? I'm just curious."

"It would take a few millennia," Ashanti says, "for us to gain that level of power again. However, Anpu can open a portal to another plane to get rid of the Lumastar before it destroys this world."

"I can," Anpu says, "but since the Lumastar is a living being, and hasn't died, it has to go willingly." They all look to Anpu before Ogun says,

"What are you waiting for? Open the portal."

Anpu slants his eye in Ogun's direction and says,

"I need everyone to stand over here," as he points to his side. They all move as he summons a portal closely behind the Lumastar. The portal grows in size and struggles to engulf the Lumastar. Anpu continues to increase the size of the portal but the Lumastar doesn't budge.

"It's not moving," he says as he turns toward them, "it doesn't want to go."

"Can you modify the plane inside the portal," says Takhor, "to one the Lumastar is familiar?"

"That may make the portal unstable, but I will try." The portal begins to flicker a bright yellow to a darkened orange. The Lumastar moves slightly but stops. Slowly dust begins to lift off the ground and flow into the portal as it grows stronger.

"Do you feel that?" Haygena asks as they all notice the pull from the portal on them. It intensifies and begins pulling everything loose off the ground. The pull becomes so great they all fight their way against the suction to hold onto various structures holding up Malkum's bungalow. Leonyx roars as she digs her claws into the earth and hunkers down.

"As I feared the portal is growing unstable and it will only get worse until it has the Lumastar," Anpu says. Ogun then says,

"You think!"

Anpu gives him a disapproving look as Rashid shouts over the noise,

"Aren't you gods? Do something."

"Like what, mortal?" Anpu says, "The Lumastar knows the portal leads to death and it clearly doesn't want to die!"

"But if it doesn't," Haygena yells, "it will blow up and still die anyway."

"Again," Anpu yells, "unless it goes willingly or you want to push it through the portal and run the risk of dying along with it, there is nothing else I can do."

They all struggle to hold on as the pull continues to grow. Xolani unties his red sash and binds it around his hands and the nearest pole.

They all adjust their grips as the pull toward the portal lifts them off their feet. Xolani holds his head down. Then in a moment of fear, courage, and love, he looks at Raine. She feels his gaze and looks over to him. She reads his face and mouths the word.

"Don't."

He smiles and whispers, "I see you, my Moon," before unbinding his hand and letting the pull take him.

"Lani!" Raine shouts as she looks back and watches him struggle to twist and turn onto his back as the pull draws him to the portal. He uses the force to position himself just right and as he draws near the Lumastar, he tackles it through the portal. It closes instantly, only leaving Xolani's sash floating to the ground.

"No!" Raine screams before they all fall back down. She quickly makes her way to where the portal was, falling to her knees as she picks up his sash.

"Lani!" she cries out. Rashid rushes over to her and sinks down beside her. Haygena looks on in disbelief as she collapses and says,

"He can't be gone." Kaleo lowers to her level and embraces her gently. She allows herself to fall into his arms.

Anger, frustration and desperation building inside Raine until she explodes up and rushes over to Anpu saying,

"Bring him back! You brought Miss Lupita back, bring Lani back!"

Anpu lowers his head and says gently,

"I'm sorry, but..." Raine cuts him off and says,

"No! Xolani's bill was not due. Bring him back. Take me!" She sobs uncontrollably as Rashid holds her.

Ashanti stops caressing Leonyx to walk over and softly says,

"Anpu, could you open a portal to that plane again?" Anpu, puzzled, says,

"I could, but why would I?" Then like a flash of lighting he knows what Ashanti is suggesting and says, "Absolutely not. You know the rules are very clear about sending mortals to the plane of non-existence." He turns to Takhor for confirmation, "Takhor, please tell her it's a bad idea."

"What's a bad idea?" Raine asks through her tears.

The gods are silent until Takhor says,

"Anpu doesn't have the ability to bring people back from the dead."

"Then how is Miss Lupita here?" Haygena asks.

"I saved her like she saved me," Anpu says.

"Yes," Takhor says. "So, Ashanti is suggesting that Anpu opens a portal to allow you to retrieve Xolani. That is if he is still alive."

"I want to go," Raine says as she shoots up and rises to her feet. "I need to go."

"It's not that easy," Anpu says.

"Correct," Takhor adds, "We have no dominion over that plane and cannot go or help you once you are there. Also, as I mentioned, we cannot guarantee Xolani is alive,"

"He's alive!" Raine says as she ties Xolani's sash around her waist.

"Raine," Rashid says.

"He's alive," she says, "I can still feel him."

"That may be," Anpu states, "but even if you find him, I can't bring you back. You will have to find Anubis. He is the only one in the plane of non-existence with that kind of power."

"Let's go," Raine says.

"Raine," Rashid says, "this is crazy, you can't."

"Watch me," Raine says and then commands, "open the portal."

"I'm going too," Haygena says, before standing next to Raine.

"I can't ask that of you Haygena."

"You're not asking," Haygena says, "he's my brother and you, are my sister."

Raine smiles and mouths thank you.

"I guess I'm going too," Rashid says as he steps up beside them. Raine looks at him kindly and says,

"Thank you. I know Xolani was your best friend but, as Niya and Keon's god-parent, I would respectfully ask you and Miss Lupita to stay behind and watch over them while we rescue Xolani."

Rashid rethinks his position and quickly says,

"Of course."

Kaleo walks over and says in a lowered voice,

"You don't think I am just going to stand by and watch you two go off alone, do you?"

Haygena hugs his arm and they look at Anpu.

"I guess it's settled then," Anpu says, "If Xolani is alive, he is mostly going to be near the Valley of Lost Souls. Once you've found him, Anubis will most likely be in the tower of Babel."

"Wasn't that the structure created to reach heaven?" Rashid asks.

"Something like that," Anpu says as he starts to open another portal. "Just remember, Anubis is not to be trifled with. He will also need that gate key to bring you back." They look puzzled before Rashid blurts out,

"The sash, it's a key to open any door." They look at Rashid and he says, "What? I know things."

"Trust half of what you hear," Anpu says, "and even less of what you see. Anubis will weigh your intentions, so make sure you go to him honestly and earnestly."

They all nod in understanding and turn to face the portal. Raine leads the way as they look ahead and walk into the void.

———◉———

END

Thank you for reading...
The Forgotten Legacy of Gods & Men:
A Scion Book Series
I'd love to hear your thoughts, so please don't forget to leave a review. Reviews help authors like me more than you may know, and they also help other readers like you find stories they may be looking for more easily.

Thank You to:

Every local coffee shop I've visited that didn't kick me out as I stayed for hours to write after purchasing several chai lattes and earl gray teas.

My fellow authors, Javier Garay, and Rosaly Aponte for helping me talk out ideas and concepts.

Every single person that has given me a word of encouragement.

Snowbird Mountain Coffee Co for providing some of the best chi lattes and specialty drinks an author could ask for while spending hours/days writing and editing in your shops.

God for giving me the talent to tell a story and the discipline to write it.

My beta readers Shelia Walker, Mandy Grooms, and my editor Kaitlyn Brown for sticking with me to make sure the story wasn't held hostage by my bad grammar.

Deranged Doctor Designs for designing such a wonderful cover.

Everyone who has read this book, because that's exactly what it's for.

My wife and kids for allowing me to take bits of our lives and fictionalize them.

My loving wife, who is my partner, and support.

Debbie Hall, for your love and support, even in the moments that you may not have even known it.

And lastly, thank you to my father-in-love, Timothy E. Hall, who sadly passed away while I was completing this book. Your guiding hand, sense of humor, and support were with me even though you physically were not. We love and miss you every day.

Final Thoughts:

Thanks for purchasing The Forgotten Legacy of Gods and Men. If you've enjoyed this book or you simply have thoughts you'd like to share about it, please be sure to give it a review. Giving reviews helps other readers like you find books they may love, and of course it also helps out authors like me more than you may know.

Also, if you'd like to connect with me to see what I've done, what I'm working on, and what's coming up next... please follow me on most social media apps @iamjayreace. Or sign up for The World Builders Newsletter at JayReace.Com

At the time of this publication, you can find the other great stories mentioned in this book, at:

E.X.O. The Legend of Wade Williams: https://www.youneekstudios.com

Aceblade, Harlem, & Luberjax: https://www.4thwallpros.com

Konkret Comic's Odina: https://www.konkretecomics.com

World Map made by Saumya Singh using Inkarnatethe. Please contact Saumya via Instagram @Saumyasvision

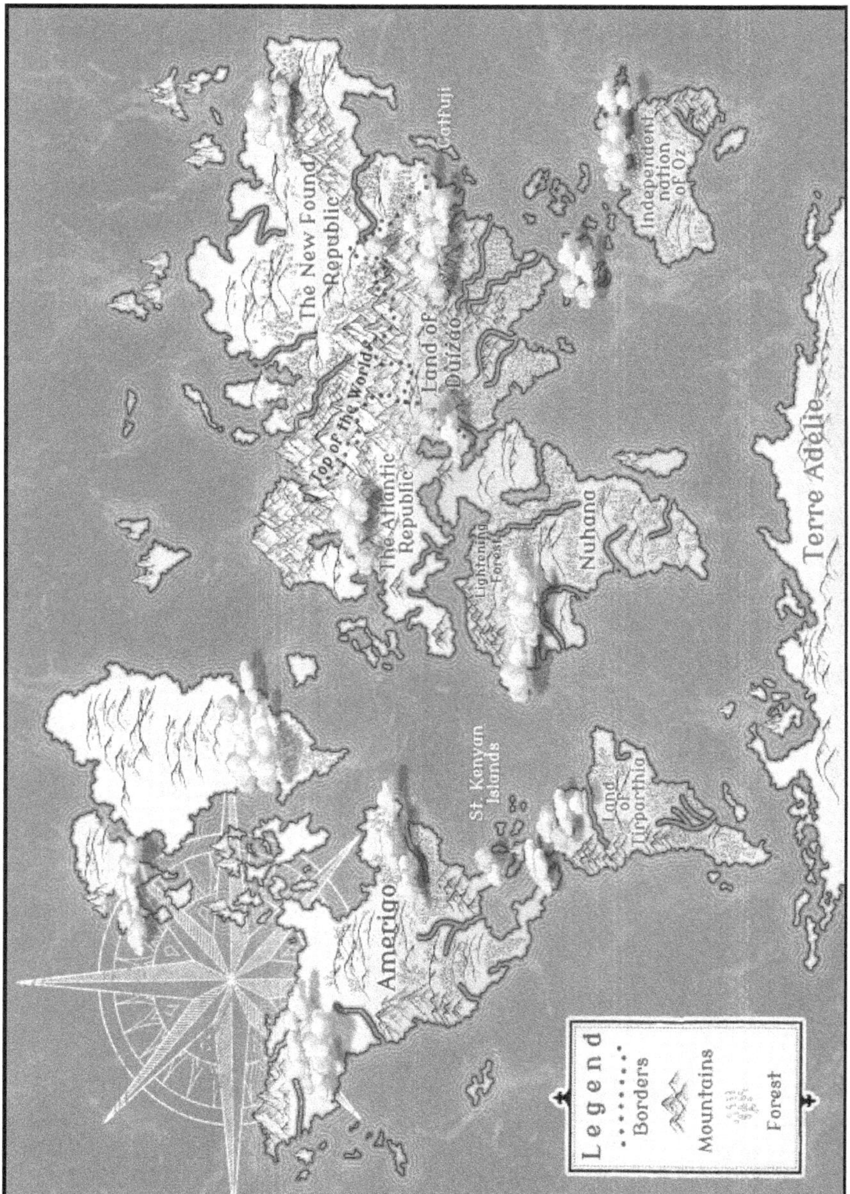
The New Found Republic
Catfuji
Independent nation of Oz
Top of the World
Land of Duizao
The Atlantic Republic
Lightening Forest
Nuhana
Terre Adelie
St. Kenyan Islands
Land of Urparthia
Amerigo
Legend
Borders
Mountains
Forest